How to Read Spook's Symbols

Boggarts

Beta for Boggart

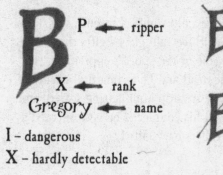

P ← ripper

B — Naturally bound boggart

X ← rank

Gregory ← name

B — Artificially bound boggart

I – dangerous
X – hardly detectable

Ghosts/Ghasts

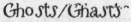

I – dangerous
X – hardly detectable

X

Gregory

Witches

O

M

Gre...

M – malevolent
B – benign
U – unaware

Character profiles

Tom

Thomas Ward is the seventh son of a seventh son. This means he was born with certain gifts – gifts that make him perfect for the role of the Spook's apprentice. He can see and hear the dead and he is a natural enemy of the dark. But that doesn't stop Tom getting scared, and he is going to need all his courage if he is to succeed where twenty-nine others have failed.

The Spook

The Spook is an unmistakable figure. He's tall, and rather fierce looking. He wears a long black cloak and hood, and always carries a staff and a silver chain. Like his apprentice, Tom, he is left-handed, and is a seventh son of a seventh son.

For over sixty years he has protected the County from things that go bump in the night.

Alice

Tom can't decide if Alice is good or evil. She terrifies the local village lads, is related to two of the most evil witch clans (the Malkins and the Deanes) and has been known to use dark magic. But she was trained as a witch against her will and has helped Tom out of some tight spots. She seems to be a loyal friend, but can she be trusted?

Mam

Tom's mam has always known he would become the Spook's apprentice. She calls him her 'gift to the County'. A loving mother and an expert on plants, medicine and childbirth, Mam has always been a little different. Her origins in Greece remain a mystery. In fact, there are quite a few mysterious things about Mam . . .

THE WARDSTONE CHRONICLES

THE SPOOK'S

NIGHTMARE

JOSEPH DELANEY

Illustrated by David Wyatt

RED FOX

THE SPOOK'S NIGHTMARE
A RED FOX BOOK 978 1 782 95252 7

First published in Great Britain by The Bodley Head,
an imprint of Random House Children's Publishers UK
A Random House Group Company
Bodley Head edition published 2010
First Red Fox edition published 2011
This edition published 2014

7 9 10 8

Penguin Random House is committed to a sustainable future for
our business, our readers and our planet. This book is made from
Forest Stewardship Council® certified paper.

MIX
Paper from
responsible sources
FSC® C018179

Printed and bound in Great Britain by Clays Ltd, Elcograf S.p.A.

Set in 10.5/16.5pt Palatino by Falcon Oast Graphic Art Ltd.

Red Fox Books are published by Random House Children's Publishers UK,
61–63 Uxbridge Road, London W5 5SA

www.randomhousechildrens.co.uk
www.totallyrandombooks.co.uk
www.randomhouse.co.uk

Addresses for companies within The Random House Group Limited
can be found at: www.randomhouse.co.uk/offices.htm

THE RANDOM HOUSE GROUP Limited Reg. No. 954009

A CIP catalogue record for this book is available from the British Library.

for Marie

THE HIGHEST POINT IN THE COUNTY
IS MARKED BY MYSTERY.
IT IS SAID THAT A MAN DIED THERE IN A
GREAT STORM, WHILE BINDING AN EVIL
THAT THREATENED THE WHOLE WORLD.
THEN THE ICE CAME AGAIN, AND WHEN IT
RETREATED, EVEN THE SHAPES OF THE
HILLS AND THE NAMES OF THE TOWNS
IN THE VALLEYS CHANGED.
NOW, AT THAT HIGHEST POINT ON
THE FELLS, NO TRACE REMAINS OF WHAT
WAS DONE SO LONG AGO,
BUT ITS NAME HAS ENDURED.
THEY CALL IT –

THE WARDSTONE.

CHAPTER 1
RED WITH BLOOD

The Spook, Alice and I were crossing the Long Ridge on our way back to Chipenden, with the three wolfhounds, Claw, Blood and Bone, barking excitedly at our heels.

The first part of the climb had been pleasant enough. It had rained all afternoon but was now a clear, cloudless late autumn evening with just a slight chilly breeze ruffling our hair: perfect weather for walking. I remember thinking how peaceful it all seemed.

But at the summit a big shock awaited us. There was dark smoke far to the north beyond the fells. It looked like Caster was burning. Had the war finally reached us? I wondered fearfully.

Years earlier, an alliance of enemy nations had invaded our land far to the south. Since then, despite the best efforts of the combined counties to hold the line, they had been slowly pushing north.

'How can they have advanced so far without us knowing?' the Spook asked, scratching at his beard, clearly agitated. 'Surely there'd have been news – some warning at least?'

'It might just be a raiding party from the sea,' I suggested. That was very likely. Enemy boats had come ashore before and attacked settlements along the coast – though this part of the County had been spared so far.

Shaking his head, the Spook set off down the hill at a furious pace. Alice gave me a worried smile and we hurried along in pursuit. Encumbered by my staff and both our bags, I was struggling to keep up on the slippery wet grass. But I knew what was bothering my master. He was anxious about his library. Looting and burning had been reported in the south and he was worried about the safety of his books, a store of knowledge accumulated by generations of spooks.

I was now in the third year of my apprenticeship to the Spook, learning how to deal with ghosts, ghasts, witches, boggarts and all manner of creatures from the dark. My master gave me lessons most days, but my other source of knowledge was that library. It was certainly very important.

Once we reached level ground we headed directly towards Chipenden, the hills to the north looming larger with every stride. We'd just forded a small river, picking our way across the stones, the water splashing around our ankles, when Alice pointed ahead.

'Enemy soldiers!' she cried.

In the distance, a group of men were heading east across our path – two dozen or more, the swords at their belts glinting brightly in the light from the setting sun, which was now very low on the horizon.

We halted and crouched low on the riverbank, hoping that they hadn't seen us. I told the dogs to lie down and be quiet; they obeyed instantly.

The soldiers wore grey uniforms and steel helms with broad, vertical nose guards of a type I hadn't seen before. Alice was right. It was a large enemy patrol. Unfortunately they saw us almost immediately. One of them pointed and barked out an order, and a small group peeled off and began running towards us.

'This way!' cried the Spook and, snatching up his bag to relieve me of the extra weight, took off, following the river upstream; Alice and I followed with the dogs.

There was a large wood directly ahead. Maybe there was a chance we could lose them there, I thought. But as soon as we reached the tree-line my hopes were dashed. It had been coppiced recently: there were no saplings, no thickets – just well-spaced mature trees. This was no hiding place.

I glanced back. Our pursuers were now spread out in a ragged line. The majority weren't making much headway, but there was one soldier in the lead who was definitely gaining on us: he was brandishing his sword threateningly.

Next thing I knew the Spook was coming to a halt.

He threw down his bag at my feet. 'Keep going, lad! I'll deal with him,' he commanded, turning back to face the soldier.

I called the dogs to heel and stopped, frowning. I couldn't leave my master like that. I picked up his bag again and readied my staff. If necessary I would go to his aid and take the dogs with me; they were big fierce wolfhounds, completely without fear.

I looked back at Alice. She'd stopped too and was staring at me with a strange expression on her face. She seemed to be muttering to herself.

The breeze died away very suddenly and the chill was like a blade of ice cutting into my face; all was suddenly silent, as if every living thing in the wood were holding its breath. Tendrils of mist snaked out of the trees towards us, approaching from all directions. I looked at Alice again. There had been no warning of this change in the weather. It didn't seem natural. Was it dark magic? I wondered. The dogs crouched down on their bellies and whined softly. Even if it was intended to help us, my master would be angry if

Alice used dark magic. She'd spent two years training to be a witch and he was always wary of her turning back towards the dark.

By now the Spook had taken up a defensive position, his staff held diagonally. The soldier reached him and slashed downwards with his sword. My heart was in my mouth, but I needn't have feared. There was a cry of pain – but it came from the soldier, not my master. The sword went spinning into the grass, and then the Spook delivered a hard blow to his assailant's temple to bring him to his knees.

The mist was closing in fast, and for a few moments my master was lost to view. Then I heard him running towards us. Once he reached us we hurried on, following the river, the fog becoming denser with every stride. We soon left the wood and the river behind and followed a thick hawthorn hedge north for a few hundred yards until the Spook waved us to a halt. We crouched in a ditch, hunkering down with the dogs, holding our breath and listening for danger. At first there were no sounds of pursuit, but then we heard voices to the north and east. They were still searching for us – though the light was beginning to fail, and with each minute that passed it became less likely that we'd be discovered.

But, just when we thought we were safe, the voices from the north grew louder, and soon we heard footsteps getting nearer and nearer. It seemed likely that they would blunder straight into our hiding place and my master and I gripped our staffs, ready to fight for our lives.

The searchers passed no more than a couple of yards to our right – we could just make out the dim shapes of three men. But we were crouched low in the ditch and they didn't see us. When the footsteps and voices had faded away, the Spook shook his head.

'Don't know how many they've got hunting for us,' he whispered, 'but they seem determined to find us. Best if we stay here for the rest of the night.'

And so we settled down to spend a cold, uncomfortable night in the ditch. I slept fitfully but, as often happens in these situations, fell into a deep slumber only when it was almost time to get up. I was awoken by Alice shaking my shoulder.

I sat up quickly, staring about me. The sun had already risen and I could see grey clouds racing overhead. The wind was whistling through the hedge, bending and flexing the spindly leafless branches. 'Is everything all right?' I asked.

Alice smiled and nodded. 'There's nobody less than a mile or so away. Those soldier boys have given up and gone.'

Then I heard a noise nearby – a sort of groaning. It was the Spook.

'Sounds like he's having a bad dream,' Alice said.

'Perhaps we should wake him up?' I suggested.

'Leave him for a few minutes. It's best if he comes out of it by himself.'

But if anything his cries and moans grew louder and his body started to shake; he was becoming more and more agitated, so after another minute I shook him gently by the shoulder to wake him.

'Are you all right, Mr Gregory?' I asked. 'You seemed to be having some kind of nightmare.'

For a moment his eyes were wild and he looked at me as if I were a stranger or even an enemy. 'Aye, it was nightmare all right,' he said at last. 'It was about Bony Lizzie . . .'

Bony Lizzie was Alice's mother, a powerful witch who was now bound in a pit in the Spook's garden at Chipenden.

'She was sat on a throne,' continued my master, 'and the Fiend was standing at her side with his hand on her left shoulder. They were in a big hall that I didn't recognize at first. The floor was running red with blood. Prisoners were crying out in terror before being executed – they were cutting off their heads. But it was the hall that really bothered me and set my nerves on edge.'

'Where was it?' I asked.

The Spook shook his head. 'She was in the great hall at Caster Castle! She was the ruler of the County . . .'

'It was just a nightmare,' I said. 'Lizzie's safely bound.'

'Perhaps,' said the Spook. 'But I don't think I've ever had a dream that was more vivid . . .'

We set off cautiously towards Chipenden. The Spook said nothing about the sudden mist that had arisen the previous night. It was the season for them, after all, and he had been busy preparing to fight the soldier at the time. But I was sure that it had appeared at Alice's bidding. Though who was I to say anything? I was tainted by the dark myself.

We'd only recently returned from Greece after defeating the Ordeen, one of the Old Gods. It had cost us dear. My mam had died to gain our victory, and so had Bill Arkwright, the spook who'd worked north of Caster – that's why we had his dogs with us.

I'd also paid a terrible price. In order to make that victory possible, I'd sold my own soul to the Fiend.

All that prevented him from dragging me off to the dark now was the blood jar given to me by Alice, which I carried in my pocket. The Fiend couldn't approach me while I had it by me. Alice needed to stay close to me to share its protection – otherwise the Fiend would kill her in revenge for the help she'd given me. Of course, the Spook didn't know about that. If I told him what I'd done, it would be the end of my apprenticeship.

As we climbed the slope towards Chipenden, my master grew more and more anxious. We'd seen pockets of devastation: some burned-out houses; many that were deserted, one with a corpse in a nearby ditch.

'I'd hoped they wouldn't have come so far inland. I dread to think what we'll find, lad,' he said grimly.

Normally he would have avoided walking through Chipenden village: most people didn't like being too close to a spook and he respected the wishes of the locals. But as the grey slate roofs came into view, one glance was enough to tell us that something was terribly wrong.

It was clear that enemy soldiers had passed this way. Many of the roofs were badly damaged, with charred beams exposed to the air. The closer we got, the worse it was. Almost a third of the houses were completely burned out, their blackened stones just shells of what had once been homes to local families. Those that hadn't gone up in flames had broken windows and splintered doors hanging from their hinges, with evidence of looting.

The village seemed completely abandoned, but then we heard the sound of banging. Someone was hammering. Quickly the Spook led us through the cobbled streets towards the sound. We were heading for the main road through the village, where the shops were. We passed the greengrocer's and the baker's, both ransacked, and headed for the butcher's shop, which seemed to be the source of the noise.

The butcher was still there, his red beard glinting in the morning light, but he wasn't carrying out repairs to his premises; he was nailing down the lid of a coffin. There were three other coffins lined up close by, already sealed and ready for burial. One was small and obviously contained a young child. The butcher got to his feet as we entered the yard and came across to shake the Spook's hand. He was the one real contact my master had amongst the villagers; the only person he ever talked to about things other than spook's business.

'It's terrible, Mr Gregory,' the butcher said. 'Things can never be the same again.'

'I hope it's not . . .' the Spook muttered, glancing down at the coffins.

'Oh, no, thank the Lord for that at least,' the butcher told him. 'It happened three days ago. I got my own family away to safety just in time. No, these poor folk weren't quick enough. They killed everybody they could find. It was just an enemy patrol, but a very large one. They were out foraging for supplies. There was no need to burn houses and kill people; no cause to murder this family. Why did they do that? They could just have taken what they wanted and left.'

The Spook nodded. I knew what his answer was to that, although he didn't spell it out to the butcher. He would have said it was because the Fiend was now loose in the world. He made people more cruel, wars more savage.

'I'm sorry about your house, Mr Gregory,' the butcher continued.

The colour drained from the Spook's face. 'What?' he demanded.

'Oh, I'm really sorry . . . don't you know? I assumed you'd called back there already. We heard the boggart howling and roaring from miles away. There must have been too many for it to deal with. They ransacked your house, taking anything they could carry, then set fire to it . . .'

CHAPTER 2
YOU AIN'T DEAD YET!

Making no reply, the Spook turned and set off up the hill, almost running. Soon the cobbles gave way to a muddy track. After climbing the hill, we came to the boundary of the garden. I commanded the dogs to wait there as we pushed on into the trees.

We soon found the first bodies. They had been there some time and there was a strong stench of death; they wore the grey uniforms and distinctive helmets of the enemy, and they'd met violent ends: either their throats had been ripped out or their skulls crushed. It was clearly the work of the boggart. But then, as we left the trees and headed out onto lawn near the house, we saw that what the butcher had said was correct. There had been too many for the boggart to deal with. While it had been slaying intruders on one side of the garden, other soldiers had moved in and set fire to the house.

Only the bare, blackened walls were standing. The Spook's Chipenden house was now just a shell: the roof had collapsed and the inside was gutted – including his precious library.

He stared at it for a long time, saying nothing. I decided to break the silence.

'Where will the boggart be now?' I asked.

The Spook replied without looking at me. 'I made a pact with it. In return for guarding the house and doing the cooking and cleaning, I granted it dominion over the garden: any live creature it found there after dark – apart from apprentices and things bound under our control – it could have, after giving three warning cries. Their blood was its for the taking. But the pact would only endure as long as the house had a roof. So after the fire, the boggart was free to leave. It's gone, lad. Gone for ever.'

We walked slowly around the remains of the house and reached a large mound of grey and black ashes on the lawn. They had taken a load of the books off the library shelves and made a big bonfire of them.

The Spook fell to his knees and began to root around in the cold ashes. Almost everything fell to pieces in his hands. Then he picked up a singed leather cover; the spine of a book that had somehow escaped being totally burned. He held it up and cleaned it with his fingers. Over his shoulder I could just make out the title: *The Damned, the Dizzy and the Desperate*. It was a book that he'd written long ago as a young man – the definitive work on possession. He'd once lent it to me when I was in terrible danger from Mother Malkin. Now all that remained was that cover.

My master's library was gone; words written by generations of spooks – the heritage of countless years battling the dark, a great store of knowledge – now consumed by flames.

I heard him give a sob. I turned away, embarrassed. Was he crying?

Alice sniffed quickly three times, then gripped my left arm. 'Follow me, Tom,' she whispered.

She picked her way over a couple of charred beams and entered the house through the jagged hole that had once been the back door. She found her way into the ruin of the library, now little more than charred wood and ashes. Here she halted and pointed down at the floor. Just visible was the spine of another book. I recognized it immediately. It was the Spook's Bestiary.

Hardly daring to hope, I reached down and picked it up. Would it be like the other book we'd found – just the cover remaining? But to my delight I saw that the pages had survived. I flicked through them. They were charred at the edges but intact and readable. With a smile and a nod of thanks to Alice, I carried the Bestiary back to my master.

'One book has survived,' I said, holding it out to him. 'Alice found it.'

He took it and stared at the cover for a long time, his face devoid of expression. 'Just one book out of all those – the rest burned and gone,' he said at last.

'But your Bestiary is one of the most important books,' I said. 'It's better than nothing!'

'Let's give him some time alone,' Alice whispered, taking my arm gently and leading me away.

I followed her across the grass and in amongst the trees of the western garden. She shook her head wearily. 'Just gets worse and worse,' she said. 'Still, he'll get over it.'

'I hope so, Alice. I do hope so. That library meant a lot to him. Preserving it and adding to it was a major part of his life's work. It was a legacy, to be passed on to future generations of spooks.'

'You'll be the next spook in these parts, Tom. You'll be able to manage without those books. Start writing some of your own – that's what you need to do. Besides, everything ain't lost. We both know where there's another library, and we'll be needing a roof over our heads. Ain't no use going south to Old Gregory's damp, cold Anglezarke house. It'll be behind enemy lines and it's no place to spend the winter anyway – no books there either. Poor Bill Arkwright can't live in the mill any more so we should head north for the canal right away. Those soldier boys won't have got that far.'

'Perhaps you're right, Alice. There's no point in waiting around here. Let's go and suggest exactly that to Mr Gregory. Arkwright's library is much smaller than the Spook's was, but it's a start – something to build on.'

We left the trees and started to cross the lawn again, approaching the Spook from a different direction. He was sitting on the grass looking down at the Bestiary, head in hands and oblivious to our approach. Alice suddenly came to a halt and glanced towards the eastern garden, where the witches were buried. Once again she sniffed loudly three times.

'What is it, Alice?' I asked, noting the concern on her face.

'Something's wrong, Tom. Always been able to sniff Lizzie out when I crossed this part of the lawn before . . .'

Bony Lizzie had trained Alice for two years. She was a powerful, malevolent bone witch who was buried alive in a pit, imprisoned there indefinitely by my master. And she certainly deserved it. She'd murdered children and used their bones in her dark magic rituals.

Leading the way, Alice moved cautiously into the trees of the eastern garden. We passed the graves where the dead witches were buried. Everything seemed all right there, but when we came to the witch pit that confined Lizzie, I got a shock. The bars were bent and it was empty. Bony Lizzie had escaped.

'When did she get out, Alice?' I asked nervously, afraid that the witch might be lurking nearby.

Alice sniffed again. 'Two days ago at least – but don't worry, she's long gone by now. Back home to Pendle, no doubt. Good riddance is what I say.'

We walked back towards the Spook. 'Bony Lizzie's escaped from her pit,' I told him. 'Alice thinks it happened the day after they burned the house.'

'There were other witches here,' Alice added. 'With the boggart gone they were able to enter the garden and release her.'

The Spook gave no sign that he'd heard what we said. He was now clutching the Bestiary to his chest

21

and staring into the ashes morosely. It didn't seem a good time to suggest that we go north to Arkwright's place. It was getting dark now, and it had been a hard journey west, with bad news at the end of it. I just had to hope that my master would be a bit more like his old self in the morning.

Now that they were in no danger from the boggart, I whistled to summon the dogs into the garden. Since our return from Greece, Claw and her fully grown pups, Blood and Bone, had been staying with a retired shepherd who lived beyond the Long Ridge. Unfortunately they'd become too much for him, so we'd collected them and were on our way back to Chipenden when we'd seen the smoke over Caster. The three had been used by their dead master, Bill Arkwright, to capture or kill water witches.

I made a small fire on the lawn while Alice went hunting rabbits. She caught three, and soon they were cooking nicely, making my mouth water. When they were ready, I went across and invited the Spook to join us for the meal by the fire. Once again he didn't so much as acknowledge me. I might as well have been talking to a stone.

Just before we settled down for the night, my eyes were drawn to the west. There was a light up on Beacon Fell. As I watched, it grew steadily brighter.

'They've lit the beacon to summon more troops, Alice,' I said. 'Looks like a big battle's about to begin.'

Right across the County from north to south, a chain of fires, like a flame leaping from hill to hill, would be summoning the last of the reserves.

Although Alice and I lay close to the embers of the fire, there was a chill in the air and I found it difficult to get to sleep, especially as Claw kept lying across my feet. At last I dozed, only to wake suddenly just as dawn was breaking. There were loud noises – rumbling booms and crashes. Was it thunder? I wondered, still befuddled with sleep.

'Listen to those big guns, Tom!' Alice cried. 'Don't sound too far away, do they?'

The battle had begun somewhere to the south.

23

Defeat would mean the County being overrun by the enemy. We needed to head north quickly while we still could. Together we went over to confront the Spook. He was still sitting in the same position, head down, clutching the book.

'Mr Gregory,' I began, 'Bill Arkwright's mill has a small library. It's a start. Something we can build on. Why don't we head north and live there for now? It'll be safer too. Even if the enemy win, they may not venture any further north than Caster . . .'

They might send out foraging patrols, but they would probably just occupy Caster, which was the most northerly large town in the County. They might not even spot the mill, which was hidden from the canal by trees.

The Spook still didn't raise his head.

'If we wait any longer, we might not be able to get through. We can't just stay here.'

Once again, my master didn't reply. I heard Alice grind her teeth in anger.

'Please, Mr Gregory,' I begged. 'Don't give up . . .'

He finally looked up at me and shook his head sadly. 'I don't think you fully understand what's been lost here. This library didn't belong to me, lad. I was just its guardian. It was my task to extend and preserve it for the future. Now I've failed. I'm weary – weary of it all,' he replied. 'My old bones are too tired to go on. I've seen too much, lived too long.'

'Listen, Old Gregory,' Alice snarled. 'Get on your feet! Ain't no use just sitting there till you rot!'

The Spook jumped up, his eyes flashing with anger. 'Old Gregory' was the name Alice called him in private. She'd never before dared to use it to his face. He was gripping the Bestiary in his right hand, his staff in his left – which he lifted as if about to bring it down upon her head.

However, without even flinching, Alice carried on with her tirade. 'There are things still left to do: the dark to fight; replacement books to write. You ain't dead yet, and while you can move those old bones of yours it's your duty to carry on. It's your duty to keep Tom safe and train him. It's your duty to the County!'

Slowly he lowered his staff. The last sentence Alice uttered had changed the expression in his eyes. 'Duty above all' was what he believed in. His duty to the County had guided and shaped his path through a long, arduous and dangerous life.

Without another word he put the charred Bestiary in his bag and set off, heading north. Alice and I followed with the dogs as best we could. It looked like he'd decided to head for the mill after all.

CHAPTER 3
THE 'OLD MAN'

We never reached the mill. Perhaps it simply wasn't meant to be. The journey over the fells went without a hitch, but as we approached Caster, we saw that the houses to the south were burning, the dark smoke obscuring the setting sun. Even if the main invading force had been victorious, they couldn't have got this far north yet: it was probably a raiding party from the sea.

Normally we'd have rested on the lower slopes, but we felt a sense of urgency and pressed on through the darkness, passing even further to the east of Caster than usual. As soon as we reached the canal it became clear that it would be impossible to travel further north to the mill. Both towpaths were thronged with refugees heading south.

It was some time before we could persuade anybody to tell us what had happened: they kept on pushing past, eyes filled with fear. At last we found an old man leaning against a gate, trying to get his breath back, his knees trembling with exertion.

'How bad is it further north?' the Spook asked, his voice at its most kindly.

The man shook his head, and it was some time before he was sufficiently recovered to answer. 'A large force of soldiers landed north-east of the bay,' he gasped. 'They took us all by surprise. Kendal village is theirs already – what's left of it after the burning – and now they're moving this way. It's over. My home's gone. Lived there all my life, I have. I'm too old to start again . . .'

'Wars don't last for ever,' the Spook said, patting him on the shoulder. 'I've lost my house too. But we have to go on. We'll both go home one day and rebuild.'

The old man nodded and shuffled across to join the line of refugees. He didn't seem convinced by the Spook's words, and judging by his own expression, my master didn't believe them either. He turned to me, his face grim and haggard.

'As I see it, my first duty is to keep you safe, lad. But nowhere in the County is secure any longer,' he said. 'For now, we can do nothing here. We'll come back one day but we're off to sea again.'

'Where are we going – Sunderland Point?' I asked, assuming we were going to try and reach the County port and get passage on a ship.

'If it isn't already in enemy hands, it'll be full with refugees,' the Spook said with a shake of his head. 'No, I'm going to collect what's owed me.'

That said, he led us quickly westwards.

Only very rarely did the Spook get paid promptly, and sometimes not at all. So he called in a debt. Years earlier he'd driven a sea-wraith from a fisher-man's cottage. Now, rather than coin, the payment he demanded was a bed for the night followed by a safe passage to Mona, the large island that lay out in the Irish Sea, north-west of the County.

Reluctantly the fisherman agreed to take us. He didn't want to do it but he was scared of the man with the fierce glittering eyes who confronted him – who now seemed filled with new determination.

I thought I'd gained my sea legs on the voyage to Greece in the summer. How wrong I was. A small fishing boat was a very different proposition to the three-masted *Celeste*. Even before we were clear of the bay and out in the open sea, it started pitching and rolling alarmingly, and the dogs were soon whining nervously. Instead of watching the County recede into the distance, I spent the larger part of the voyage with my head over the side of the boat being violently sick.

'Feeling better, lad?' asked the Spook when I finally stopped vomiting.

'A bit,' I answered, looking towards Mona, which

was now a smudge of green on the horizon. 'Have you ever visited the island before?'

My master shook his head. 'Never had any call to. I've had more than enough work to keep me busy in the County. But the islanders have their fair share of troubles with the dark. There are at least half a dozen bugganes there . . .'

'What's a buggane?' I asked. I vaguely remembered seeing the word in the Spook's Bestiary but I couldn't remember anything about them. I knew we didn't have them in the County now.

'Well, lad, why don't you look it up and find out?' said the Spook, pulling the Bestiary from his bag and handing it to me. 'It's a type of daemon . . .'

I opened the Bestiary, flicked through to the section on daemons and quickly found the heading: BUGGANES.

'Read it aloud, Tom!' Alice insisted. 'I'd like to know what's what too.'

My master frowned at her, probably thinking it was spook's business and nothing to do with her. But I began to read aloud as she'd asked:

'The buggane is a category of daemon that frequents ruins and usually materializes as a black bull or a hairy man, although other forms are chosen if they suit its purpose. In marshy ground bugganes have been known to shape-shift into wormes.

'The buggane makes two distinctive sounds – either bellowing like an enraged bull to warn off those who venture near its domain or whispering to its victims in a sinister human voice. It tells the afflicted that it is sapping their life force, and their terror lends the daemon even greater strength. Covering one's ears is no protection – the voice of the buggane is heard right inside the head. Even the profoundly deaf have been known to fall victim to that insidious sound. Those who hear the whisper die within days unless they kill the buggane first. It stores the life force of each person it slays in a labyrinth, which it constructs far underground.

'Bugganes are immune to salt and iron, which makes them hard both to kill and to confine. The only *thing they are vulnerable to is a blade made from silver alloy, which must be driven into the heart of the buggane when it has fully materialized.'*

'Sounds really scary,' said Alice.

'Aye, there's good reason to be both afraid and wary where a buggane is concerned,' said the Spook. 'It's said they have no spooks on Mona, but from what I've heard they could certainly do with some. That's why bugganes flourish there – there's nobody to keep them in check.'

It suddenly began to drizzle and my master quickly seized the Bestiary from me, closed it and put it in his bag, out of harm's way. It was his last book and he didn't want it damaged any further.

'What are the islanders like?' I asked.

'They're a proud, stubborn people. They're warlike too, with a strong force of paid conscripts called "yeomen". But a small island like that would have no chance if the enemy looked beyond the County and chose to invade.'

33

'The islanders ain't going to welcome us, are they?' Alice said.

The Spook nodded thoughtfully. 'You could be right, girl. Refugees are rarely welcome anywhere. It just means extra mouths to feed. And a lot of folks will have fled the County and headed for Mona. There's Ireland further to the west, but it's a much longer journey and I'd prefer to stay as close to home as possible. If things are difficult, we could always head west later.'

As we approached the island, the waves became less choppy, but the drizzle was heavier now, and blowing straight into our faces. The weather and the green rolling hills ahead reminded me of the County. It was almost like coming home.

The fisherman put us ashore on the south-east of the island, tying his boat briefly to a wooden jetty that jutted out over a rocky shore. The three dogs leaped off the boat in turn, happy to be back on dry land, but we followed more slowly, our joints stiff after being confined in the boat for so long. It was just minutes before the fisherman put out to sea again. Silent and grim on the voyage across, now he was almost smiling. His debt to the Spook was paid and he was glad to see the back of us.

At the end of the jetty we saw four local fishermen sitting under a wooden shelter mending their nets; they watched us draw near with narrowed hostile eyes. My master was in the lead, his hood up against the rain, and he nodded in their direction. He got just one response: three of the men kept their eyes averted and continued with their work; the fourth spat onto the shingle.

'Right, wasn't I? We ain't welcome here, Tom,' Alice said. 'Should have sailed further west to Ireland!'

'Well, we're here now, Alice, and we'll just have to make the best of it,' I told her.

We advanced up the beach until we came to a narrow muddy path, which ran uphill between a dozen small thatched cottages, then disappeared into a wood. As we passed the last doorway, a man came down out of the trees and barred our path. He was carrying a stout wooden cudgel. Claw bounded forward and growled at the stranger threateningly, her black fur bristling.

'Call the dog back, lad. I'll deal with this!' the Spook shouted over his shoulder.

'Claw! Here – good girl!' I called, and reluctantly she came back to my side. I knew that even by herself, she was well able to deal with a man carrying only a club for a weapon.

The stranger had a tanned weather-beaten face and, despite the chilly damp, had his sleeves rolled up above his elbows. He was thick-set and muscular, with an edge of authority about him, and I didn't think he was a fisherman. And then I saw that he was actually wearing a military uniform: a tight brown leather jerkin with a symbol on the shoulder – three running legs in a circle; legs that wore armour. Under it was a Latin inscription: QUOCUNQUE JECERIS SABIT. I suspected that he was one of the island's yeomen.

'You're not welcome here!' he told the Spook with a hostile glare, raising his club threateningly. 'You should have stayed in your own land. We've enough mouths of our own to feed!'

'We'd little choice but to leave it,' said the Spook mildly. 'Enemy soldiers burned my house and we were in peril of our lives. All we ask is to stay here for a short while until it's safe to return. We come prepared to work and earn our keep as best we can.'

The man lowered his club and nodded. 'You'll work all right, if you're given the chance – just as hard as all the others. So far, most seeking refuge from the County have been coming ashore at Douglas, to the north. But we knew some would try to sneak in like you lot, so we've been keeping watch,' he said, looking first at the Spook and then at me. I saw him note our distinctive hooded cloaks, then our staffs and bags. Even those on Mona would recognize the garb and accessories of our trade.

Next he studied Alice, looking down at her pointy shoes, and I saw his eyes widen. He quickly crossed himself. 'What's a spook doing in the company of a witch?' he demanded.

'The girl's no witch,' the Spook replied calmly. 'She's been working for me copying books. And this is my apprentice, Tom Ward.'

'Well, he won't be your apprentice while he's here with us, old man. We've no call for those of your trade and have our own ways of dealing with witches. Once sorted, those chosen will all work on the land. It's food we need, not your hocus-pocus.'

'*Sorted*?' asked the Spook. 'Explain what you mean by that!'

'We didn't ask you to come here,' growled the yeoman, lifting his club again. 'The lad's young and strong, and will certainly be put to work. But some go back into the sea – and we might have different remedies for others . . .' His gaze fell on Alice.

I didn't like the sound of that, so I stepped forward to stand beside my master.

'What do you mean by "back into the sea"?' I demanded.

The Spook rested his hand on my shoulder. 'Take it easy, lad. I think we both know what he means.'

'Aye – those who can't work are food for the fishes. Old men like you. And as for witches,' the yeoman said, scowling at Alice, 'you're not the first to have tried to sneak ashore this past week. You'll all get what's coming to you. We have our own way of dealing with your kind!'

'I think we've heard enough,' said the Spook, rain dripping off the end of his nose. He lifted his staff and held it across his body in the defensive position. The man gave a mirthless grin and stepped forward aggressively.

Everything happened very fast then. The stranger swung his club at my master's head, but it didn't make contact. The 'old man' was no longer there. The Spook stepped to one side and delivered two rapid blows. The first cracked his assailant on the wrist to send the club spinning from his hand and a cry of pain bursting from his lips. The second thwacked him hard on the side of the head to drop him unconscious at our feet.

'Not exactly the best of starts, lad!' said my master, shaking his head.

I looked back. The four fishermen had come out of their shelter and were staring at us. The Spook followed my gaze, then pointed up the hill. 'Best we put some distance between ourselves and the shore,' he said immediately, striding out at a furious pace that had Alice and me struggling to keep up.

CHAPTER 4
RATS WITH WINGS

We climbed up through the trees, the Spook some distance ahead.

For the next half-hour or so my master did his best to take a route that would throw any trackers, even hounds, off our trail. We walked up to our knees in two different streams, once leaving by a different bank, the next time by the same. When he was finally satisfied, the Spook led us northwards at a slower pace.

'We'd have been better off taking our chances in the County,' Alice remarked. 'Don't care how many streams we cross, they'll hunt us down now for sure. Soon find us on an island this size.'

'I don't think Mona's that small, Alice. There'll be

plenty of places to hide,' I told her. I hoped I was right.

The Spook had reached the summit of a hill and was staring off into the distance.

'Think they'll make a serious effort to find us?' I asked him, catching up at last.

'Could do, lad. I reckon our friend back there will wake up with a bit of a headache – he certainly won't come after us alone. Those fishermen didn't chase after us, so he'll need to find himself some proper help and that'll take time. Did you see that symbol and sign on his shoulder?'

'Three armoured legs in a circle,' I replied.

'And the Latin underneath means ...?' my master asked.

'Wherever you throw me I'll stand?'

'Aye, that's near enough – it suggests self-reliance, lad. They're a tough, resilient people, and we've clearly come to the wrong place. That said, I reckon we've shaken 'em off our trail now. Besides,' he continued, pointing down the hill, 'they've got more than just us to worry about!'

Far below I could see a large town and a harbour full

of boats of all sizes. Beyond that lay a wide half-moon bay with a scattering of larger vessels, some of them a good distance from the land. Smaller boats were ferrying people to the shore. A huge flock of seagulls circled over the harbour, making a racket that we could hear up on the hill.

'That's Douglas, the largest town on the island. More people seeking refuge like ourselves,' said the Spook. 'Some of those ships will be sailing away again soon, but most probably not back to the County. I might just have enough money to get us a passage further west to Ireland. We should receive a warmer welcome there. It certainly couldn't be any worse.'

'But will they let us leave?' I asked.

'Best if we go without 'em noticing, lad. We'll wait until nightfall, then you go down into the town. Most sailors like a drink or two – you'll find them in the waterfront taverns. With a bit of luck you'll be able to hire someone with a small boat.'

'I'll go with Tom,' Alice said quickly, 'and keep my eyes peeled for danger—'

43

'No, girl, you stay with me and the dogs. The lad will be better off alone this time . . .'

'Why can't Alice come with me? Two pairs of eyes are better than one,' I suggested.

The Spook glared at us in turn. 'Are you two bound by an invisible chain?' he asked, shaking his head. 'You've hardly been apart lately. No, I've made up my mind. The girl stays here!'

Alice glanced at me and I saw fear flicker in her eyes as she thought of the blood jar, the only thing keeping the Fiend at bay. Inside that jar were six drops of blood: three of hers and three of mine. Alice was safe too – as long as she stayed close to me. But if I went down into the town alone, there was nothing to stop the Fiend taking his revenge upon her. So I knew that, although she didn't argue now, she'd disobey the Spook and follow me.

I set off down the hill soon after dark, leaving my cloak, bag and staff behind. It seemed that the islanders didn't welcome spooks – or their apprentices. By now they could be searching for us in the town. The clouds had blown away and it was a clear starry night with a pale half-moon high in the sky. Once I'd walked a hundred yards or so I stopped and waited. It wasn't long before Alice was by my side.

'Did Mr Gregory try to stop you?' I asked.

Alice shook her head. 'Told him I was off hunting for rabbits, but he shook his head and glanced down at my feet so I know he didn't believe me.'

I saw that her feet were bare.

'I sneaked my shoes into your bag, Tom. Less chance of anyone thinking I'm a witch that way.'

We set off down the hill and soon emerged from the trees onto a grassy slope made slippery by the recent rain. Alice wasn't used to going barefoot and slipped onto her bottom twice before we reached the first of the cottages and found a gritted track.

Ten minutes later we were in the town, making our way through the narrow cobbled streets towards the harbour. Douglas thronged with sailors, but there were a few women about too, some of them barefoot like

Alice – so apart from being the prettiest by far, she didn't stand out in any way.

There were almost as many seagulls as people and they seemed aggressive and fearless, swooping down towards people's heads. I saw one snatch a slice of bread from a man's hand just as he was about to take a bite.

'Horrible birds, those,' said Alice. 'Rats with wings, they are.'

After a while we came to a broad, busy thoroughfare in which every fifth house seemed to be an inn. I glanced through the window of the first tavern. It looked full, but I didn't realize how full until I opened the door. Warm air and a strong odour of ale wafted over me; the loud, boisterous crowd of drinkers inside were standing shoulder to shoulder. I saw that I would have to push my way in forcefully, so I turned, shook my head at Alice and led the way further down the street.

All the other inns we passed looked equally busy, but then I glanced down a side street that sloped away towards the harbour and saw what looked like another tavern. When I opened the door, it was almost deserted, with just a few men sitting on stools at the bar. I was about to step inside when the proprietor shook his fist at me and Alice.

'Be off with you! We don't allow riff-raff in here!' he shouted.

I didn't need telling twice – the last thing I wanted was to draw attention to myself. I was just about to head back towards the main thoroughfare when Alice pointed in the opposite direction.

'Try there, Tom. Looks like another tavern further down . . .'

She was soon proved right. It was right at the end of the narrow street, on the corner, the main door facing towards the harbour. Like the last tavern, it was almost empty, with just a few people standing at the bar clutching tankards of ale. The proprietor looked across at me with interest rather than hostility, and that curiosity quickly decided me – it was better to get out. But just as I turned to go, a voice called my name.

'Well, if it isn't Tom Ward!' And a large red-faced man with side whiskers strode towards me.

It was Captain Baines of the *Celeste*, the ship that Mam had chartered for our voyage to Greece the previous summer. He operated out of Sunderland Point. No doubt he'd sailed here with a hold full of those fleeing the invaders.

'It's good to see you, lad. The girl too!' he said, looking at Alice, who was standing in the open doorway. 'Come across and warm yourselves by the fire.'

The captain wore a long, dark, waterproof coat with a thick grey woollen jumper underneath: sailors certainly knew how to dress for cold weather. He led the way back to a bare wooden table in the corner, and we sat down on stools facing him.

'Are you hungry?' he asked.

I nodded. I was starving. Apart from a few mouthfuls of cheese, the last thing we'd eaten had been the rabbits that Alice had cooked the previous night.

'Landlord, bring us two steak and ale pies and make them piping hot!' he called out towards the bar, then turned back to face us. 'Who brought you across the water?' he asked, lowering his voice.

'We came in a small fishing boat. We were dropped south of Douglas but ran into trouble right away. We were lucky to escape. A man with a club tried to arrest us but Mr Gregory knocked him out.'

'Where's your master now?'

'He's up on the hillside south of the town. He sent me down to see if I could hire a boat to take us further west to Ireland.'

'You've little chance of that, young Tom. My own ship, the *Celeste*, is impounded and has armed guards on board. As for the people I brought here, they're all in custody. Same with the refugees from the other ships. You can't really blame the islanders though. The last thing they want is for the invaders to come here. They're scared of witches fleeing the County too – and with good reason. A small fishing boat came ashore to the north. Both crew members were dead – they'd been drained of blood and their thumb-bones cut away.'

At that Alice gave a little gasp. I knew what she was

thinking. The Pendle witches would no doubt stay put and wait to see what happened. But this could well be the work of another witch – some would have fled the County – and what if it was Alice's mother?

What if Bony Lizzie was at large on the island?

CHAPTER 5
THE ABHUMAN

We both tucked into our hot steak and ale pies while the captain told us what he knew. It seemed that almost all the refugees were being returned to the County. The leaders of the island's Ruling Council were afraid that if they weren't, Mona would be the next place to come under attack.

'That's why the *Celeste* is impounded. Soon I'll be sailing back to Sunderland Point, returning those who fled to the tender mercies of the enemy. There'll still be armed guards on board to make sure that I do just that. The only ones who'll stay here are the witches they find – not that I was carrying any. Mind you, some who aren't really witches will be tested and found guilty. No doubt innocents will suffer . . .'

He was referring to what the Spook called the 'falsely accused'. He was right: no doubt at least one real witch had reached Mona, but many other innocent women would be forced to pay a terrible price for what she'd done.

'My advice would be to head inland, then towards the south-western coast. There's a fishing town, Port Erin, and lots of small villages further south on that peninsula. Refugees aren't likely to put ashore there, so there'll be fewer people watching out for them. You might get yourselves a passage to Ireland from there . . .'

'Sounds like good advice to me, Tom,' Alice said with a smile.

I smiled back, but then the expression on her face changed to one of fear and horror. She was staring at the door, as if sensing danger.

Suddenly it burst open and half a dozen large men brandishing clubs surged in. They wore leather jerkins with the three-legged insignia – yeomen. A tall man with a dark moustache and carrying a sword at his hip – clearly their leader – followed them inside. They all halted near the door, their eyes sweeping the room, looking at the occupants of each table as well as those standing at the bar. It was then that I noticed they had a prisoner.

He also wore a leather jerkin with the badge. It accentuated his bulk; he was tall and very thick-set. Why would they hold one of their own captive? I wondered. What had he done wrong? Then I saw that the man was bound, but in a strange, cruel way. A length of fine silver chain ran from each ear to the hands of the two guards who flanked him. His ears had been pierced very close to his head and the holes through which the chains passed were red and inflamed.

The prisoner sniffed loudly three times and spoke, his voice as harsh as a file rasping against metal. 'I smell woman! There's a woman here, Commander Stanton,' he said, turning towards the tall man with the moustache.

The guards all stared at Alice. She was the only female in the room.

The prisoner started to approach our table, the two flanking guards keeping pace, with Stanton further to one side. As he did so, I noticed two things simultaneously: the first was that he was blind, his eyeballs milky-white; the second sent a tremor of fear down my spine and I felt the hairs on the back of my neck rise.

He had dark, curly, matted hair – more like the hide of an animal than human hair. Through it, very high on his forehead, protruded two very short curved horns. They were white, and each came to a sharp point. This wasn't a man; it was an abhuman, the result of a union between the Fiend and a witch.

'This is no woman!' laughed Stanton. 'It's just a scrawny girl with dirty feet. Try again!'

This time the abhuman didn't sniff; he just peered at Alice as though his blind eyes could actually see her. A puzzled expression creased his face.

'Well, come on,' the commander demanded in an impatient voice. 'Is the girl a witch or not?'

'She has darkness inside her!' cried the abhuman. 'Dark power!'

'Well, that's all we need to know! Seize her, lads!' he cried, and two men stepped forward and dragged Alice off her stool. She didn't try to struggle – her eyes were wide and filled with fear.

I knew just one thing – wherever they took Alice, I had to go too. If she was separated from the blood jar, the Fiend would take his revenge on her. However, as it turned out, I didn't need to do anything.

'Check the other two!' Stanton commanded. 'They were talking to a witch. Could be they're in league together. Maybe one of them's a warlock . . .'

The abhuman looked at Captain Baines next. 'No darkness here,' he growled.

'What about the boy, then?'

Now it was my turn, but after studying me with his blind eyes, the creature looked even more puzzled. His mouth opened twice to reveal two rows of sharp yellow teeth, but no words came out.

'We haven't got all day. What's the problem?'

55

'A sliver of darkness is buried deep within his soul. A very small piece . . .'

'It's enough! Bring him along!' snapped Stanton. 'It's a long time since we tested a male witch. They're very rare.'

I just had time to glance back at Captain Baines's anxious face before I was seized too, and moments later my hands were tied behind my back and I was outside the tavern with Alice, being dragged by rough hands up the hill towards the main thoroughfare.

After a forced march through the busy streets, during which we were jostled, jeered and spat on, we arrived at last at the outskirts of the town and were pushed aboard a dray-cart pulled by four sturdy shire horses. The driver cracked his whip and we set off along a track; having glanced up at the stars and noted the position of the Plough constellation, I judged it was taking us roughly north-west. Alice and I weren't alone in the cart. We were guarded by three thick-set men with clubs who looked more than willing to use them. Our hands were still tied and there wasn't the slightest chance of escape.

The men didn't speak at first and seemed content to stare at us. We both lowered our eyes, not wanting to give them any excuse for violence, and kept quiet, but after a little less than an hour, I judged, one of them nudged me with his club.

'See that, boy?' he said, pointing to his right.

In the distance, lit by the moon, was some sort of fortification. I could see a tower surrounded by castellated walls, with a mountain beyond it.

'That's Greeba Keep,' he continued. 'You might just live to see it again!'

The other yeomen laughed. 'But once in there you'll wish you'd died! It's the lucky ones who are pulled out dead!' said one.

I didn't bother to ask him what he meant and remained silent until the cart finally came to a halt. We seemed to have reached a village. It was surrounded by trees, and hills rose up on either side. We were pulled down from the cart and taken past a large, curious mound of earth. It was shaped like a barrow but had four tiers. I'd never seen anything quite like it. Beyond stood another stone tower – this one much smaller than the first. I wondered if it was for holding prisoners, and was soon proved correct.

We were dragged up some steps to a door about halfway up the tower, and after our hands had been untied we were thrust inside. The door clanged behind us, a key turned in the lock and the guards went back down the stairs, their footsteps echoing off the stones.

I looked about me. A single candle stood in a recess in the wall, flickering in the draught from a narrow window far above. The cell was circular, with no furniture and only dirty straw covering the damp flags of the floor.

'Don't like this place much,' said Alice, her voice hardly more than a whisper.

'You may not like it, girl,' said a voice from the shadows to our right, 'but you'd better make the best of it. It's the most comfortable you'll ever be again. This is the Tynwald witch tower – after you leave here, there's only pain and death to look forward to.'

Someone stepped out of the shadows to confront us. It was a tall girl of about eighteen or nineteen with dark glossy hair which reached down to her shoulders. She wore a pretty blue dress and her skin was clean and shining with health. She didn't look much like a prisoner.

'Came across the water from the County, did you?' she asked.

I nodded. 'My name's Tom Ward and this is my friend, Alice.'

She glanced at Alice then gave me a warm smile. 'My name's Adriana Lonan,' she said. 'I was born and bred on Mona and they've left me alone until now. But everything's gone crazy and they're testing even their own folk to see if they're witches.'

'Are you a witch?' I asked.

Adriana nodded. 'I'm a bird witch,' she said.

'You mean you have a bird for a familiar,' Alice corrected her.

The girl tossed her hair and frowned. 'I don't have a familiar. Don't give my blood to anything. Not dark

59

stuff like that. I'm a bird witch. Birds are my friends. We help each other. What about you, Alice? Are you a witch?'

Alice shook her head. 'I come from a clan of Pendle witches and I was taught the dark craft for two years. But no, I'm not a witch. Ain't right that we've been brought here, especially Tom. He's a spook's apprentice and fights for the light. They say he's a warlock, but that ain't true.'

Adriana stared at me, her face very serious. 'Did Horn sniff you out?'

'The abhuman? Yes,' I told her. 'He said Alice had darkness inside her and that I had a sliver of dark too.'

'Then maybe you do,' Adriana murmured. 'None of us are perfect. But whatever we are won't count for much when we're tested tomorrow.'

'What'll they do?' asked Alice. 'Will they swim us? Ain't going to use the press, are they?'

Swimming was the most popular way of testing to see if someone was a witch or not. Your hands were tied to your feet and you were thrown into a pond.

Sometimes your right thumb was bound to your left big toe, left thumb to right toe. It was a funny name for the test – how could you swim like that? If you sank and probably drowned, you were innocent. If you somehow managed to float, then you were considered guilty, taken away and burned at a stake.

Pressing was even worse. You were chained to a table, and over a period of time heavy stones were placed on your body, often as many as thirteen. After a while you could hardly breathe. If you confessed because of the pain, they burned you. If you didn't, you were slowly crushed to death. And if you managed to stay alive for more than an hour it was assumed that the Fiend had saved you and you were burned anyway.

'No, we islanders have our own way of doing things,' Adriana replied. 'Someone suspected of witchcraft is taken to the summit of Slieau Whallian, a large hill to the south, and sealed inside a barrel – one with sharp iron spikes inside. Then she's rolled down the hill. If she's still alive at the bottom, they think she's been protected by the dark and she's taken away and . . .' Her voice faded away before she'd finished the sentence and I saw that her eyes were filled with fear.

'Do many survive?' I asked.

'The guard told me that two survived – and one of them was badly spiked – out of the seven who were rolled yesterday. I tried to tell them what to do. There is a way to get to the bottom without being cut too badly. Not all the barrels are the same so you'd need a bit of luck, but if you can find space between the spikes, you can use your arms and legs to brace yourself against the inside. As the barrel spins, centrifugal force presses you into the spikes so you have to hold yourself clear. Then, providing the barrel doesn't hit a big bump on the way down, you don't bounce around inside and get jolted onto the spikes.'

'How do you know it works?'

'I know a man at the brewery who makes some of the special barrels to order. When a new apprentice cooper starts, they have a ritual. They put him in a spiked barrel and roll him slowly from one side of the work-shop to the other while all the other craftsmen bang their hammers on the bench tops and cheer. But first he's shown how to wedge himself in. At the worst he might suffer a few cuts, that's all. But I've never managed to talk to anyone who's survived to the bottom of Slieau Whallian. If they're still alive, they're taken away immediately.'

'Big difference between being rolled slowly and bounced about,' said Alice. 'If you told them what to do, why didn't more survive yesterday?'

'Some were probably too scared and upset to listen to what I told them,' Adriana explained. 'Maybe they *wanted* to die in the barrel . . .'

'Why would they want that?' I asked.

'Because of what happens to you if you *do* survive. That's even worse than being rolled. They feed you to the buggane . . .'

CHAPTER
6
ANOTHER DEAD ONE!

'There are several bugganes on Mona,' Adriana continued, 'but they feed you to the most dangerous one of all. It haunts the ruined chapel near Greeba Keep.'

'And it eats you?' asked Alice, her eyes wide with fear.

Adriana nodded. 'They lock the victims in the dungeons in the south wing of the keep, which is right on the edge of the buggane's domain. It slowly draws the spirit from each body and stores it somewhere under the chapel. After that the body still walks and breathes, but it's empty. That's until the buggane, walking on two legs, looking like a big hairy man, comes to

64

drink its blood and eat its flesh. It even eats some of the bones, crunching them with its big teeth – that's why we call it the *Cruncher*. Afterwards what's left is buried in a lime-pit in the yard.'

We fell silent, thinking of the grim fate that awaited us, but then something began to puzzle me. Adriana had said she'd tried to tell the other prisoners how to survive being rolled in the spiked barrel – but why hadn't she been rolled too?

'Adriana, why didn't they test you yesterday with the others?'

'Because Lord Barrule – he's the lord of Greeba Keep, and head of the Ruling Council of the island – gave me one last chance to change my mind: if I do as he asks, he'll save me. Otherwise he'll let me be tested . . .' Adriana's bottom lip began to quiver and tears sprang to her eyes.

'Change your mind about what?' I asked.

'I want to marry Simon Sulby, a cooper – the one who told me about the barrels – but Lord Barrule wants me for his wife. He's lived alone for ten years since his first

65

JOSEPH DELANEY

wife died. He's never looked at another woman but it seems that I look very like his dead wife – the spitting image, he says. That's why he wants me. He's very powerful, and he's used to getting his way. I refused and kept refusing – until finally he lost his temper and denounced me as a witch.

'He could still save me if he really wanted – he's a powerful man. One word from him and they'd let me go. But he's very proud, and can't bear being denied anything. He'd rather I was dead than belonged to another. Soon it'll be too late. They started off doing the testing in the evening, but it attracted large crowds and they became unruly. They'll roll us down the hill when it's quiet, just before dawn.'

Following those words, neither Alice nor I spoke for a long time. Things looked really bleak.

I wondered what the Spook would be doing now. He'd be worried about me and wondering why I hadn't returned. No doubt he'd have realized that Alice had followed me. I just hoped he wouldn't venture down into the town. He was sure to be captured.

* * *

The long silence was suddenly ended by the harsh metallic grate of a key turning in the lock. Had they come for us already? I wondered. It was still several hours until dawn.

The cell door opened slowly and just one figure stepped inside. It wasn't a yeoman or a guard. It was Horn, the abhuman. The chains were gone from his ears and he was stripped to the waist, wearing only a pair of breeches and heavy boots. His chest was matted with dark hair, and muscles bunched on his broad shoulders and long arms. He looked strong and dangerous; capable of killing with his bare hands.

As he lumbered into the room, we stood up and, retreated until our backs were against the wall furthest from the door. What did he want? I didn't like the expression on his face. Even without the horns, it would have been a face with more than a hint of the beast.

He advanced directly towards Alice. When I tried to get between them to protect her, he took a swing at my shoulder. It was like being struck with a table leg and I was knocked clean off my feet. I fell, but scrambled back up as quickly as I could and moved towards Alice again. The abhuman twisted round to face me, his feral eyes gleaming dangerously; he lowered his head so that his horns were pointing at me. I continued to approach him more warily, but Alice held out her hand to ward me away.

'No, Tom! Stay back!' she cried. 'He'll kill you. Let me deal with him.'

I obeyed, but readied myself to attack the creature at the first sign of danger to Alice – though without my staff and chain there was very little I could do. I had the gift of being able to slow time, inherited from my mam, but it was extremely difficult to use and I decided to attempt it only if Alice seemed in real danger.

The abhuman turned back towards her. Less than the length of his arms separated them.

'Sister?' he said, his voice a low rumble.

'I ain't your sister!' Alice said, shaking her head angrily.

The abhuman put his head on one side and sniffed three times. 'We have the same father. You must be my half-sister. Do not deny it. I wasn't sure back in the town but I am now. There's no doubt about it.'

It was true. Both had different human mothers but the Fiend was father to them both.

Alice suddenly gave him a little smile. 'Well, if we be brother and sister, you'll want to help me, won't you? Won't want me to die, will you? Big and strong, you are. Can't you get us out of here?'

'I can't do that. Commander Stanton would punish me. He'd have me whipped.'

'We could run away, escape together,' Alice suggested.

'I can't leave my master, Lord Barrule. He's been good to me.'

'Good to you?' I asked. 'What about having you dragged through the town with chains strung from your ears? That's not good.'

The abhuman growled in displeasure. 'Commander Stanton does that because he's afraid of me, but Lord

Barrule never hurts me. No, not him. He could have had me killed, but instead he allowed me to serve him. He's a good master.'

'So what's your business?' demanded Alice. 'You must want something or you wouldn't be here.'

'Just wanted to see you, that's all,' he replied. 'I just wanted to see my little sister.'

With those words he turned and began to head back towards the door.

'Hope it makes you happy seeing me, 'cause I'll be dead soon,' Alice shouted. 'Fine brother you are. Brothers and sisters should stick together!'

But he closed the door behind him and we heard the key turning in the lock once more.

'Well, it was worth a try,' said Alice. 'Wonder how many abhumans there are . . . Wonder if all the rest are like him and Tusk . . .'

Tusk was the son of Old Mother Malkin, an abhuman with big teeth – too many to fit into his mouth, hence his name. The Spook had killed him with his staff, stabbing him through the forehead.

Just how many abhumans had the Fiend fathered? That was an interesting question. Tusk was evil. He'd helped Mother Malkin kill mothers and their babies – that was how the witch had got her name. She'd run a home for destitute mothers. But lots of them had gone missing, and when the locals had finally summoned the courage to investigate, they'd found a field full of bones. Most of the women had been crushed to death, their ribs cracked and broken – that had been the work of Tusk. Abhumans were incredibly strong and Horn looked very dangerous.

'No use denying it,' Alice went on. 'I shared the same father as Tusk too, but I never considered him my half-brother for a moment.'

'Horn doesn't seem anywhere near as bad as Tusk. I think he's had a hard time,' I said.

'That's certainly true,' said Adriana. 'Stanton is cruel to him, but I don't understand why he remains so loyal to Lord Barrule. Can't he see that his master permits Stanton to do that? Some people say Horn's loyal because Barrule lets him be the buggane's keeper.'

'His keeper?' I asked.

'Horn works with the buggane, they say. He helps it choose its victims . . .'

The night passed quickly, and long before dawn there were three other prisoners sharing the cell with us: two were refugees from the County, young girls still in their teens; the other was an older local woman.

Adriana wasted no time in explaining how you could wedge yourself in the barrel. The two girls from the County listened to her with interest but the local woman just started to cry. She'd heard too many tales about what she faced. The idea of being fed to the buggane terrified her so much that she almost preferred the prospect of being spiked.

Just before dawn the guards – a couple of dozen of them – came for us and dragged us back down the tower steps and across the village, heading south. Adriana accompanied us – evidently Barrule had run out of patience with her. Then they forced us up a big hill, which must have been Slieau Whallian.

It was a long steep climb. Were they going to roll us down this? If so, we surely had little chance of survival.

To the east the sky was beginning to redden while, low on the horizon, a single bright star was visible. There was no wind and the air was chilly, and we stood there shivering next to a row of big barrels. A line of torches on poles went down the hill, marking the course that the barrels would take, but they weren't needed – there was already plenty of light to see by. Most of the guards waited with us at the summit. At the bottom, at the edge of a big wood, we could see only six men; one had a sword at his belt, and I guessed it was probably Stanton, the commander of the yeomen who'd arrested us.

'She's first!' cried one of the guards, pointing at the older woman; as they seized her, she began to sob hysterically, her whole body shaking and trembling.

'Cowards!' Adriana exclaimed angrily, shaking her fist at the men. 'How can you do that to a woman – and one of our own islanders too?'

'Keep your mouth shut or we'll gag you!' the largest of the yeomen shouted back. Another seized her by the shoulder, but she shook him off.

The barrel was now in position, ready to be rolled; when they lifted off the lid I saw the sharp spikes within. Immediately I felt that Adriana had been optimistic about our chances of survival. How could you wedge yourself safely into that?

They forced the woman to her knees in front of the barrel. 'Right! In you get!'

She stared at the spikes, her face twisted in horror, certain that she was looking at her own death.

'It'll be all the worse for you if we have to push you in!' the guard threatened, his voice harsh.

The woman responded by crawling in, crying out as the sharp spikes pierced her flesh. Once she was inside, they put the lid back on and fixed it in place with just two nails.

Rap! Tap!

One push, and the barrel set off, rolling down the hill. The yeomen had worked really fast, I reflected, worried now. You'd have only a few seconds to wedge yourself into position.

Three terrible shrieks issued from the barrel before it reached the bottom and came to rest hard against a tree trunk. Two men approached it, one carrying a crowbar. There was a grating, crunching sound as he prised off the lid.

We were too far away to see clearly, but when they pulled the woman out of the barrel, she didn't seem to be moving. They threw her body aside like a sack of potatoes.

'This one's dead! Send down the next!' Commander Stanton called up the hill.

The two County girls were weeping and trembling; they'd been holding hands, but now, as the guards approached, they clung tightly to each other and had to be dragged apart.

I watched, horrified, as the first of them received the same treatment, the poor girl shrieking and struggling as she was thrust inside. This time the barrel hit a rock on the way down and left the ground briefly, coming down again with a crash. When it came to a stop, the guards pulled the girl's body out and threw it down next to the other one.

I was appalled by what had just happened and my heart was pounding with fear. Was it really possible to wedge yourself in and survive?

But the third woman to be 'tested' was still alive when she reached the bottom of the hill. As two of the yeomen led her away, I could hear her sobbing and gasping. She was clearly hurt, but at least she had survived. So it *was* possible . . .

Adriana turned back to face Alice and me. Her bottom lip was trembling and her former courage had suddenly deserted her; she looked terrified. 'Can you sense when you're about to die?' she asked. 'Because that's how I feel now – as if I don't have long for this world . . .'

'My master doesn't believe in that,' I told her. 'He doesn't think anyone can foretell their own death.'

'But I feel it so strongly,' she sobbed. 'I sense that it's coming very soon!'

I leaned forward and whispered in her ear. 'You'll be all right,' I reassured her. 'Just wedge yourself into the barrel like you told us.'

Before she could reply, the guards came for her. She gave us a nervous smile, then went over to the barrel and crawled inside without a word.

Rap! Tap!

Now the barrel was on its way down. It was a smooth descent with no bumps. Had she survived? Again there was a sound of splintering wood as they prised off the lid.

'Another live one here! This one's a witch for sure!' shouted Stanton.

As soon as Adriana crawled out of the barrel, she was hauled to her feet and marched away by a further two guards. I noticed that she was limping, but she too had survived the descent. I suddenly felt more optimistic. We could worry about the buggane later.

Alice gave me a little smile as they dragged her away. It seemed that I would be the last to be tested. Alice crawled into the barrel quickly, like Adriana. As soon as they tapped on the lid, she'd wedge herself into position.

This time the descent was rough, the barrel bouncing twice – though at least it didn't hit a tree. When it reached the bottom, my heart was in my mouth. Had Alice managed to position herself properly? The remaining guard took off the lid and I waited expectantly for her to emerge. Instead there was a pause before he dragged her out of the barrel.

'Another dead one!' shouted the commander. 'Send down the little warlock. Let's get it over with! I'm ready for my breakfast!'

My throat constricted and a huge sob built up in my chest. Down below, they were laying Alice's body out alongside the other two corpses.

CHAPTER 7
THUMB-BONES WERE TAKEN

I couldn't believe she was dead. We'd gone through so much together, survived so many dangers . . . As my eyes filled with tears, I was seized and pushed to my knees in front of an open barrel.

'In you get, lad. Stop blubbing and make it easier on yourself!'

Blinded by tears, I started to crawl into the barrel, the spikes jabbing painfully into my hands and knees as I did so. No sooner was I in than the lid was clamped on top, plunging me into darkness.

Rap! Tap!

The barrel began to move and, just in time, I used my elbows and knees to brace my body against the inner curve of the wood, somehow managing to find gaps amongst the murderous spikes. The barrel began to spin faster and faster, the force pressing me harder against the points. There was a jolt, and I was almost shaken onto the barbs. Then I slowed and finally came to a halt. I didn't move until the lid was forced off, filling the inside of the barrel with light.

A face peered in at me. It was Commander Stanton. 'Got another live one here!' he shouted. Then he spoke to me, his voice lower but filled with sneering contempt. 'Out you come, you little warlock! It's the buggane for you . . .'

I crawled out, the spikes jabbing painfully into my hands and knees. Suddenly I heard a dull thud and a cry of pain. As I got shakily to my feet, Stanton spun away from me, reaching for his sword. He started to draw it, but then there was another thud and he fell to his knees, blood flowing down over his forehead.

'Alice!'

She was standing facing me, holding a rock in her left hand. She'd used it to fell both Stanton and the remaining guard. A mixture of emotions came over me in waves: shock, relief, happiness and then fear again . . .

I heard shouts from the top of the hill and glanced up to see some of the guards heading towards us.

'Run, Tom!' Alice cried, throwing down the rock and sprinting into the trees.

I followed at her heels. The trees were old and mature to begin with, well-spaced with big branches. I glanced back and saw figures less than a hundred yards behind us now. We splashed across a stream and headed towards a denser part of the wood where the saplings hadn't been coppiced. Before we entered the thicket, I looked behind again and saw to my satis-faction that our pursuers were no nearer. Now it would be a question of who had the greater endurance – or perhaps we could somehow lose them in the dense wood.

We ran on for five minutes, thin branches snapping as we passed, dead twigs crunching underfoot. We were making a lot of noise, but so were those following us, and they seemed to be falling further and further behind.

Suddenly Alice halted and pointed to our left. She dropped to her knees and began to crawl into an even denser thicket. For some time we moved forward on all fours, doing our best to make as little noise as possible. Then we waited, listening out for our yeomen. We heard sounds in the distance, but they grew fainter and fainter and finally faded away altogether.

Alice reached across and took my hand. 'Sorry, Tom. Did I give you a scare?'

'I thought you were dead, Alice,' I said, filling up with emotion again. 'Don't know how that guard made such a mistake . . .'

'Didn't make a mistake – not really. I stopped my own heart and breath. Easy when you know how. Lizzie used to make me practise it – it's very useful when talking to spirits. Dangerous though. Some witches forget to start breathing again and never wake up!'

'I wish I'd known what you intended to do,' I said, squeezing her hand.

'I didn't know myself until I got into the barrel. No sooner wedged myself in than I thought of that and did it as soon as the barrel came to rest at the foot of the hill. Better than being taken to the buggane, ain't it? Mind you, we didn't get off scot-free!'

I smiled. She was right: we were both covered in gashes from the spikes and there were ragged tears in my shirt and breeches and Alice's dress.

'We both look like Mouldheels now!' I joked, looking down at Alice's muddy feet. The Mouldheel witch clan were well-known for their bare feet and ragged clothes.

'Well, Tom, you certainly know how to make a girl feel good about herself,' she said sarcastically. My face dropped, but then she gave me a warm smile and squeezed my hand again.

'Poor Adriana,' she went on after a while. 'Told us how to survive but it ain't done her much good. They'll feed her to the buggane now for sure.'

We waited for about an hour before leaving our

hiding place, then headed south-east, towards the hill where the Spook had waited while we went down into Douglas. We just had to hope that he'd still be there.

We hadn't been walking long when we heard dogs barking in the distance. 'Sounds like tracker dogs!' I said.

The animals seemed to be approaching us from the east. Just when we thought we were safe, the pursuit had begun again. If we were caught, we'd no doubt receive a good beating because of what Alice had done – before being taken to the buggane. We could expect little mercy.

Once again we began to run, but this time the sounds of pursuit drew steadily closer no matter how quickly we sprinted. At one point I glanced back and saw three men in the distance; however, the dogs were gaining fast.

I had no staff, no weapons to fight off the dogs. In minutes they would catch us and we'd feel their teeth for sure. They might do us a lot of damage before their handlers caught up.

It was then that something cut right through my fear and panic and brought me to a breathless halt. Alice turned to look back at me and stopped too.

'It's all right, Alice!' I said, struggling to get the words out as I fought for breath. You see, I'd recognized the barks at last. 'They're Bill Arkwright's dogs!'

Theirs was a distinctive harsh sound, accompanied by the occasional howl. And I was soon proved right. It was Claw and her pups, Blood and Bone. They bounded towards me, and moments later were in competition to lick my face and hands. But who were the three men following them? There should just be one – my master . . .

I peered at them carefully. One was indeed the Spook, I realized, and he was carrying both our bags and staffs. As they approached, I recognized the second as Captain Baines. He must have found my master and told him about our capture and what we'd faced. But who was the third? He was a young man no older than twenty or so, with fair hair and an open, honest face.

'Well,' said the Spook when they finally reached us, 'you certainly led us a merry dance.'

'We've been chased already,' I told him. 'We thought it was more of the same lot from Greeba Keep . . .'

'How did you get away?' asked the captain.

'We were tested in the barrels on Slieau Whallian – we wedged ourselves in and managed to survive in one piece. Then Alice pretended to be dead and knocked the guards out with a rock.'

I couldn't tell the Spook that she'd used dark magic to stop her heart and breathing, so I left that bit out. He'd already be angry that she'd come with me after he'd forbidden it.

'They've rolled you already?' the fair-haired man demanded, speaking for the first time. He looked distraught. 'They weren't supposed to do the next batch until late evening!'

'They did it early – just before dawn, to stop too many people coming to gawp,' I told him.

'Then what happened to the others? Did they escape

too? Was there a girl there called Adriana?' he asked anxiously.

I nodded. 'There were six of us in all. Adriana was alive when she reached the bottom and was taken away with another survivor. Two other women died in the barrels.'

'Then I'm too late to save her,' he groaned. 'Now they'll take her to the buggane at Greeba Keep . . .'

'This is young Simon Sulby,' explained the captain. 'He was on his way to try and rescue his lady friend when the dogs sniffed him out and our paths converged, so it seemed wise to proceed in convoy. Sadly, it seems that we're too late.'

'I'll head for the keep!' said the young man, his face twisted with desperation. 'I've got to *try* and save her—'

'No, that's madness,' said Captain Baines, seizing him by the arm. 'No good setting off alone and half-rigged.'

'Aye, I agree with that,' said the Spook. 'But in the meantime we could all head towards Greeba. That will give us time to collect our thoughts. I'd also like to tell you all I know about bugganes – it might just help. And here, lad, you can carry these. I've lugged them around long enough!'

So saying, the Spook handed me both bags and my staff; then, after Alice had put her shoes on, we set off for Greeba Keep.

The most direct way was to follow the narrow track the cart had used. But to avoid bumping into the yeomen, we took a more round-about route. The country was hilly, with mountains in the distance; the wooded valleys reminded me of the County. The journey was pleasant but overshadowed by Simon Sulby's grief; he was near to despair. After all, what hope did he have of rescuing Adriana from those dungeons?

In the early evening we halted for the night in a small wood overlooked by Greeba Mountain. I made the fire, and Alice went off and caught three rabbits and a large hare. While she cooked them, we gathered around the fire and talked over what had happened in more detail.

'So a real County witch came ashore,' said the Spook. 'One or more?'

Captain Baines shrugged. 'Who knows? But there were two men dead, and it gave the Ruling Council just the excuse they needed to authorize the testing.'

'And thumb-bones were taken, you say?'

'Aye, and both fishermen were dead and drained of blood. Their throats had been cut.'

'That *could* suggest two witches,' said the Spook; 'a bone witch and a blood witch . . .'

'Or it could be Lizzie,' said Alice, turning the hare on the spit. 'She uses both blood *and* bone magic. She had a familiar once too, but it was killed. Maybe she was cut off from Pendle after she escaped from the pit – and headed west towards the coast!'

'It's a possibility, girl, I'll grant you that, so we must be on our guard.'

Soon we were tucking into our supper – I shared the hare with Alice, but Simon stared at his rabbit for a long time before pushing it away.

'Eat up, Simon. Try a little bit at least. You need to keep your strength,' advised Captain Baines.

'No,' he said, getting to his feet. 'I've got to press on towards the keep. Once it's dark, the buggane will go into the dungeons and Adriana—'

'Sit yourself down,' said the Spook. 'She's in no danger tonight – and perhaps not for several nights to come either. Trust me, although I've never had to deal with one directly, I know as much about bugganes as anybody. No doubt there are still things to be found out, but I know that they concentrate on one victim at a time and usually drain them over several days. How many prisoners have already been taken to the keep?'

'They've been testing for almost a week,' Simon answered. 'At least seven or eight have been pulled alive from the barrels. A couple may have died of their injuries though . . .'

'Are they all County refugees?'

'All but Adriana. But for Lord Barrule's interest in her she'd be safe at home.'

'Well, that makes my mind up for me,' said the

Spook. 'We need to help those people. I serve the County and its inhabitants, whether at home or abroad. It's my duty.'

'So we're going to try and rescue them from the dungeons?' I asked.

'Maybe we will in time, lad, although at present I can't see how. No, we're going to make them safe from the dark in another way. We're not going to the keep. If the ruined chapel is where the buggane is to be found, that's where we're going!'

After supper we sat around the embers of the fire and continued to discuss what we faced. The sun had gone down and the stars were starting to appear overhead. There was no wind and the wood was very quiet. The loudest sound was the panting of the dogs.

'Just how dangerous is a buggane?' Captain Baines asked.

'Well, you might as well all know the worst,' the Spook replied. 'And you get your notebook out, lad, and jot down some of what I say. There are a few things that needed adding to my Bestiary so you don't know it all. This is all part of your training . . .'

He waited while I got the bottle of ink, pen and notebook out of my bag, then he began.

CHAPTER 8
BUGGANE LORE

'A buggane is a daemon that usually lurks near a ruin,' the Spook began, 'but it can roam quite a distance from this central point. They're immune to salt and iron, which makes them hard to deal with – though they're vulnerable to a silver-alloy blade. You have to thrust it into the heart of the creature when it's fully materialized. The good news is that we spooks have such a blade . . .'

By way of demonstration, he reached across for his staff, and pressed the recessed switch so that the blade emerged with a click.

'As my apprentice already knows, they usually

confine themselves to two shapes – a black bull and a huge hairy man.'

'What's the main threat when it's in the form of a bull?' I asked.

'It bellows loudly and the sound draws upon the dark energy at its disposal. It often fills its victims with such dread that they're unable to move. Then it charges, goring and trampling anything in its path.'

The Spook fell silent and seemed deep in thought. After a while I prompted him: 'What about the hairy man? They call it the Cruncher here.'

'That's an apt name for it, lad. The buggane takes on that shape to dig its tunnels. Its sharp claws and teeth can chomp through tree trunks or roots that it finds in its path. I've just been searching my memory for any snippets of information . . . That's why the burning of my library is such a tremendous loss. There are things that only exist in my head now, and when I die, they're gone for ever . . .'

'Then you need to write 'em down again, Mr Gregory. Soon as possible,' Alice told him.

'Aye, you're right, girl,' the Spook acknowledged. 'Just as soon as I get the chance, I'll do exactly that.' He sighed, then continued staring into space as he pulled the details from his memory. 'The buggane does its most deadly work in its invisible, spirit form—'

'It's worse than just dying!' Simon interrupted, his voice full of emotion as he thought of the fate that awaited Adriana. 'The buggane sucks the victim's soul right out of its body!'

The Spook shook his head. 'No, that's not so – even though it's what most people believe. The soul survives and moves on. What the buggane sucks out is the *animus*, or life force, which is quite a different thing. It feeds on the energy that gives a body and mind strength; it consumes its vitality so that it dies. It's just that the mind dies first, and that's why the person seems to be just an empty vessel.

'There are mages known as *shamans* who practise the same sort of magic, which we call *animism*. A buggane may gain strength from an alliance with a shaman: in return for human sacrifices it will destroy an enemy or share its store of *animas* with the mage.

'And that's what I fear most – that we may not just be dealing with a buggane alone. There may be a dark shaman involved. Let's face it, in supposedly dealing with the dark – testing and killing falsely accused witches – the dark itself is being used: not only the buggane, but also an abhuman. So tell me, Simon, when did all this start?'

'Well over twenty-five years ago, before I was born, a witch landed on our western shore in company with that abhuman. Turned out it was her son. She was fed to the buggane and he was imprisoned and used to hunt down other witches. Potential witches have always been tested using spiked barrels, but the guilty were formerly burned at the stake. They've always picked on foreigners – immigrants who've come ashore and tried to make this their home. Adriana is one of the first to be accused from among our own people . . .'

At that point Simon's voice failed him and he choked back a sob. The Spook waited patiently for him to regain his composure before questioning him further.

'I know this is hard, Simon, but anything you can tell me will give us a chance of dealing successfully with what we face. You say "they", but who's behind it all? Who's in charge of what goes on?'

'The head of the Ruling Council is Lord Barrule of Greeba Keep, the one who condemned Adriana. It was his decision to let the abhuman live and use him to search for witches. He also said that nothing could be done about the buggane; however, feeding it witches, rather than burning them, would keep it quiet, and our own folk safer.'

'Then *he* could well be the dark shaman,' said the Spook. 'It couldn't be worse – he's a man of power and influence. But if we can destroy the buggane, that'll undermine him. What sort of a man is he?'

'"Cruel" is the word that best sums him up,' Simon replied. 'He's a man who likes to get his own way – and he's a big gambler. There are all sorts of tales about gambling parties in the keep. They often bet on fights between dogs. They say Barrule once had a bear shipped in and made it fight a pack of wolves.'

We all fell silent on hearing that. I hate cruelty to animals, and I was thinking of Claw and her pups being in that situation.

'It must be terrible when the buggane approaches in its spirit form,' I said at last.

'In the open, your only hope is to get away from it just as fast as you can,' the Spook told me. 'Trapped close to one, you have no chance at all, lad. It whispers to its victims in a sinister human voice until they see images in their heads – pictures of the very worst things they've experienced or done during their lives. The daemon is sadistic – it loves to inflict pain – and it forces them to re-live those events over and over again.

'You hear the whispering right inside your head. Some folks have been driven mad, forcing sharp sticks into their ears to make themselves deaf, but that doesn't help – the whispering still goes on. Over the course of a few days the creature sucks out the whole of your life force. It stores the animas of its victims in an underground labyrinth.'

'You mean a labyrinth like the one behind the silver gate under Priestown Cathedral?'

'No, lad, this is very different. The Bane was bound there, and that labyrinth had been dug out by the Little People and lined with cobbles. A buggane digs its own labyrinth, which weaves in and out between the roots of trees. It controls the trees and makes their roots move – sometimes with devastating effects for those who are close by. The first time I attempted to deal with the Bane, as a young man, I tied a ball of twine to the silver gate. I unravelled it as I explored the tunnels and followed it back again. But you couldn't do this here: those buggane tunnels shift and change, sometimes overnight. They can also collapse, suffocating any who venture inside. There's one record of a buggane being slain by a spook far to the south of the County. About three months after the daemon died, its tunnels collapsed, causing subsidence over the whole area.

'A buggane should never be confronted in its tunnel system,' continued the Spook, 'so going underground is the very last thing we should be thinking about! It won't show its face in the daytime, but just venturing near the chapel after dark should be enough to tempt it out into the open. So that's what I intend to do . . .'

I slept well that night before being woken a couple of hours before dawn to take my turn on watch. I thought the dogs would be sufficient to keep guard, but the Spook was taking no chances. He said that shamans had a special power over animals and, no matter how well trained they were, could force them to do his bidding.

At last the sun came up through the trees to the east and soon the birds were singing, the wood slowly coming to life around us.

There was no sense of danger at all. It was hard to believe that, just a mile or so to the north, we would enter the domain of the buggane. We had a late breakfast – some mushrooms, again supplied by Alice. It was too risky to buy food in a tavern; neither the

Spook nor I ate much anyway. We were about to begin a fast, our preparation for facing the dark.

Later, the four of us set off for the chapel. Captain Baines was to stay behind with the dogs.

'Stealth is the key to success here,' my master told him, 'and I don't want those animals anywhere near the ruin in case a shaman is involved. However, I'm reasonably confident that the buggane poses no threat during the hours of daylight. We're just going to observe for now, so that we're better prepared once night falls.'

By the time we arrived, rain clouds were billowing in from the west and the chapel looked forbidding in the grey light. It stood on a hillside, surrounded on three sides by a wood that extended down the slope. All the walls were standing, but there was no roof. The door had been removed from its hinges so we went inside and stared up at the ancient stone walls, which were patterned with moss and lichens.

'Some believe that a buggane haunts a ruined chapel to prevent it being rebuilt,' said the Spook, 'although there's no evidence for that. However, many creatures of the dark shun places where people gather to pray. Some boggarts move the foundations of churches as they're being built – they can't bear the sound of prayers. But what concerns me here is the extent of its territory. How far does it roam?'

'There's the keep!' I said to Alice, pointing towards the grey tower just visible above a distant wood. Behind it loomed the forbidding Greeba Mountain.

She stared at it but said nothing.

'That it is,' Simon said mournfully. 'The dungeons where they keep the victims for the buggane are on this side, just to the south of the moat . . .'

'If the buggane's territory extends that far in every direction, it's got itself a sizeable domain,' observed the Spook. 'Let's take a walk in that direction so we better know the lie of the land.'

He led the way south from the chapel ruins. We began to descend the hill, going deeper into the woods, the murmur of running water increasing in volume with every step we took. The ground was saturated and our boots made squelching sounds as we walked.

'That should be the Greeba River down there in the valley,' the Spook said, coming to a halt. 'We've gone far enough. This is dangerous terrain – not a place we'll risk entering after dark. If the buggane does take a different form, it's likely to be one suited to this boggy environment.'

'Could it take the shape of a worme?' I asked. Wormes were really scary. When I was working with Bill Arkwright, we had to hunt down one that had killed a child. It had dragged the boy from his bed and eaten him. All that was left was a few blood-spattered pieces of nightshirt.

'It's possible, lad – but let's hope not. Wormes are dangerous creatures – sometimes as big as a carthorse. They love marsh and water. This place would suit one all right.' The Spook turned to Simon. 'Their bodies are covered with scales that are very difficult to penetrate with a blade. Moreover, they have powerful jaws and a mouthful of sharp teeth, and when on land they spit a deadly poison that's absorbed through the victim's skin. What results is a very unpleasant death indeed . . .'

I remembered the worme we'd finally cornered. It had spat at Bill, but luckily the venom had landed on his boots. I looked down through the trees and thick vegetation. It was so dense I couldn't even see the river. Alice and I looked at each other, both thinking the same thing. This place gave us a bad feeling.

We returned to the copse, where Captain Baines was waiting with the dogs. Soon after dark we prepared to set off back to the chapel. It had been raining heavily, but now the moon flickered fitfully through tattered clouds, driven across the sky by a blustering westerly wind.

'Well, lad, let's get it over with,' said the Spook, handing me his bag.

The captain and Simon Sulby were to remain behind with the dogs. I suppose the Spook expected Alice to do the same because he first looked surprised, then frowned as she started to follow us.

'Stay where you are, girl,' he said. 'This is spook's business.'

'I've been useful enough in the past,' Alice replied.

My master glanced at us in turn, his eyes full of suspicion. He certainly didn't know about the blood jar, but I could tell that he thought something was wrong.

'Joined at the hip, are you?' he asked, frowning.

I smiled and shrugged. With a shake of his head, the Spook set off for the chapel; we both followed behind. We were still quite some distance from the ruins when he brought us to a halt. 'Keep your wits about you now, lad,' he said softly.

We continued forward, but much more slowly and cautiously, every step bringing us towards the chapel walls. Eventually we were standing close enough to touch the damp stones.

'I think it's near by,' said the Spook. 'I can feel it in my bones . . .'

I knew he was right. A chill was moving down my spine, a warning that something from the dark was very near. The Spook led the way forward along the wall, heading for the trees.

Moments later we were amongst them, a breeze in our faces, shadows dappling the ground briefly each time the moon emerged from behind the clouds. We'd taken another couple of dozen steps when my master came to a sudden halt. There were two men standing amongst the trees about fifty yards ahead of us. One was a thin, tall, scarecrow-like figure in a long dark gown; the other appeared squat and muscular, with a large head and no discernible neck.

The moon came out again and lit them, showing the true horror of what we faced. The tall man had a hard, cruel face, but it was the other figure that filled my heart with dismay and started my knees trembling. It wasn't a true man at all. The creature had appeared squat because it had been on all fours. Now it suddenly stood upright to reveal its immense size. The face was hairy, as was the rest of the body, but it was more like fur than human hair. We were facing the buggane in the shape of a hairy man – the Cruncher. Its companion had to be the shaman.

No sooner had those thoughts flicked through my head than the buggane dropped onto all fours once more. The moon went behind a cloud, plunging us into darkness, and all I could see was a pair of glowing red eyes. Then it bellowed loudly – a fearful cry that made the ground – and the very trees – shake. So terrifying was that cry that I was rooted to the spot, unable to move.

I heard a click as the Spook released the blade from the tip of his staff, and he began to stride purposefully towards our enemies. But when the moon came out again, we saw only the buggane ahead. The shaman had vanished.

The daemon had now taken the shape of a muscular black bull with enormous horns, its huge front hooves pawing the ground in anger, its nostrils snorting clouds of steam. It was getting ready to charge.

It galloped towards the Spook, hooves drumming on the earth. My master took up a defensive position, holding his staff diagonally across his body. Compared to the buggane he appeared small and frail and looked certain to be gored and trampled underfoot. My heart was in my mouth. I stood there, terrified. My master was about to die.

CHAPTER 9
THE ATTACK OF THE BUGGANE

It was all so quick that at first I didn't register what had happened. The daemon completely missed the Spook, who had stepped aside at the last moment, stabbing at it with his staff. But then, as it passed, the buggane lunged with its huge head, catching my master with its left horn and tossing him sideways. He fell hard, then rolled over and over before coming to a stop.

He wasn't moving. Was he dead? If he wasn't now, he soon would be. The buggane ignored Alice and me and came round in a wide circle, lowering its head so that its sharp horns pointed straight at the prone figure of my master. My heart lurched. It was going to charge him again.

For a moment I was unable to move, but then Alice gave a cry and started to run forward. She was waving her arms, trying to distract the buggane and make it attack her instead.

It stopped and stared at her with its huge red, baleful eyes. Then it charged at her!

All at once I was free to move again. I dropped the bags and sprinted towards Alice in an attempt to get between her and the fearsome creature. I released the blade in my staff as I ran, shouting out to distract it. 'Here!' I cried. 'Here! It's me you want!'

It ignored my shouts, and my heart was in my mouth: it was upon Alice before I could get into a position to defend her. For one awful moment I thought it had trampled her, but I saw her drop to her knees and roll clear just in time.

The buggane came about again. Once more it pawed the ground and snorted hot breath through its nostrils. This time it was looking at me. I'd got what I wanted. Now *I* was the target!

It rushed at me, red eyes locked with mine, sharp

horns ready to impale me. But I concentrated hard, sucking in a deep breath, trying to slow the flow of time outside myself. It was a gift I'd inherited from Mam – something that I'd only recently discovered I possessed. I'd used it to defend myself against the Ordeen – she'd said I had 'a speed that mocks the tick of time'.

If so, I certainly wasn't mocking time now. The gift wasn't easy to use and I was far from being in full control of it. I tried my best, but if time *did* slow, it didn't seem to bother the buggane much. It was upon me in seconds, and as I stepped clear and dropped to one knee, its right horn missed my head by a fraction of an inch.

I'd barely time to get back on my feet before it charged at me again. This time it shook its head, sweeping its horns wide. But I'd already anticipated that, jumped clear and stabbed at it with my staff. The blade cut it just below the ear and the creature bellowed with pain and seemed to stagger slightly before turning to attack again.

The silver blade had hurt it. If the daemon assumed the form of a worme, its armoured scales would make it hard to kill, but now I had an opportunity to plunge my blade into its heart and put an end to it. I felt more confident now and began to focus.

Concentrate! Squeeze time. Slow it. Make it halt!

It was working. The buggane really did seem to be slowing. Before, its legs had been a blur, but now I could see the individual movement of each one. As it came within reach of my staff, it was almost frozen in time, its breath in a still cloud, its red eyes like glass. Seizing my chance, I stepped to one side and raised my staff, ready to stab behind its shoulder and down into its heart. It was almost completely still now. I'd nearly done it – stopped time! One thrust of my blade and the daemon would be no more. I thrust downwards, but, to my intense disappointment, met only empty air.

The buggane had vanished!

The surprise disappearance broke my concentration and I lost my grip on time. I felt the breeze on my face again, heard it sighing through the branches; the moon sent brief shadows flickering across the ground before being obscured by cloud once more.

I stood there, letting my breathing return to normal after the exertion of the struggle. Would the creature rematerialize? I'd hurt it, but not that badly. Perhaps it had sensed what I was attempting to do with time; realized the threat I posed. Would it come back – this time in a more dangerous shape? Or would it whisper to me in its spirit form and start to drain my animus?

I glanced across at my master. He still wasn't moving. How badly was he hurt? It was only then that I realized that there was no sign of Alice.

'Alice! Alice!' I called, but there was no reply. Fear clutched at my heart. Had the shaman seized her?

'Alice!' I shouted again, desperation in my voice. The only answer was a groan from the Spook, so I went over to see how he was.

As I knelt down beside him, he sat up with a grunt of pain. 'Here, help me to my feet, lad . . .'

I laid my staff down on the ground, put my arm around him and helped him up.

'How badly are you hurt?' I asked anxiously. There was no sign of blood but he was deathly pale.

'Fortunately the point of the horn missed me, but it whacked me hard on the shoulder and knocked me clean unconscious. I'll live – but with a headache and a few bruises to remember it by. What happened?'

I told him about my fight with the buggane and how it had vanished. 'But Alice is missing,' I continued. 'When you were down, the buggane was about to charge you again and she distracted it. She saved your life. That's the last I saw of her. Maybe the shaman's got her? That *was* the shaman next to the daemon, wasn't it?'

'Most likely it was, lad – especially as he vanished like that. But don't worry about the girl. She can look after herself. If she's got any sense she'll put some distance between herself and the buggane. And so should we.'

'But what if the shaman feeds her to the buggane?'

The Spook didn't answer but we both knew he might well do that. After all, the abhuman had sniffed Alice and found darkness within her. But there was something more immediate that put a terrible fear into my heart. She was now beyond the protection of the blood jar.

Despite the Spook's warnings of the risks, I insisted on searching the area but found nothing, and finally I was forced to abandon it.

I was scared for Alice – there was a lump in my throat as I left, following my master. The Fiend might appear at any time and take his revenge. He could slay Alice and drag her soul off into the dark for ever.

Back at the camp, racked by fears for Alice, I found it impossible to sleep. I thought dawn would never arrive, but at last morning came – a bright, beautiful one, totally unsuited to my mood.

The day started badly. No sooner was I up and about than I realized that the dogs were missing. Of Claw, Blood and Bone there was no sign – nor did they answer my call. They were generally obedient and it was unusual for them to wander off for so long. Was it the shaman's doing?

There was no real breakfast – just a nibble of cheese. Everyone was in a sombre mood, and Simon Sulby in particular was desperate to do something, aware that each day that passed increased the danger to Adriana.

'I can't just sit around here!' he said, his voice filled with anguish. 'What if you fail again tonight?'

'I can guarantee nothing,' the Spook replied, clearly irritated, 'but I'll tell you one thing – go off alone in some foolish attempt to rescue her from that keep and there'll be one more person in those dungeons, ready to feed to the buggane. And that'll be you!'

'I might have little hope of rescuing Adriana, but there's one other thing I could do. I could walk to St John's and appeal to the Tynwald.'

'The Tynwald?' I asked. 'Is that the island's Ruling Council?'

Simon shook his head. 'No, it's the Parliament, an elected body, but they appoint the Council and have the power to overrule them. They'll be meeting in a few days in St John's – the village by the witch tower where they imprisoned you. The Tynwald could order Lord Barrule to free Adriana.'

'Are they likely to listen to you?'

'They'll listen, though they rarely interfere once the Council is appointed. But what else can I do? Citizens have a right to be heard by the Tynwald. Adriana's not a witch and never was. She understands birds – that's all. It's a special talent and it worries some people. Why do things have to be like this? Why do people like Barrule make life so hard for others? Adriana and I just want to get married, have children and be happy. Is that too much to ask? I know one thing for sure: without her my life would be over. I couldn't live without her.'

The Spook shook his head sadly and said nothing for a while. 'Look,' he said at last, 'just give it one more night. If we can put an end to the buggane tonight, it takes her out of any immediate danger.'

Simon didn't respond. He didn't look convinced.

'Do you think the shaman did capture Alice?' I asked my master. I was sad for Simon and concerned about Adriana, but the plight of Alice was uppermost in my mind.

'Could well be, lad. He might have lured her away somehow by using dark magic, but he couldn't have physically carried her off. You see, he wasn't there in person last night. That's why he seemed to vanish. A shaman can project his spirit from his body, and to those like us with the gift to see it, it looks just like him. The dogs are a different matter, though: as I said, he has a special power over animals. Bill Arkwright had them well-trained and it's not like them to go off like that.'

'I'd like to visit St John's myself to buy a few provisions,' Captain Baines interrupted, 'and I might be able to find out what's going on.'

He left soon after that and then, despite all our attempts to persuade him otherwise, Simon set off for St John's too, intending to find accommodation and work on his appeal. But before he left he drew us a map. He marked in Greeba Keep, the ruined chapel and Douglas. He also included the small town of Peel on the west coast of the island, indicating the mill where Adriana lived with her parents.

I studied it carefully, committing it to memory.

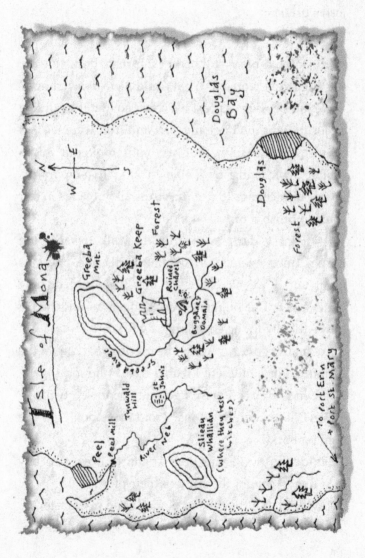

At dusk the captain still hadn't returned, and we were starting to get worried. What could have delayed him?

We hid our bags as best we could so that it would be easier to fight the buggane. Salt and iron were useless against this daemon, but we both took our silver chains, which might be able to bind it temporarily, giving us a chance to use the silver-alloy blades in our staffs to finish it off.

As it grew dark, we started to walk towards the chapel ruins again. It had gone badly the previous night and I wasn't confident that we could do any better now. The buggane was dangerous and had a powerful ally in the shaman.

We hadn't gone far when I heard dogs barking in the distance. For a moment I feared tracker hounds again, but then I relaxed. I wasn't going to be fooled twice.

'It's Bill Arkwright's dogs,' I told the Spook. 'They're coming back!'

Suddenly the distant dogs began to howl and bay as if they'd caught the scent of their prey.

'Aye, lad, but they're not alone!' cried my master.

The dogs were racing towards us, and at their heels was a large group of armed men, maybe twenty or more.

'Run for it, lad!'

We set off as fast as we could, our feet flying over the rough grass, but after several minutes we still hadn't put any distance between ourselves and our pursuers.

'Split up!' the Spook shouted. 'Divide them, and maybe they won't catch us both!'

I obeyed, peeling off to the left while he went right. For either of us to be captured was bad enough, but what he'd suggested certainly made good sense.

For a few moments I sprinted off and the sound of the dogs actually started to fade. But just when I thought I was getting away, I heard a single bark close behind me. I looked back to see Claw closing on me fast. Beyond her were half a dozen men with clubs. They didn't seem to be gaining on me, but the dog certainly was.

I stumbled on a tussock of grass, went down on all fours, and immediately jumped to my feet again. But before I could go anywhere Claw was on me, her teeth clamped on my breeches just above the ankle.

'Let go, Claw! Let go!' I shouted, but she growled and began to shake my leg as she would a rat.

I couldn't believe she was behaving like this. She'd always obeyed Bill Arkwright, and had once saved my life when I'd been seized by the water witch, Morwena. Since Bill's death I'd thought of her as my own dog. How had the shaman managed to turn her against me like this? She seemed like a different animal.

She was a big, powerful wolfhound and the only way to make her let go was to whack her hard with my staff – though even that might not be enough. I raised my arm, but then hesitated . . . I couldn't bring myself to do it . . . And then it was too late. The first of the yeomen – a big, burly man – was upon me.

He swung his club at my head. I used my staff against him rather than the dog, and he went down at my feet with a grunt. I felled a second assailant, but then I was surrounded. What happened next was bad. Claw snarled and transferred her grip from my breeches to my ankle. I felt her teeth sink in. My sense of shock at her behaviour was worse than the physical pain. Then a whack to my head brought me to my knees and my staff fell to the ground. The blows rained in hard; someone booted me in my stomach and I doubled up in pain, fighting for breath.

I was hauled roughly to my feet, my hands were tied behind my back and I was marched off through the trees. Every so often someone would direct a kick at my back or my legs. That was bad enough, but soon the grey stone of the keep loomed up through the trees. I knew where they were taking me – down into the dungeons to feed me to the buggane.

Greeba Keep had a wide moat full of murky water, but rather than a drawbridge like Malkin Tower, this fortification had a simple wooden approach ramp and a metal portcullis between two small gatehouses that were scarcely higher than the outer wall. I stood there, suffering kicks and thumps as we waited for it to be raised.

Once inside, I saw that the walls enclosed a flagged area full of stone buildings. The tall tower was right at the centre, protected by another portcullis. Two yeomen, each furnished with a flickering torch, dragged me along beneath the strong metal grille, then down some steep spiral steps until we reached a guard-room, where half a dozen men sat eating while others cleaned boots and polished armour.

I was taken through a doorway opposite them and down more steps into the damp darkness. Eventually we emerged in a narrow passageway dripping with water, with soft mud that squelched underfoot. At one point I saw water cascading down the wall – I assumed we were passing under the moat, heading for the deep dungeons to the south, within the buggane's domain. Every so often other passageways led off to our right and left.

I'd expected to be held in a chamber similar to the one in the Tynwald witch tower, along with the other prisoners, including Adriana, but we went straight past a row of narrow cells: I heard no sounds or movement so it was impossible to tell if any were occupied. One of the yeomen unlocked the door of the one at the end and, after cutting the ropes that bound my hands, thrust me inside. Once the metal door clanged shut, I was plunged into complete darkness.

I waited for the footsteps to die away and then reached into my pocket for my tinderbox and candle stub. I always carry them with me because spook's business often means working after dark or in underground chambers. I also checked on the blood jar, relieved to find that it was still safe. But poor Alice – she was beyond its protection. I could hardly bear to think about the risk she faced from the Fiend.

I was surprised that I hadn't been searched and still had my silver chain – not that it would be any use against the buggane in its spirit form as it came to draw the life from my body.

I managed to light the candle, but the underground cell proved even worse than I'd expected. Not even straw to lie on. There was an oddity too: three of the walls were made of damp stone but the fourth was just earth – hard-packed sub-soil. My hands began to tremble, making the candle flame flicker – because low down, in the centre of that earthen wall, was the dark entrance to a tunnel.

Was it one of the buggane's tunnels? I bent low and peered in. The rear part was still in partial shadow, but it seemed to come to a dead end no more than fifteen feet inside. Had someone tried to dig an escape tunnel and been discovered? If so, why hadn't the guards filled it in again?

I had another way out of the cell; one other item in my pocket that might prove useful – my special key. It had been crafted by the Spook's brother, Andrew, and could open most locks. Not that I'd be in a rush to use it. I could probably get out of the cell easily enough, but then there was both an inner and an outer portcullis controlling access to the keep. The mechanisms to raise them would be guarded, so escape from the keep seemed out of the question.

Of course, there were other cells nearby, and one of them might hold Adriana. If they caught the Spook, they might bring him here too – but I'd probably hear them in the passageway outside, so it was best to bide my time. Several of us working together would have a better chance of getting out.

I waited for long time but heard nothing. Surely, if they'd caught the Spook, he'd have been brought here by now? Perhaps he'd managed to escape? Eventually I blew out the candle to save it for future use, then curled myself up into a ball on the earth floor and tried to sleep. It was cold and damp, and soon I began to shiver. I was aching all over and covered in bruises from the beating I'd suffered. There was no Alice here to offer relief from pain with her herbs – only time would heal me.

Several times I dozed off, only to wake up with a jerk. But the final time I awoke, it was for reasons other than cold and discomfort.

I could hear the patter of earth falling onto the floor. Someone or something was emerging from the tunnel . . .

CHAPTER 10
A DANGEROUS OPPONENT

I opened my tinderbox, and despite the trembling of my hands managed to light the candle stub. I stared at the earthen wall in horror. A hairy head, arms and upper torso were visible at the entrance of the tunnel and the creature was looking directly towards me. It was huge.

My worst fears were realized: it was the buggane, once again in the shape of the Cruncher. The daemon was squat and bulky, with virtually no neck, its front limbs ending in broad claws clearly shaped for burrowing. Its massive body was covered in long black hair which shone in the candlelight as if slick with oil. At close quarters, the most striking thing about it was its face. It had the large, close-set staring eyes of a cruel predator, but when its gaze turned towards the candle, the lids narrowed into a squint. In this form the buggane had created and now inhabited a labyrinth of dark tunnels. I wondered if the light bothered it?

The creature had a slimy wet quivering snout, from which drops of moisture fell and splattered on the floor; it suddenly growled low in its throat and opened its mouth to reveal teeth that looked capable of biting off an arm, a leg or even a head. It had a double row of teeth: those at the front were sharp and triangular like the teeth of a wood-saw; those to the rear were broad, like human ones, but far larger – molars shaped for grinding and chewing. No wonder they called it the Cruncher.

But why was it visiting me like this? Wasn't it supposed to approach in its spirit form and whisper as it drew out my life essence? I slipped my left hand into my pocket and readied my silver chain. I wondered if the chain would hold it – and, if so, for how long?

My staff had been taken by my captors. I had nothing with me that could kill it.

The buggane pulled itself into the cell and moved towards me on all fours, panting like a dog. It was maybe twice the size of a fully grown man. How had it fitted into the tunnel? I saw now that its fur was shining with beads of water. Luckily it didn't come too close but I could still smell its foul breath, making me retch. As I struggled to hold down the contents of my stomach, it began to circle me slowly, still on all fours, and as it did so, the panting gave way to a deliberate sniffing. Was it about to attack? I wondered. If so, what was it waiting for? Or was it like a witch, short-sniffing, trying to find things out about me?

I turned slowly on my knees so that I was always facing towards it as it circled menacingly. The candle was dancing in my trembling hand, and at one point, unintentionally, I jerked the flame towards the creature. It seemed to flinch, its eyes narrowing again – or had I just imagined it?

Most denizens of the dark both feared and avoided

daylight but were not usually troubled by the light of a fire or a candle. In its present form the buggane was certainly bothered by the candlelight. But how would it cope with fire? Would a torch be a real threat to it? I tried moving the candle towards its face. It retreated and gave a threatening growl, so low that it seemed to come from deep within its belly. Next it showed me its sharp teeth and I immediately moved the candle back again.

'I wouldn't do that if I were you!' warned a deep voice from the tunnel entrance. 'One bite and he'd have your arm off. Or maybe your head – that would make a good mouthful.'

It was the abhuman, Horn: he was staring at me and shaking his head.

I turned my gaze back to the buggane. Having completed a full circle, it was surely planning to attack now. I waited tensely, mouth dry with fear, left hand still gripping my silver chain. But to my surprise the creature crawled back towards the wall of earth. It halted beside Horn, who began to pat its forehead, then whispered something into its ear before moving aside. The daemon squeezed its bulk into the tunnel. For a while I could hear it scuffling and grunting as it made its way along. Then the sounds faded away altogether.

Horn was still gazing at me. 'He wants you, boy. Knows what you are – a seventh son of a seventh son. Likes the smell of your blood and would love to eat your flesh and crunch your bones. I've rarely seen him so eager!'

Then he turned and followed the buggane into the tunnel. I waited until the noise of his departure faded away into absolute silence. Only then did I rise to my feet and approach the tunnel entrance. I held up my candle and peered inside. It still seemed to come to a dead end. So where had the buggane and Horn gone? Had the creature filled the tunnel in behind them? It didn't seem possible – I was facing what looked like solid earth.

I was nervous but curious. I listened. There wasn't the faintest sound. Was it waiting for me in the darkness somewhere ahead? Common sense told me that if it had wanted to harm me, it could easily have done so in the cell. So, holding the candle in my right hand, I scrambled into the tunnel and began to crawl forward. As soon as I reached what, from the cell, had appeared to be a dead end, I saw that the tunnel angled off at ninety degrees to my left. It ran parallel to the other cells: that was what the earthen wall was for – so that the buggane could reach its victims in its physical form. No doubt each cell had a short tunnel connecting it to this one.

So was it a means of escape? Not for most people. They'd be terrified after such a visitation and wouldn't dream of venturing inside. But could it be for me? I was a spook's apprentice and had been in some scary situations before. My instinct as a trainee spook was to follow the tunnel. It was part of the job. Then I remembered my master's warning about the labyrinth created by the buggane amongst the roots of trees. They moved and shifted and sometimes collapsed without warning. That thought filled me with panic. What if this tunnel collapsed now? And what if I got lost in the labyrinth or

JOSEPH DELANEY

suddenly came face to face with the buggane or Horn?

No, I wasn't ready to take such a risk yet. So I slowly backed my way out and was soon sitting on the floor of the cell again.

I blew out my candle and tried to sleep once more. This time it was more difficult. I was finally dropping off when I heard footsteps approaching along the corridor. Had they captured the Spook? But then a key turned in my lock, and two burly yeomen carrying torches came into my cell.

'On your feet, boy!' one of them commanded. 'We're taking you to the long room.'

The other walked over to the tunnel entrance. 'Well, what have we here?' he remarked, looking at the scattering of soil on the cell floor. 'Looks like you've had a hungry visitor! Likes to take a good look at each victim first, but he'll be back tomorrow night to start the real business, you can be sure of that!'

They marched me back along the passage with the cells to our right. Again, no sounds came from them. Were they empty? I wondered what had happened to

Adriana. Where was she being kept? Had the buggane already begun the process of devouring her? I shuddered at the thought. The poor girl didn't deserve that. Nobody should have to suffer such a fate. But then, instead of heading for the steps, we turned left, then left again into a much wider, stone-flagged passageway, lit by torches set in wall brackets. It seemed to me that we were still south of the moat and within the buggane's domain.

I could hear dogs barking in the distance, the sounds increasing in volume as we approached a door at the end of the passageway, and then I was pushed into a large oblong chamber. There were dozens of torches on the walls, and I could clearly see what was going on there. About two dozen men sat on bales of straw near the right-hand wall; perhaps another five or six armed yeomen stood nearby. In the doorway stood their commander, Stanton, scowling at me, a bandage wrapped round his head – clear sign of the damage Alice's rock had done to him. At the far end, against an earthen wall, stood a large, ornately carved wooden chair, and seated on it was the gaunt figure of Lord Barrule, the shaman, who was presiding over events. Behind him, to his left, was the entrance to a dark tunnel, similar in size to the one in my cell.

Large steel cages lined the left-hand wall – I counted fourteen. Inside each but the last was a dog. There were a variety of breeds but all were big and fierce. My eyes swept down the line. I knew what I would see but it was still a shock when I saw Claw, Blood and Bone there. I felt sick to my stomach.

In the middle of the room was a large empty space, where the floor was covered in sawdust that was dotted with patches of fresh blood. They were clearly staging dog-fights there. I saw money changing hands – men gambling on the outcome of each fight.

Lord Barrule got to his feet and raised his hands high. As he did so, the tumult of barking ceased and, but for a faint whimper here and there, all the dogs fell silent.

As I watched, horrified, two of the cages were opened and the dogs dragged into the centre of the chamber by their leather collars; they were forced to face each other, their noses almost touching. Although powerful, big dogs, they appeared cowed and terrified. Their handlers left them there and retreated back towards the doorway where we were standing. The shaman suddenly brought his hands down and clapped loudly three times. On the third clap, the dogs were instantly transformed from timidity to aggression and leaped forward savagely.

The fight was fast and furious: they tore at each other with their teeth, the first blood being drawn in just seconds. It was cruel and horrible and I couldn't bear to look, so I cast my eyes down to the ground. Unfortunately my ears were still open to what was happening. Eventually one of the dogs let out a shrill cry and then fell silent. There was a burst of applause, a few cheers and the odd curse of disappointment from the losers. When I looked up, the winning dog was being led back to its cage; the losing animal was lying on its side with its throat torn out, fresh blood soaking into the sawdust.

* * *

I was forced to witness another three contests, each
time terrified that one of Bill Arkwright's dogs would
be dragged out to fight. And what if they made two of
them fight each other? I'd no doubt that the shaman
had the power to make them kill their own kin.

But, to my relief, the fighting was at last over for the
night and the gamblers got to their feet and started to
leave. I was frog-marched back to my cell and left in the
darkness once more. Why had I been taken to watch
that cruelty? I wondered. Was it simply sadism – a wish
to make me suffer in anticipation of what was going to
happen to Claw, Blood and Bone? It wasn't long before
my question was answered . . .

There was a shimmer in the darkness by the tunnel;
a luminosity in the air. I stood up in alarm. Was it the
buggane in its spirit form? But the shimmer quickly
assumed an appearance of solidity, taking a shape I
recognized: a tall, skeletal figure with a cruel
expression, dressed in a dark robe. It was the shaman,
Lord Barrule. Although somewhere else within

Greeba Keep, he was projecting his spirit into my cell.

'The buggane certainly wants you, boy,' the apparition said. 'It likes what it sniffed, but it doesn't have to be that way. Did you enjoy what you saw tonight?'

I shook my head.

'It could have been much worse. I could have pitted your own dogs against each other. The mother against her whelps perhaps. It could still be done . . .'

I didn't reply. I had rarely seen such malevolence and cruelty in a face. This man was capable of anything.

'I'd spare your dogs if you were willing to put your own life on the line. You've seen my gambling friends – I'd like to offer them some special entertainment tomorrow night: a spook's apprentice in combat with a witch. Who would prove victorious? The outcome is uncertain enough to make it interesting, even though the odds are firmly on the witch. But you'd be free to use the tools of your trade. I've left you your silver chain and I'll return your staff. Defeat the witch and I'll let you go. You can even take your dogs with you. But lose and I'll make them fight to the death!'

'You want me to fight Adriana?' I asked. I couldn't believe what he was asking me to do.

'No, you young idiot! Not that foolish girl. I've got other plans for her! You'll face a much more dangerous opponent – one who's from your own neck of the woods. I mean Lizzie, the bone witch!'

CHAPTER 11
THE WITCH'S PET

'**B**ony Lizzie's here?' I asked in alarm.

'She's my prisoner, boy. And soon she'll be dead – that's if you have the skill and guts to put an end to her! What do you say?'

I didn't reply. Was it a trick or a real chance of freedom?

'Of course, if you lose, you'll forfeit your own life. I've made the witch the same promise. And I'll let her take her pet away with her too; lose, and it dies with her. Come on, make up your mind. Don't keep me waiting!'

'Her pet?'

'The other witch. The one she controls. No doubt she

came with her from over the water. Together they cut the throats of those poor fishermen. For that they both deserve to die. My own money will be on you. I like to bet on long shots . . .'

What choice did I have? I gave the merest of nods to signal my acceptance of his offer. Immediately the image of the shaman began to fade as he withdrew his spirit back into his body.

The next day they fed me well. The first meal was a hot plate of lamb with roast potatoes and carrots.

'Eat up, boy! My master wants you fighting fit!' jeered the mocking guard who handed me the meal. 'And you'll need every last ounce of strength to face what he's got planned!'

He and his companion left, laughing as if at some private joke, and were back just over six hours later with a delicious venison stew. I ate sparingly – despite the fact that I had eaten little the previous day and was very hungry. I needed to prepare myself to face the dark – though I also knew I would need all my speed and strength to overcome Lizzie: it would be a difficult test. I could use my staff and chain against her, but no doubt she'd be armed too; a bone witch like Lizzie was skilled in the use of blades. And if she won, she'd take my bones . . .

And who was this other witch, the 'pet' whom she'd brought over from the County with her? She was a completely unknown entity – probably a young witch Lizzie had taken under her wing to train. Maybe it was one of the witches who'd released her from the pit in the Spook's garden. She would be dangerous too – one more servant of the dark to worry about.

I had plenty of time to think. Mostly I worried about Alice. What had become of her? I took the blood jar out of my pocket and held it in the palm of my right hand for a while. How long would it be before the Fiend realized that she was no longer protected? I couldn't bear it if anything happened to Alice.

Then there was my master. Had he managed to escape? I wondered. If so, I knew he'd be planning to rescue me. It seemed hopeless – most probably he'd be imprisoned himself. Could I escape from Greeba Keep before that happened? Would the shaman really let me go if I defeated Lizzie? Was he likely to keep his word?

There was poor Adriana too. What did the shaman mean by saying he had 'other plans for her'? How could I just abandon her?

My fruitless speculations were brought to a halt by the arrival of the guards, this time to take me to face Lizzie. When we entered the long room, I noticed that there were a lot more men sitting on the straw bales. Many were standing too, and money was changing hands, but they all fell silent when I was brought in, staring at me in silent appraisal.

The dogs were in their cages against the left wall of the room, and to my relief Claw, Blood and Bone were still amongst them. Would the shaman really let me take them with me if I won? I'd no choice but to fight anyway. If I did nothing, Lizzie would soon put an end to me.

It was then that my eyes settled on the furthest cage,

the one nearest the entrance to the buggane's tunnel. Yesterday it had been empty; now there was something inside it – but not a dog. At first glance it looked like a bundle of dirty rags. But then I made out a figure curled into a ball, hands gripping ankles, head resting on knees.

Lord Barrule got to his feet and came across the saw-dust floor towards me. 'Are you ready, boy?' he asked. 'I have to tell you that most of the sensible money is on the witch. We all saw what she was capable of when we captured her. Five of my men died; another two lost their minds. So we've tried to give you a fighting chance. We've done the same to her as we've done to her pet. Come and see . . .'

He led the way to the furthest cage, the guards pulling me after him. He halted there and pointed down at the bundle of rags on the filthy straw. I saw the pointy shoes even before she raised her head.

It was Alice, and at the sight of her my throat constricted with emotion. She looked up at me, her eyes filled with tears, and her expression was one of

145

pain and hopelessness. They had stitched her mouth shut with thin brown twine. Her lips were tightly bound together so that she couldn't speak.

'I've had the same done to her mistress. The witch can't utter spells now, boy! But no doubt Lizzie will still manage something . . .'

At that moment, had my staff already been in my hands, I would have thrust its silver-alloy blade into his heart without a moment's hesitation. I was furious at what had been done to Alice. But then despair took over: if I won and the shaman kept his word, I'd be free to take the dogs with me; but Lizzie would die and so would Alice. Either way, I'd lose.

Still, at least I knew that she hadn't been seized by the Fiend and dragged off to the dark. Things looked grim, but as my dad used to say, while there's life there's hope.

'Right! Let's make a start!' Lord Barrule said, and as he returned to his seat, the guards dragged me to the very centre of the long chamber. A dozen yeomen came in, each gripping a long spear, and formed a wide circle about me; then each went down on one knee, facing me, so that the gamblers behind would still have a clear view. Their spears were pointing inwards, and it was clear that their purpose was to mark the boundary of the arena and prevent any escape or retreat from the contest.

Lord Barrule stood up and raised his hand, and I heard a commotion from the doorway; the same one from which I'd entered. Bony Lizzie was brought into the room, kicking and struggling – it took four men to control her.

Two of the yeomen guards moved aside to allow them into the circle, and she was forced to face me. It was the Lizzie I remembered – almost the spitting image of Alice, but older, in her late thirties perhaps, and with shifty eyes and a sneering expression. Her lips were stitched together just like Alice's. The moment she saw me, the witch stopped struggling and a strange, sly look came into her eyes; one of calculation and cunning.

Someone behind me pushed my staff into my left

hand. Instantly I transferred it to my right, feeling in the left pocket of my cloak to check my silver chain. That would offer me the best chance of victory. One disadvantage was that I still ached from the beating I'd received when I was captured. The food I'd eaten had made me stronger physically but I was far from my best.

One of the yeomen handed Lizzie two long knives, each murderously sharp. Our eyes met again and I released the retractable blade on my staff with a click and held it diagonally across me. Lizzie might not realize that I had the chain. For now, I would keep it in reserve.

Lord Barrule clapped his hands three times, and silence fell over the gathering. I could hear Lizzie breathing hard through her nose, almost snorting. I suddenly remembered something about her: in the past she'd always seemed to have her mouth slightly open – no doubt she naturally breathed through it. Or maybe she had a cold? Either way it would be to my advantage if she were struggling for air.

'Let the contest begin!' cried Lord Barrule. 'A fight to the death!'

Wasting no time, Lizzie lunged at me with the blade in her left hand, but I parried it with my staff and began to retreat widdershins, against the clock, moving warily in a slow circle. Her face began to change, eyes bulging. Now, instead of hair, a nest of black snakes writhed from her scalp, forked tongues flickering, their fangs spitting a cloud of venom towards me. A wave of fear washed over me, and I staggered and took a step backwards, a chill gripping my heart.

She was using *dread* against me – the enchantment used by malevolent witches to make themselves terrifying, freezing their helpless opponents to the spot. Such was Lizzie's power that she could cast it without the incantation. What would she be capable of if her mouth were not stitched?

I took a deep breath and resisted. I'd faced worse than this last summer in Greece when I'd tried to enter the Ord, the terrifying citadel of the Ordeen. If I could withstand that terrible pulse of fear – it had caused the instant death of brave warriors – I could overcome whatever Lizzie could throw at me.

I stepped forward and swung my staff at her head. She leaned back, almost overbalancing, and retreated. Now the snakes had disappeared, to be replaced by hair again; her face almost human. The spell was fading. And then a voice spoke right inside my head . . .

Fool! We should work together!

Was it the buggane? But it was a harsh, sibilant voice – not the insidious whisper that I'd been told about. Then I heard it again:

Neither of us can win here. He intends to slay us both!

It had to be Lizzie. But how was she doing it? What spell could grant her that power?

I refused to listen and whirled in fast, avoided a stab from her left hand then cracked her on the right wrist to send the blade spinning from her hand.

There were loud whoops of excitement from the spectators – along with a few groans. I wondered what Lizzie was doing. How could we work together? Was she mad? How could we hope to escape from this room together?

Help me! Do it for my daughter, Alice, or we'll all die here!

Her use of Alice's name angered me, and I thrust my left hand into my pocket and coiled the silver chain about my wrist. As I did so, Lizzie attacked, moving in quickly and catching me off balance. I leaned away but I wasn't fast enough. I felt a sharp pain as her blade slit my forehead below the hairline. I staggered backwards, just managing to block the next blow with my staff, and felt warm blood running down into my left eye. How bad was the cut? I wondered. How deep?

I used the back of my hand to wipe it from my eye, but it only made it worse. I could hardly see out of it now. You needed both eyes to judge distance correctly so I knew I'd have to use my silver chain quickly now, or it would be too late. Once again I thrust my left hand into my pocket and coiled the chain about my wrist.

It was easier to cast a chain about a witch when she was moving right, left or away from you. But Lizzie was attacking again, running straight for me: this was the most difficult shot of all. I had no choice but to attempt it, so I cracked the chain, sending it spiralling towards her.

It dropped over her head, then down over her body, bringing her to her knees. The remaining knife fell from her grasp as the chain tightened. It wasn't a perfect shot because it had dropped over her from shoulder to knee, leaving her head free. Usually a spook needed to bind a witch's mouth so that she couldn't chant dark magic spells, but this time it didn't matter because her mouth was already stitched shut. A wave of relief washed over me. Under the circumstances the shot wasn't so bad after all. I'd won. Throwing the chain was a skill I had honed to a fine art. All those long hours of practice with the post in the Spook's garden had paid off again.

And then there was a brief moment of doubt. Had it been a little *too* easy? I thought to myself. Was this defeat serving Lizzie's purpose in some way?

'Kill her!' shouted the Lord Barrule, rising to his feet.

I lifted my staff and pointed the blade at Lizzie's

heart . . . But then I hesitated . . . I couldn't do it. I'd killed other creatures of the dark before, but never in cold blood like this. Usually, whether bound or not, they'd still presented a threat to me and I'd had to do it quickly. But Bony Lizzie was secure. There was no way she could hope to free herself. Not only that – she was Alice's mother. There was no love lost between them but it made it hard. So I lowered my staff . . .

Well done, boy! I heard Lizzie hiss. *Now see what I've got planned!*

I looked up at Lord Barrule, who was shaking his head. 'Can't bring yourself to do it?' he called out, his voice echoing around the chamber. 'I'm surprised. What sort of master trained you? What kind of a spook's apprentice are you? That was our bargain: kill the witch to gain what I promised. Now you'll have to do something else to earn your freedom. You'll fight the witch's pet!'

My heart sank right down into my boots. He was going to make me fight Alice and there was no way out of it. Two yeomen went over to the far cage. I stared in horror as they pulled her out. The sight of her twisted my insides, wrenching my emotions. Her eyes were wild and full of pain, and what had been done to her mouth was cruel beyond belief. The twine that bound her lips together was cutting into the soft flesh, making them red and swollen.

They dragged her into the circle of spears to face me. Lizzie's blades were pushed into her hands. There was a murmur of conversation from the gamblers and the chink of money as the bets were placed once more. I struggled to think of some way out of our predicament but nothing came. It seemed hopeless. Whatever happened, one of us would die.

Our eyes met. Alice's were glistening with tears. Blood was still running down my forehead and I brushed it away with the back of my hand. How could I fight Alice?

The shaman clapped his hands three times to signal the beginning of the contest. Nothing could have prepared me for what happened next. Alice raised her blades, then rushed towards me as if to take me by surprise. I couldn't believe it. Would she really hurt me after all we'd been through together?

Horrified, I stepped back, instinctively holding my staff across my body, preparing to meet her attack.

CHAPTER 12
THE BONE-YARD'S EYE

I should have known better than to think Alice would attack me.

I wasn't called on to use my staff because she simply brushed past me to reach Lizzie, who was still bound by my silver chain. She knelt down beside her and, before I could react, used a blade to slit through the twine that stitched her mother's lips together.

Had Lizzie been waiting for this to happen all along? If she'd tried to free her own lips with her knife during our struggle, I'd have immediately attacked her with my staff. Had she planned to wait for Alice to do it?

The witch was still on her knees, still bound with my silver chain, but a gloating expression now settled across her face. It puzzled me – for despite her predicament and the armed yeomen who surrounded us, it was a look of triumph.

The yeomen tightened their circle, moving towards us with spears at the ready.

'Kill them all!' shouted the shaman. 'All bets are off. Take no chances. Kill them now!'

In response, Lizzie uttered just one word, almost under her breath. It was indistinct but it sounded like something from the Old Tongue.

Immediately a wave of cold fear rushed towards me – though this was nothing compared to its effect upon the guards around us. Rarely have I seen such panic and terror on so many faces. Some threw down their spears and ran. Others simply fell to their knees and started to sob. All the dogs started whining at once, and there were shouts and cries of fear from the gamblers to my right.

Whether it was a more powerful form of *dread* or some other spell, with just one word Lizzie had, in the space of a few seconds, reduced the yeomen to a cowering rabble. She was now staring at Lord Barrule. I followed her gaze and saw that apart from us three, he was the only person in the room not gripped by terror. Instead he was glaring at us, his face twisted with malevolence. What would he do – use his own dark magic against us? Maybe summon the buggane to his assistance? The threat was palpable in the air. Lizzie hadn't won yet . . .

'Release me from the chain!' she shouted, turning her attention back to me.

It was a command; there was no magic involved. But I didn't hesitate. Instinctively I knew it was the right thing to do. Lizzie represented the only hope Alice and I had of getting out of Greeba Keep alive. I went over to her, picked up the end of the chain, flicking it to uncoil it from her body. She was on her feet even before I'd returned it to my pocket.

With the long nails of her left forefinger and thumb, like a bird tugging worms from wet soil, Lizzie drew the two pieces of twine from her flesh; first the top, then the bottom lip. Next she licked away the drops of blood, pointed her forefinger towards the ceiling and arched her back. Then she shouted three words and stamped her foot.

Instantly there was a crackling roar like a thunderbolt right inside the room. All the torches flickered and died, and we were plunged into absolute darkness. For a moment there was silence; then a small light flared close by. Lizzie was holding a black candle. The dogs started barking and I heard running feet receding into the distance. The yeomen and gamblers were fleeing for their lives – but what about Lord Barrule? Had he gone too, or was he still lurking in the darkness?

'We'll leave by the tunnel, boy!' Lizzie said, taking a step towards me.

'What about the buggane?' I asked.

'Leave the worrying to me,' she replied.

I looked at Alice. She was using one of the blades to cut the twine from her own lips. With a groan of pain she tugged it out. Beads of blood oozed from the wounds.

Lizzie led the way towards the tunnel entrance. What had happened to Barrule? I wondered. Had the witch defeated him so easily? I could see nothing beyond the small circle of yellow light cast by the candle. But as we passed the cages that held Arkwright's dogs, I hesitated. I wanted to free them and take them with me.

When I reached Claw's cage, however, she snarled and hurled herself at me in a fury and was only prevented from sinking her teeth into me by the bars.

'Leave her here, Tom,' Alice said, gripping my arm. 'Ain't worth the risk. We'll find a way to get 'em all out later.'

I nodded and followed her into the tunnel. The three dogs were still under the control of the shaman. The danger in leaving them behind was that he might still make them fight to the death – probably against each other – in revenge. But what choice did I have?

We started to crawl forward along the earthen tunnel. I couldn't see much – Lizzie had the only candle, and she and Alice ahead of me were obscuring most of its light. I still had my candle stub but hadn't time now to use my tinderbox to light it. For the witch it had been but the work of a second to ignite hers by means of dark magic.

The tunnel twisted and turned and went up and down, sometimes quite steeply. Occasionally the roots of a tree would almost block our way, huge woody claws grasping the soil. At one point I thought I saw a thin one twitch. It was probably just my imagination, but I remembered what the Spook had said about the buggane's tunnels moving or collapsing suddenly. I thought I glimpsed bones too – it was hard to tell in the dim flickering candlelight – but at one point I felt sure my fingers had brushed against a cold human skull.

Finally the tunnel headed up towards the surface and we emerged inside a hollow tree. We sat down facing each other with our backs to the inner trunk. There was a smell of damp rotten wood. Above us, patterned with dead flies, spiders' webs hung like curtains, while below, insects scuttled away from the flickering candle.

Lizzie had clearly known exactly where she was heading. 'We're safe enough now!' she said. 'Nowt can get at us here.'

'Not even the buggane?' I asked.

The witch shook her head and gave me an evil smile. 'Find us it will eventually, but I've hidden this place well – right in the middle of its labyrinth. There'll be time enough to sort it out. Though first I'll put an end to its master. Are you hungry, boy?'

I shook my head. I'd eaten a little before the fight with Lizzie, but now I needed to fast to ready myself for any dark magic she might use against me.

'Well, I certainly am. I could eat a bullock, hooves and all!' She pointed upwards into the darkness. 'Climb up there!' she commanded: I could feel the compulsion in her voice and had to resist. 'It'll bring you out onto a branch. It's just a short drop to the ground. Bring me back a couple of rabbits – and make sure they're still alive—'

'No, Tom!' Alice cried in alarm. 'Don't listen to her. She's created a bone-yard here and this tree's right at its centre. You'll be crushed as soon as you touch the ground!'

Although I'd never encountered one, I knew what a bone-yard was from my reading of the Spook's Bestiary. Crafted by dark magic, it made the bones of any creature that entered it very heavy. They were unable to move and were trapped until the witch came, either to collect them for food or harvest their bones for dark magical purposes. Near the centre, the pressure was so great that the victim was crushed to death – though only something very fast, like a hare, would get that far before the magic forces took effect. But here we were right at its centre, in its *eye* – safe from its forces. If I left the hollow tree, however . . .

'You've got a big gob on you, girl!' Lizzie said angrily. 'Wants stitching up again . . .'

Alice ignored her and pulled a small leather pouch from the pocket of her skirt. It contained the herbs she used for healing. She crawled towards me and peered closely at my forehead.

'Nasty cut, that, Tom,' she said. The inside of the tree

trunk was wet in places and Alice collected some moisture with her fingers and used it to dampen a leaf before pressing it firmly against my skin. 'That should do it, keep infection away – but you'll have a scar. Nothing I can do about that.'

So I'd have another scar to add to the one on my ear where Morwena, the water witch, had once hooked me with her finger, driving the nail right through the flesh. It was all part of the job; to be expected when training for the dangerous job of spook.

Next Alice licked her lips and pressed small pieces of leaf against the holes around her mouth left by the twine. When she'd finished, she held a leaf out towards her mother, but Bony Lizzie shook her head.

'I'll heal myself, girl. Don't need your help,' she sneered, getting to her feet. 'I'll go and get my own rabbits. You two stay here if you know what's good for you!'

With that she began to climb up the inside of the tree, pushing her head through the curtain of spider webs. She was soon lost to view in the darkness, but we could hear her pointy shoes scrabbling on bark, and then a soft thud as she dropped to the ground outside. Lizzie would be safe enough in her own bone-yard: a witch usually left a secret twisty path so she could move through it unharmed. She could also guide others through – but how could we force her to do that? Our only real option was to go back into the tunnels, but I didn't fancy our chances against the buggane one bit.

'Oh, Tom, is the blood jar safe? Do you still have it?' Alice asked, her eyes full of anxiety.

'Yes, it's safe. I wasn't searched. Barrule even let me keep my silver chain – but how were you caught, Alice?' I wondered. 'I saw you roll over and avoid the buggane, but then you just disappeared.'

'I hid behind a tree so it couldn't charge me again, but then Lizzie stole up on me – clamped her hand over my mouth, she did. I never sensed her coming – must have used some really powerful magic. She dragged me away and brought me here. Before that she'd been hidden here for days. They'd never have found her, but she took a risk because she wants Old Gregory really badly. Wants him dead, she does, in revenge for binding her in that pit in his garden. Wants to give him a slow, painful death.

'So later that night we set off hunting for him. She had me bound fast under a spell and only half my head was working. Couldn't object to anything she did or said. But she was too confident – didn't even bother long-sniffing for danger. Thought she could deal with anything. When we were out in the open, the shaman's men attacked us. She used *dread* and killed several of the yeomen, she did – some with her knives, a couple with curses – but there were too many of them. Eventually they beat her unconscious with the ends of their spears and dragged us to Greeba Keep.'

'Did you see any of the other prisoners?' I asked, thinking about Adriana.

Alice shook her head. 'Saw nobody – put us in separate cells. They brought me up to the cage just before you came in. Didn't see her again until they dragged her in to fight you. It's been bad, Tom, really bad – especially when they stitched my lips together. But the worst part of all was when the buggane crawled out of the tunnel and sniffed at me. All hairy, it was, with big sharp teeth. I thought I was going to die and would never see you again . . .'

She began to sob, so I put my arms round her and hugged her tight. After a while she calmed down, and we sat there, holding hands for comfort.

'Do you know anything about the spell that controls a bone-yard, Alice?' I asked at last. 'Could you find Lizzie's secret path through it?'

'Wouldn't want me to use dark magic, Tom, would you? Can't be asking me to do that . . . ?' There was an edge of sarcasm in Alice's voice.

For a long time I had avoided using the dark in any way, even when I was fighting for my life. Alice had struggled to persuade me to use the blood jar. But my worries about my recent separation from her had largely been unfounded. She'd been close to Lizzie, and the Fiend couldn't approach a witch who'd had a child by him.

'It was just a thought, Alice. I can't think of any other way of getting out of here. Not unless we risk the tunnels . . .'

'We'd be better off doing that than tampering with Lizzie's yard. It's true that there's a path through it, but it's hard to find. Dangerous things to meddle with, they are. Make one mistake and you're dead—'

Suddenly we heard a noise outside. Someone had started climbing down the tree. Moments later, Lizzie's pointy shoes came into view and she dropped down the last few feet to stand before us, clutching something in her left hand.

'Couldn't find any rabbits so these will have to do,' she spat, holding up three dead rats by their tails. She tossed one at our feet.

'I can spare one but I'll need the other two. Need to build up my strength for what's ahead, and rat's blood is as good as anything. It'll do until I take your thumbs, boy!'

CHAPTER 13
MY GIFT TO THE COUNTY

'Over my dead body!' Alice shouted, rising angrily to her feet.

Bony Lizzie gave a wicked smile. 'Let's hope it don't come to that, girl. Calm down. I've another use for the boy that should allow him to keep breathing a little while longer – that's if things go well.'

The witch sat down and, setting one rat aside, lifted the other by its long thin tail. She bit its head off and spat it out, then started to suck the blood from its neck; some dribbled out of her mouth and down her chin. She drank noisily, and the unpleasant sounds made me feel sick to my stomach. I shuddered, and Alice reached across and squeezed my hand.

169

Lizzie looked at our joined hands, lowered the rat and smirked. 'What a fool you are, girl!' she told Alice. 'No man's worth a second glance. Never get too close to 'em. This boy will bring you down for sure. Be the ruin of you. Many a good witch has gone soft because of a man.'

'Me and Tom are good friends,' Alice retorted. 'That's something you know nothing about. Eating rats and killing people – that's all you're good for. Why did I have to have a mother like you? What did you want with the Fiend? Couldn't you find a normal man?'

Lizzie's expression hardened and she glared at Alice. 'I've had men, but none of 'em have lasted long. They liked pretty young things, they did. Know why? Because they're scared. Scared of a real woman in her prime. They look at me, see what I am and run back to their mothers. Know how old I am, girl?'

Alice shook her head and squeezed my hand again.

'I turned forty just a week ago, the day after Old Gregory's house burned and I got out of the pit. A Pendle witch comes into her prime at forty and inherits her full power. Now I've got the strength to deal with anybody. You, daughter, could be even stronger one day.' Lizzie gave me an evil smile, staring straight into my eyes. 'Know what Alice is, boy? She's my gift to the County . . .'

She smirked meaningfully when she uttered that last bit. It was what Mam had once said about me in a letter to the Spook. Could Lizzie read my mind now? Pluck things out of it as if she were rifling through an open drawer?

'She's my special gift to the Pendle clans,' the witch continued after a pause. 'One day she'll unite 'em once and for all, and then the world had better watch out!'

She went back to drinking the rat's blood. Once it was drained she started on the second, sucking and slurping until there wasn't a drop left. Seeing that we hadn't touched the third, she took that one too.

Gradually it began to lighten inside the tree trunk, indicating that the dawn was close.

'Are you thirsty?' I asked Alice.

She nodded. 'My throat's parched.'

'It'll rain soon,' Lizzie said, with an evil laugh. 'Have all the water you want then!'

She was right. Within the hour it began to rain. First a light pitter-patter against the tree, soon followed by the drumming of a heavy downpour. Hour after hour it went on, and water began to drip into the tree, eventually cascading down the inside of the trunk.

It was running water, and Lizzie didn't like that, so she moved away from the trunk, but Alice and I caught enough in our cupped hands to slake the worst of our thirst. It must have been early in the afternoon when the rain eased. It was then that we heard the dogs.

Lizzie gave a gloating smile and moved across to lean against the wood once more. 'Dogs got our scent,' she said. 'Not that it'll do 'em much good. Not when they enter the yard . . .'

I pictured the dogs running towards the bone-yard, heading towards the tree at its centre. Their speed would carry them close before the pressure crushed them.

'Claw and her pups . . .' I said, looking with dismay at Alice.

'He won't be using them, boy, you needn't fear. He's another use for those dogs,' said Lizzie. 'He'll want you to fight 'em – and to the death!'

'How can you know that?' I asked angrily.

She smirked. 'Easy to read, he is. That's what he had planned last night. First you'd fight me, then, if you won, Alice. Finally your own dogs. Sniffed it out, I did. They call that type of bet a treble. Each win is carried forward to the next stage. Gives you a big pay-day if you win all three. Odds were against you, but the shaman liked those odds. Didn't work out for him, did it? But given half the chance he'll still pit you against those dogs. Just you wait and see . . .'

The barking was getting closer, but the sound quickly turned to yelps and whines as the first of them blundered into the bone-yard and started to feel the pressure exerted by Lizzie's dark magic.

'Won't get too close so they won't know our exact hiding place,' she said. 'Wouldn't help them if they did

173

though. We're safe enough here – at least from the likes of them.'

Now I heard men shouting and cursing in the distance, calling their dogs back. Then there was suddenly a louder scream. This time it came from a human throat and Lizzie smiled. It went on for a long time and Alice covered her ears. At last, except for the patter of light rain, there was silence.

The time passed slowly but my mind raced. I was desperately trying to think of a way out of this. I still had my staff and my chain, but even if I could bind Lizzie again, what could Alice and I do against the buggane?

As it started to get dark, we heard a noise emanating from the tunnels. Had the shaman's men found us? But as the sounds drew closer, they became more disturbing. I'd heard them before.

'It's found us at last,' said Lizzie. 'Certainly took its time.'

Now I could hear a snuffling: the buggane had

174

arrived. Lizzie crawled to the centre of the hollow tree, pulled out the stub of her black wax candle and said a word under her breath. It ignited just in time to illuminate the monstrous hairy head of the buggane as it protruded from the mouth of the tunnel. Its big cruel eyes looked at us one by one, finally settling on Bony Lizzie. Rather than retreating, the witch shuffled forward on her knees and slowly stretched out her hand.

The buggane opened its mouth wide and growled, showing its two rows of teeth, but Lizzie's hand continued to advance.

'There, there, what a good boy you are,' she said in a soft, husky voice. 'What a handsome hairy thing you be, your coat all fine and glossy . . .'

Her left hand was actually touching the buggane now; she was stroking its hideous head just above its wet snout.

'There, there, my sweet,' she crooned. 'We could help each other . . .'

With those words, Lizzie raised her left hand and pierced her wrist with the long sharp nail of her right forefinger. She positioned the wound above the creature, and drops of blood began to fall onto its snout. Suddenly, from between the sharp triangular teeth, a long purple tongue emerged and began to lick up the blood with an unpleasant slurping sound.

She was feeding the buggane, trying to make it her familiar.

'Good boy! Good boy! Lick it all up. There's more where that came from. Now go back to your master and tell him exactly where we are. It's time we had a little chat . . .'

The buggane slowly backed away into the tunnel and Lizzie turned towards us triumphantly. 'That's a good start! Soon we'll put it to the test. But our next visitor prefers the dark – so let's oblige him!'

With those words she blew out the candle, plunging us into darkness.

It wasn't long before a luminous shape began to form in front of the tunnel. It was the tall, gaunt figure of the shaman.

'I've found you at last,' he said, his cruel eyes looking only at Lizzie. 'I'll make you pay for leading me such a merry dance!'

'There's no need for harsh words between us,' Lizzie replied, a crafty look coming over her face.

'No? There's another good man dead, plus five of my best dogs. I owe you for that!'

'How about what you done to me?' the witch accused. 'You stitched my lips together. No man ever shut me up like that before. I should kill you for that, but if we can settle it another way, I'll let bygones be bygones—'

'It'll be settled all right. Within an hour I'll show you what I can do. I'll send the buggane – this time in its spirit form. I'll start with your pet, the girl. By the end of the night she'll be as good as dead. Next the boy. I'll save you until the end so you'll have time to dwell on what's going to happen—'

'Suppose the buggane listens to *me*!' Lizzie shouted. 'Suppose it whispers inside *your* head? Maybe then you'll be ready to talk terms . . .'

177

The shaman scowled and his lips curled disdainfully; then his image faded and disappeared altogether.

'Can you do that?' Alice asked out of the darkness. She sounded scared.

'Can't make it whisper inside his head yet, but he doesn't know that, does he? I said enough to make him think, though. You needn't fear, girl. I've already done enough to keep it away from us. It won't be sure what to do for a while yet. When Lord Barrule finds out it won't do his bidding, he'll be back, just you mark my words!'

Alice's hand found mine again in the darkness and I squeezed it in reassurance. After that nobody spoke for a long time. Lizzie's strength was being put to the test. Could she really keep the buggane away from Alice? I wondered.

After a couple of hours, the image of the shaman began to form again.

'You're soon back!' Lizzie crowed. 'No whispering inside the girl's head yet, is there, my sweet?' she said, turning towards Alice.

'Ain't heard a thing,' Alice said.

'What do you want, witch?'

'Our lives and a safe passage from Mona. West to Ireland, across the sea to the Emerald Isle – that's where we want to go.'

'What's in it for me? You mentioned terms. So what do I get?'

'First you get to keep your power over the buggane. Longer I stay here, more likely it is to be mine. So it's in *your* interests to get me off this island. Next I'll give you the boy. Last thing I want travelling with me is a spook's apprentice. Betting man, aren't you? So make him fight his own dogs – to the death. That should be interesting!'

'No!' Alice cried.

'I won't do it!' I protested.

'Shut your face, girl! Silence! You can both be quiet!'

And then Lizzie said a word under her breath, something guttural in the Old Tongue. My throat tightened, and for a moment I couldn't breathe. I managed to draw in a breath, although I still couldn't speak. I'd always had some degree of resistance to the dark – being a seventh son of a seventh son had given me that – but I seemed helpless in the face of Lizzie's dark power. I tried to stand but my limbs didn't respond. It was as if I were made of stone. I saw Alice start towards me, but then she too was gripped by some dark spell.

'In return, you pull all your men away from the area around here,' she continued, turning her attention back to the shaman's spirit. 'Call them back into the keep. Once the boy starts to fight, I'll leave this tree, but only when I'm safely off this island will the buggane do your bidding again. Are we agreed?'

The apparition glared at the witch for quite a while without speaking, then gave just the slightest of nods.

Lizzie smiled. 'Knew you'd see the sense of it. Rare thing, that. Not many sensible men about. Now send two more sensible men through the tunnels for the boy – that's if you can find any. If they ain't sensible, they'll be dead! So no funny business . . .'

* * *

It was a matter of minutes before I heard the shaman's men crawling through the tunnel towards the hollow tree. I was still holding hands with Alice, my left hand in her left hand, gasping for breath.

Lizzie lit her candle again and held it up as the first of the men emerged. He looked scared and stood, uncertain what to do. But the witch instantly took command.

'That's the boy you've come for!' she cried, pointing at me.

They dragged me towards the dark entrance of the tunnel. My paralysis was passing, giving way to painful pins and needles, but I was still weak and unable to resist.

'Don't forget his staff!' cried Lizzie. 'Be needing that, he will! It's dead dogs or a dead boy. One or the other, that's for sure!'

CHAPTER
14
FIGHT TO THE DEATH

They pulled and pushed me back along the claustrophobic system of earthen tunnels, until I heard the sound of barking in the distance and we finally emerged in the long room with the cages. I felt depressed and angry. After all I'd gone through defeating Lizzie and finally escaping, I'd been returned to the same point.

There were plenty of yeomen armed with spears and clubs, but only a few gamblers now sat on the straw bales. Lord Barrule was waiting in the middle of the room, standing on the blood-splattered sawdust with folded arms.

'If I weren't a betting man, I'd take your life now, boy,

182

and do it very slowly,' he said. 'But for a good fight you need some incentive so I'll still let you go if you win. This time, of course, you won't be able to take your dogs with you – you'll already have killed them. What do you say?'

I hung my head, appalled at what I was being asked to do.

'Suit yourself – but I think you'll fight anyway in self-preservation. Who wouldn't? Anyway, you'll have time to think. I'm waiting for a few more people to arrive. Can't pass up the chance to take their money – and it's the taking rather than the money that's important to me. And who do you think *my* money's on this time?'

Again I didn't reply. Their gambling fun would go on, and here on this spot there would be more deaths to add to all the ones they'd already witnessed. For how many years had the shaman and his cronies carried on in this way? I wondered.

'Most of the money will be on you because they saw how you defeated the witch. But I disagree. I've changed my mind because you're too soft – I can see that now. If you couldn't kill the witch, then you certainly won't be able to kill your own dogs. They'll rip out your throat. So I'm betting on the dogs, boy!'

The shaman walked away, and the two men dragged me to one side and forced me to squat down on the floor while we waited for the proceedings to begin. It took over an hour as, one by one, other gamblers entered the room and placed their bets. Who were these people – upright members of the local community who had this secret vice? Not all those present looked equally happy. No doubt most were afraid of Barrule and had little option but to join him here; others seemed as enthusiastic as he was, their faces eager.

Some of the latter walked over to assess the dogs; a couple even came to look at me.

'Make him stand,' one said. 'Not injured, is he?'

'Up you come, lad!' commanded the yeoman. When I hesitated, he bunched his fist in my hair and dragged me to my feet.

'Will he be armed like last time?' another asked.

'That he will, staff and all! But that silver chain won't be much use against the dogs!' The guard laughed, then pushed me to my knees again. 'Get all the rest you can,' he advised mockingly. 'You're going to need it. Those teeth will be taking pieces of you soon – starting with the tender bits!'

The caged dogs were barking and whining, and I glanced over to where Arkwright's three were confined. What was I going to do? How could I kill them? The mother, Claw, had saved my life in the past and, but for the dark power of the shaman, would be on my side rather than his, as would her pups. I had no illusions about what would happen if I did win. The shaman would not keep his word. He'd either kill me or devise some other gambling entertainment in which I would play a central and painful role.

I also found it hard to believe that he'd grant Bony Lizzie free passage from the island. He might pull back his men while she went through the bone-yard and west towards the coast. But he'd hunt her down long before she reached the sea. Whatever her fate, poor

Alice would share it too. If the Fiend didn't find her first.

What of the Spook? Where was he? I wondered. I hoped for his sake that he wouldn't attempt to rescue me. What chance did he have? And if he fell into Lizzie's hands, he would die the slowest and most terrible death imaginable.

I'd been in many dangerous situations before, but this was one of the worst: I was caught between two powerful dark adversaries, a witch and a shaman, and could see no way to triumph over either of them.

My gloomy thoughts were interrupted by a clank of metal. The sporadic barking gave way to the odd whimper. Claw, Blood and Bone were being released and dragged by their collars towards the centre of the sawdust arena.

'On your feet, boy!' snapped one of my guards, tugging me up by my hair again.

As a hushed expectancy descended on the room, I was pushed forward to face the three dogs. I gazed down at them in sorrow. Their coats were matted with dirt and they clearly hadn't been fed in days. Not one of them could meet my eye. They looked abject and defeated before we started – though I knew that was the shaman's doing. In a moment he would ready them to fight.

I noticed that this time there was no circle of spearmen. It was the witch that had worried them last time. The dogs would fight me to the death, and anyway, where could I possibly run to?

Barrule was seated on his wooden throne again, and I watched in dismay as he got to his feet and clapped his hands three times. Instantly the dogs were transformed: they locked eyes with me and began to growl, their jaws opening, ready to bite and tear. Their nervous handlers released their collars and the three wolfhounds instantly leaped towards me like furies.

I whirled away as they attacked, swinging my staff to keep them at bay. I kept my blade retracted; there was no way I intended to employ it here. Blood and Bone came straight for me, and for the first time I used my staff to fend them off. I jabbed Blood in the neck and cracked Bone across the head, trying not to put too much force into either blow. But in that moment of distraction, Claw leaped at me from behind. The weight of her knocked me to my knees and I almost let go of my staff. That brought a groan from some sections of the crowd.

I was up in an instant, whirling my staff again desperately, trying to fend the three dogs off. But they were brave hunters, trained by Bill Arkwright to hunt dangerous water creatures across the marshes north of Caster. If they could attack a water witch, despite the threat from her deadly talons, they would certainly not fear me. This was to the death. It was them or me.

Then I surprised even myself. With a click I released the retractable blade in my staff. It wasn't a conscious decision: something deep inside me had chosen not to die. Not here. Not now.

I was shocked at what I'd done. Could I really bring myself to kill these dogs? My head was suddenly filled with justifications for my instinctive act . . .

I had work to do, the County to defend. Then

a whole new terror gripped me. If I died now, I remembered, the Fiend would take my soul! I had to destroy him before that happened or my fate would be an eternity of terror and torment in the dark.

All three dogs now attacked together, and before I could use my staff, they were upon me. Their combined weight brought me to my knees again. My staff was knocked out of my hand with the force of the blow. Bone fastened his teeth on my ankle; Claw had a grip on my shoulder; and Blood went straight for my throat. I thrust out my right hand to fend off those huge jaws, and the teeth closed around my hand, biting hard. I had to get up or I was finished . . .

But suddenly the dogs released me. Simultaneously I heard a gasp of fear from the audience and the lights in the long room flickered and dimmed. I moved into a crouch and picked up my staff again.

The torches were threatening to go out at any moment. In the gathering darkness, close by, a luminous spectral shape was starting to form. It was man-shaped but at least twice normal size, and it was glowing an ominous blood-red.

I gazed at it in awe, but those feelings quickly gave way to shock and surprise. The figure was in the garb of a spook and was holding a staff in his left hand – a staff that was blackened and burned; so too was the left side of the face – terrible disfiguring burns, with one eye gone. The cloak was in tatters, the hands covered in blisters.

It was the ghost of Bill Arkwright!

CHAPTER 15
THUMB-BONES

I'd last set eyes on Bill Arkwright the previous summer, in Greece, when he'd stayed behind in the Ord, volunteering to hold off a cluster of fire elementals while we made our escape.

We had assumed he'd made the ultimate spook's sacrifice and died, and now we were proved correct. He'd been burned to death, as was now horribly plain to see. But what was he doing here? Had Bill Arkwright been trapped in the dark when the Ord had collapsed back through its fiery portal? Or was he in Limbo, that fringe area between life and death where traumatized spirits sometimes linger for years before finding their way to the light?

At first I thought Arkwright's ghost was looking at me. But no – his one eye was staring directly at the dogs. And although the room was emptying fast, filled with the cries of men driven close to insanity by fear, all three were wagging their tails with pleasure at the sight, grim though it was, of their former master.

Out of the corner of my eye I saw the shaman slowly rise to his feet and take a step towards us, a look of puzzlement on his face.

The figure suddenly stretched out its right arm and pointed directly at me, and then Arkwright's voice cried out, filled with the power of command, echoing around the room.

'That boy is your friend, not your enemy!' he told the dogs.

The ghostly arm swung slowly to the right to indicate the shaman. *'The man over there! That's your true enemy! Kill him now!'*

As one, the dogs surged forward and leaped at the shaman, their jaws open. He raised an arm to defend himself, his mouth wide in shock, but it was hopeless.

All his power over the animals was now useless. The three wolfhounds dragged him to the floor and began to savage him, their teeth biting and tearing at his flesh. He screamed – and the long drawn-out sound could be clearly heard over the snarls of his attackers. I began to retch at the sight and sound of his agony.

As the ghost of Bill Arkwright slowly faded away, the torches guttered out, plunging us into total darkness. The dogs had finished their grim work and, but for their panting, there was silence. I knelt, utterly spent and shaking all over. After a while there was a noise from the tunnel. Someone was approaching. Was it the buggane?

Shakily I got to my feet, but the figure that emerged was Bony Lizzie, clutching her lit candle stub. Behind her was Alice.

'That went well, boy,' said the witch, staring down at the shaman, her face exultant. 'Wasn't as strong as he thought, was he? Doesn't pay to mess with me! Well, waste not, want not – that's what Old Mother Malkin used to tell me . . .'

And with those words Lizzie placed the candle on

the floor, then pointed at the two nearest wall-torches, which obediently flared into life. Next she pulled a knife from the hip pocket of her dress and lifted the shaman's left hand. I heard Alice groan, and we both turned our backs on the grisly sight as Lizzie took the thumb-bones of her dead enemy.

She must have planned this all along, I realized. She'd never intended to make her escape. Never for a moment had the shaman suspected that she'd attack rather than retreat. And she'd used the ghost of Bill Arkwright to achieve her aim. That meant his spirit must be in her power. After all, she was a powerful bone witch, and necromancy – control of the dead – was amongst her dark weapons.

While she crouched down to take the shaman's bones, Lizzie was a perfect target for my silver chain. But when I reached for it, I could get my fingertips nowhere near my pocket. I tried with all my strength, and although my hand strained and trembled, I could not reach the chain. Lizzie was still exerting some special power over me.

She looked up at me and Alice, clutching the bloody bones, an ecstatic expression on her face. 'Feel good, these do!' she cried, stuffing them into her pocket along with the knife and rising to her feet. 'There's power here all right! Now, let's take a little walk upstairs and see what's what! But first we'll get the dogs back into their cages . . .'

She clapped her hands three times, just as the shaman had done, and Claw, Blood and Bone emerged from the shadows and trotted back to their cages obediently. 'Right, boy, fasten them in!'

It was clear that the witch could control the dogs now, but did she have all the shaman's powers? With his death, had they passed to her? As if in a dream, unable to resist, I went over and closed the cage doors, snapping the clasps across. As I attended to Claw's cage, she gave a little whine and tried to lick me through the bars. I felt a surge of hope. Had that been Arkwright's doing? Although forced by Lizzie to make the dogs kill the shaman, his ghost had first pointed to me and said: *That boy is your friend, not your enemy!*

With those words, had he given the dogs back to me? Had he done his best to help?

Alice and I followed Bony Lizzie along the damp corridors. As we reached the stone steps and started to climb, I felt the pulse of fear radiate from the witch once more. She was using it as a weapon to clear the areas ahead of any opposition to our progress. Three flights up, we emerged in the guardroom that I'd crossed on my way down to the cells. Spears, pikes and clubs stood in racks along the wall and a fire blazed in the grate; half-eaten meals had been abandoned on a long table. The plates were still steaming. The occupants of the room must have fled very recently.

I'd expected Lizzie to lead us out of Greeba Keep, and wondered if the inner portcullis would be raised. Even if it was, there was still the one barring the main entrance to contend with. But, to my surprise, Lizzie continued up into the tower. She seemed supremely confident: with the shaman dead, perhaps she was no longer in any danger. As we climbed, she tried every door and peered into the rooms: bedrooms, drawing rooms and the extensive kitchens – all deserted. Then, at the top, we came to the largest room of all. It was clad in white marble and the walls were hung with tapestries. A long narrow crimson carpet ran the length of the room, right up to a dais seven steps high; atop it was an ornate throne made of jade.

This must be the throne room where the shaman, Lord Barrule, had held court and meted out his rough justice. It was impressive – fit for a king, never mind a lord. From the doorway, Lizzie gazed at that throne for a long time, then went over to the only window. It had a recessed seat, and she sat and looked out for a while without speaking. Alice and I came up behind her and followed her gaze downwards.

Far below, people were still fleeing the keep. The outer portcullis was raised, and beyond the bridge over the moat, groups of yeomen were staring up at the tower. With them was Stanton, their commander, sword at his hip: there was no hope of escaping that way.

Lizzie turned away from the window with a faint

smile on her face, then slowly walked the length of the carpet, heading for that green throne. With each step the heels of her pointy shoes made deep indentations in the crimson carpet and their soles soiled it with mud from the tunnels.

Then, very deliberately, she sat herself down on the throne and beckoned us forward. Alice and I moved closer, until we were standing at the foot of the steps.

'I could rule this island,' Lizzie said. 'I could be its queen!'

'A queen? You? You're no queen,' Alice sneered. 'Look like you been dragged through a hedge backwards and rolled in a midden!'

It was true. The witch's clothes were splattered with mud; her hair was caked with it. She scowled and stood up, anger flickering in her eyes. Alice took a step backwards, but then Lizzie smiled. 'We'll see, girl. We'll soon see about that.' She pointed to a door behind the throne. 'Let's see what we've got here . . .'

We followed her through the door and discovered

that we weren't at the highest point in the tower after all. There was yet another flight of steep steps, which led up to a circular antechamber with eight doors. We entered the rooms in turn, moving anticlockwise. Like the throne room, each had a large curtained window with a seat recessed into the outer wall. The first had a tiled floor and a large wooden bath. Lizzie gazed at the bath and smiled. The next five were luxurious bedrooms, hung with ornate mirrors and rich tapestries.

The seventh was the shaman's study: three rows of shelves held his books – mostly grimoires – and on a large wooden table a big notebook lay open next to a human skull. Other shelves contained bottles and jars of potions. In the corner was a large chest, but when Lizzie tried it, she found it was locked.

'I could get it open myself, but that'll take time and be a waste of power. Why bark yourself when you've got a dog to do it for you? Come on, boy, get out that key of yours and open this up.'

How did Lizzie know about my key? I wondered.

What else did she know? Could she read all my thoughts?

But the chest had belonged to the shaman – it might well contain things that would increase the witch's power – so I shook my head.

'Refusing, are you? I'll show you what happens to those who disobey me . . .'

Lizzie's face darkened and she started to mutter a spell; in an instant the room grew cold, and fear constricted my throat. And there seemed to be things moving in the darkest corners – threatening, shadowy forms. I gripped my staff tightly, my eyes darting this way and that. When I looked directly at the creatures, they disappeared; when I looked away, they grew and moved closer.

'Do what she wants, Tom. Please,' Alice begged.

So I nodded and pulled the key from my pocket.

I'd have to make a stand against Lizzie soon, but I'd do it when she was least expecting it. I just hoped that whatever was in the chest would be of no use to a bone witch.

The special key, crafted by the Spook's brother Andrew, a master locksmith, didn't let me down this time. I lifted the lid and saw that the chest contained money: bags of both gold and silver coins.

I thought Lizzie would be disappointed, but she only smiled again. 'Useful thing, money,' she said. 'Put it to good use, I can. Lock it up again, boy. We don't want anyone else to get their thieving hands on it.' She looked around the room, her eyes settling on the bottles and jars, then finally on the open notebook. 'I'll be having a good root around in here before long,' she muttered. 'See what he's been up to. Who knows – I might learn something new.'

How long did Bony Lizzie intend to stay? I wondered. Was she serious about ruling the island? If so, how did she plan to do so with her enemies gathered beyond the keep? They'd been badly frightened, but that wouldn't last for ever. Soon they'd come back in force. They'd captured her before; if enough of them could summon up the courage, they could do it again. Then Alice and I would suffer as her accomplices.

The eighth door led to a large dressing room containing clothes – rich, elaborate gowns, suitable attire for a royal court. They must have belonged to Barrule's wife.

'They look just my size,' Lizzie smirked. 'Know what you two are going to do next?'

We didn't answer.

'Fill my bath!' she cried. 'Heat the water in the kitchen and bring it up. Half an hour and I want it done!'

'Washing behind your ears ain't going to turn you into a queen!' Alice snapped.

Lizzie hissed furiously and Alice gave a cry of fear and backed away. I gripped her hand and quickly led her back into the antechamber, then down the steps to the throne room.

'What we going to do, Tom?' she asked.

'Escape and find the Spook,' I told her, 'though I don't know how yet. We can't go that way . . .' I pointed at the window. Down below, the courtyard was empty. There seemed to be nobody at all within the walls of Greeba Keep, but there were still plenty of men beyond the open gate. They'd lit fires and were standing or sitting around them.

'I wouldn't like to risk the tunnels,' Alice said. 'I know what Lizzie's capable of. The buggane's as good as hers already. She'd send it after us for sure.'

'Then there's only one thing we can do for now,' I told her. 'Get Lizzie's bath ready . . .'

Alice nodded. 'At least it'll make her smell better!' she retorted.

So we went down to the kitchen and, after helping ourselves to some cold chicken, prepared Lizzie's hot water. The cooking fires were still burning and there were barrels of water there. Soon we had water heating in three big cauldrons. That was the easy part; getting it up the stairs and into Lizzie's bath was back-breaking work.

Down in the throne room again, we sat in the window seat and looked out. Beyond the moat nothing had changed, but spits had been set up above each fire; the yeomen camped around them were preparing to eat.

There seemed to be no immediate danger from them.

'Alice, why is Lizzie suddenly so strong?' I wondered. 'She stopped me from using my chain against her earlier – I couldn't even get my hand into my pocket. She seems so confident. Look at the way she's allowed us to roam free while she bathes – as if she has nothing to fear from us – and she's right. I can sense her new strength.'

'Some truth in what she said before about her age,' Alice answered. 'Pendle witches reckon to come into their full strength when they turn forty. But Lizzie's always been powerful and dangerous. I know what she's capable of. Got fresh bones too – a shaman's – so that's bound to help her. Tricked him and beat him good and proper, she did. Rare and hard to get, a shaman's bones. No knowing how strong that might make her— Look, Tom!' Alice cried, pointing towards the portcullis. 'Something's happening down there. Looks like they're getting ready to attack . . .'

But it was only two yeomen crossing the bridge, and they seemed to have a prisoner between them, his hands bound behind his back. Once in the courtyard, they cut the ropes and freed him, then thrust something at him – a staff.

It was the Spook.

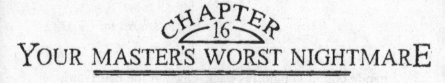

CHAPTER 16
YOUR MASTER'S WORST NIGHTMARE

'Quick, Tom. Go down and warn him!' Alice cried as she saw the Spook walking towards the tower. 'What chance has he got against Lizzie now?'

'Come with me,' I said, tugging at her arm.

'No, I'll stay here and keep her royal highness occupied. I'll ask her if she wants more hot water. The longer we keep her in that bath, the more chance Old Gregory will have. Don't you worry, I'll be fine.'

I didn't like leaving her with Bony Lizzie but I had little choice. What Alice said made sense. Maybe she could distract the witch. I knew I had to warn my master. If he came up not realizing how strong Lizzie

206

was now, he could end up either dead or in the dungeons, food for the buggane.

So I left Alice and began to run down the steps as fast as I could. I met the Spook as he was coming through the guardroom. We almost collided.

'Steady on, lad!' he cried.

'Lizzie's really powerful now!' I said, struggling to catch my breath. 'She can freeze you with a word. She stopped me from getting my chain out of my pocket!'

The Spook leaned his staff against the guardroom table and took a seat. 'I thought there must be something different about the witch. There's a small army out there and yet they don't feel able to walk in through the gate and deal with her. They think the shaman's dead. Is that so?'

I nodded. 'Lizzie took his bones.'

'So that's one less servant of the dark to worry about ... Lizzie's got the yeomen scared all right – they've resorted to sending me in to deal with her – a spook, and a foreigner to boot. These people have always been fiercely independent, so they must be desperate.'

'She's talking about becoming Queen of Mona . . .' I told my master.

He raised his eyebrows at that. 'So tell me all about it. Take your time and leave nothing out—'

'But she's having a bath right at this moment. This could be your best chance!'

'Bony Lizzie having a bath? Now I've heard it all!' said the Spook, giving me a rare smile. 'But I won't take another step until I know what's what. Sooner you start, lad, the sooner you'll finish!'

So I did as he asked. I told him about Alice and Lizzie's lips being stitched and the buggane's tunnels leading into each cell. Then about the fight and our escape, and then how she'd crooned to the buggane; finally about facing the dogs, the appearance of Bill Arkwright's ghost and the shaman's death.

My master shook his head. 'She's certainly got delusions of grandeur – though she's dangerous all right. Poor Bill . . . at least once we've sorted Lizzie, he'll be able to break free.

'But this is as bad as it could be, lad. I've been sent

in here to sort out that witch, but once it's done, they won't need me any more. There'll be a new master of Greeba Keep and things will go on much the same as ever. We might well end up in the dungeons again. They'll carry on appeasing the buggane even though the shaman's dead. They'll be back to their old tricks. It's the way of the world, I'm afraid. History repeating itself.' My master sighed deeply, lost in thought for a moment.

'I've faced similar situations before. I'm getting weary of it all, lad – tired in body, mind and spirit. Still, we'll worry about that later. First we must sort out Lizzie,' he finished, getting to his feet.

'What if she's too strong? What if—?'

'Look, lad, don't you worry – I've faced many a witch before and come out on top. You're young and still an apprentice. That's why she was able to control you. Let's go and get this over with! Lead the way to Lizzie . . .'

I didn't like it one bit, but I did as my master ordered. I just hoped that the witch was still in her bath. But as soon as we entered the throne room, I knew I'd been right to be pessimistic.

Bony Lizzie was seated on the throne and Alice was standing on the steps, looking terrified. Lizzie was dressed in a long purple gown, her hair wet but combed straight so that it framed her face, her lips painted red. She looked imposing – if not quite a queen, then certainly like a woman accustomed to life at court. But what really frightened me was her manner and the expression on her face.

She looked in total control, and I felt waves of cold malice radiating from her. However, the Spook looked resolute, and he began to stride down the carpet towards the throne.

He halted at the foot of the steps. I was close behind him, and I saw him ease his left hand into the pocket of his breeches to curl the silver chain about his wrist. I remembered the last time my master had faced Lizzie, right at the very beginning of my apprenticeship. He'd killed Tusk, her powerful abhuman accomplice, and then bound the witch with his silver chain before carrying her over his shoulder back to a pit at Chipenden. Could he do it again? He certainly thought so. And surely Lizzie must remember what had happened last time?

I soon realized that she wasn't the least bit concerned. In fact she wasn't even looking at the Spook. She was looking at me, her eyes filled with malevolence.

'Can't be trusted, can you, boy? Soon as my back's turned you run off to get your master. I should kill you now . . .'

Wasting no time, the Spook spun the chain, casting it towards Lizzie. She was still on the throne; it was an easy shot – the witch was as good as bound. I watched the chain shape itself into a gleaming, deadly spiral – but to my dismay it fell harmlessly to the floor a foot to the right of her.

How could he have missed? Powerful dark magic had to be the answer. Or maybe something else . . .

My heart sank right down into my boots. Alice was right to doubt my master's powers. I was beginning to see the truth. The Spook was a man in decline. His strength was going. The John Gregory I'd first became apprenticed to would have bound Lizzie with no trouble, no matter how strong the magic she used against him.

He frowned, and an expression of bewilderment came over his face. He staggered and seemed about to speak, but then his hand went to his throat and he started to choke. His knees gave way, then he fell forward, his forehead missing the bottom step by inches. I quickly went to kneel beside him. He lay there, face down, barely breathing.

'He's not dead, don't you worry!' cried Lizzie, getting to her feet. 'Old Gregory isn't going to enjoy an easy death like that. Not after the painful years I spent trapped in that pit. I owe him for that, and he'll suffer before he dies. I'll give him pain like he's never known before, just see if I don't! This is going to be your master's worst nightmare.'

Her words reminded me of my master's dream about Lizzie, where she'd been seated on a throne, the floor flowing with blood. It was all coming horribly true.

She walked down the steps and raised her foot as if to kick him with the pointy toe of her shoe, then stopped and shook her head. 'What's the point of kicking him if he can't feel it?' she muttered. 'Now, boy, I've got a job for you. I want you to go out and talk to those men beyond the gate. Tell 'em they work for me now: they should choose one of their own, a sensible man with experience, to be my seneschal – the servant who will give orders to the others on my behalf. He should come up to the throne room for an audience with me.

'And one other thing – I don't like being kept waiting. They have ten minutes to decide. Every five minutes over that time, and one of their number will die. So get you gone and tell them that, boy!'

I glanced down at my master and then at Alice, but that moment of hesitation angered Lizzie. She took a step towards me, her eyes flashing dangerously.

'Thinking of disobeying me, boy? Well, think again. You see, I know all about the blood jar—'

'I'm sorry, Tom, I'm sorry. She made me tell . . .' cried Alice.

'It's just a case of who the Fiend comes for first. If Alice here displeases me, I'll throw her in the dungeons. Without me by her side, she wouldn't last five minutes. And as for you – well, that's simple. I'll deal with you right now. Take that blood jar out of your pocket and smash it on the floor! Go on! Do it!'

I tried to resist, I really did, but I found my hand obeying the witch. Alice's eyes widened in terror, and I felt the sweat oozing from my brow. My heart pounded as I found my hand moving, as if of its own volition, to pull out the jar and lift it high, preparing to dash it to the floor.

'Stop!' Lizzie cried, just in time. She gave me an evil smile. 'Now you can put it back in your pocket because you know what I'm capable of. Next time you disobey me again I'll make you smash that jar and I'll put you in the deepest, darkest, dampest dungeon. Then we'll see which of them comes for you first – the buggane or the Fiend.'

I picked up my staff, turned and went to do her bidding. What choice did I have?

As I passed under the first portcullis and went across the yard towards the main gate, the yeomen got to their feet, gathering just beyond the moat.

'What have we here?' said Commander Stanton, walking towards me. 'She's bewitched you all right! We sent you in old and tall and you come back young and a good few inches shorter!'

They all laughed at his joke, but some of the guffaws were forced, the amusement hollow.

'My master's hurt,' I told him, and then went on to deliver Lizzie's message, worried about how Stanton might react to her instructions. He didn't look like the sort of man who would take kindly to her plan to rule Greeba Keep. It also seemed highly unlikely that he'd agree to choose a seneschal for her. I just hoped that he wouldn't get it into his head to punish me, her messenger.

Stanton looked unimpressed. 'We're to work for her,

are we? And what if we've got plans of our own?'

'She said you've just ten minutes to decide. If you don't respond in that time, some of you will die – one for every five minutes you keep her waiting.'

Some of the men around him began to mutter and look apprehensive. I could sense the fear passing from one to the other like a disease.

At first Stanton didn't reply. He looked thoughtful and gazed up at the tower. Then he turned back to me again. 'You're a spook's apprentice, so you know about these things. Could she do it? Could the witch really kill some of us from a distance like that?'

'It's not easy,' I admitted. 'Witches often use curses and try to kill their enemies from afar – though it doesn't always work. But Bony Lizzie is a really strong witch. She's done things I wouldn't have believed possible. A spook has some immunity against witchcraft, and my own master has practised his trade successfully for many years. That didn't help him though,' I went on, shaking my head sadly.

'She used dark magic and he fell unconscious at her feet. So who knows what she is capable of?'

He nodded and looked at his men. 'Well, I say we put her to the test. We'll let the minutes pass. Maybe she's only bluffing.'

Not everyone was happy but nobody challenged his decision. I turned to walk back over the moat, but Stanton grabbed my arm. 'No, lad, you're staying with us until we know what's what.'

He made me sit down by the fire and knelt beside me, warming his hands before the flames. 'Who else is in there besides the witch and your master?' he asked.

'My friend, Alice.'

'Alice? You mean the little witch who survived the testing in the barrel? The sly one who hit me with that rock?'

'She's not a witch—'

'Barrule thought so, and he knew about such things,' he interrupted.

'She really isn't a witch,' I insisted.

Stanton looked at me long and hard, as if making his

mind up about something, and then he said, 'What's your name, boy?'

'Tom Ward.'

'Well, Tom Ward, my name's Daniel Stanton, the commander around here – I served Lord Barrule for fifteen years, and sometimes did things I didn't like on his behalf. Still, a man knows which side his bread's buttered, and from time to time we all do things we're not entirely happy with. Not sure being seneschal to a witch appeals to me much though.

'This is the situation. Barrule didn't leave an heir. About ten years ago his wife died in childbirth and the baby only lived a few hours after her. So the Parliament, the Tynwald, will decide next week who'll be appointed to take his place and become leader of the Ruling Council. As I see it, my duty now is to secure that keep for its next master, who'll be my new employer. That means dealing with that witch one way or another—'

There was a sudden cry of pain from someone by the next fire. Daniel Stanton jumped to his feet. I followed him and saw a man lying on his back close to the flames: he was writhing in pain, his hands at his throat as if he were choking. His face was turning purple. Someone sat him up and tried to help him, lifting a cup of water to his lips. But suddenly the man gave a gasp, shuddered and went limp.

'He's dead!' the cry went up.

I was looking at lots of scared faces. Some of Stanton's men looked ready to run.

'The witch did it!' someone shouted.

'Aye,' agreed a second voice, 'and what if she does it again? Any one of us could be next!'

The yeomen milled about, their faces tense. Stanton was the only one who didn't look scared. He stood there impassively, his arms folded and head held high.

Five minutes later a yeoman close to us gave a groan, clasped his hands to his throat, then staggered and fell stone dead at our feet. Stanton's men were now terrified. These were yeomen, soldiers used to facing violent death, but this was not natural. They were beginning to panic.

Stanton held his hand up for calm and addressed his men in a loud clear voice. 'We'll do as the witch demands!' he cried. 'I'll go and talk to her myself.' He put his hand on my shoulder. 'Right, boy, I take it you'd like to put an end to her if you could?'

I nodded.

'Well, why didn't you finish her off when you had the chance the other night? I was there and saw what happened.'

I shook my head. 'Lots of reasons . . . I couldn't bring myself to kill her in cold blood.'

'That's a hard thing to do,' he agreed with a nod, 'and you're just a boy. But if I get the chance, I won't hesitate. So we'll work together on this, agreed?'

'The first thing is to try and get my master to safety. He'll work out what to do.'

'We'll go and see what the witch has to say,' Stanton said. 'We'll play along with her for a while and wait for an opportunity to present itself.'

CHAPTER
17
STONE DEAD

Together we went through the gates, into the tower and up the steps to the throne room. Lizzie was waiting for us on the throne, looking imperious. There was no sign of Alice or the Spook.

Daniel Stanton gave her a low bow. 'I'm at your service, ma'am,' he told her.

It was exactly the right thing to do; the witch positively glowed. 'What do they call you?' she asked.

'Stanton, ma'am. I was the commander of the Greeba Guard. I served Lord Barrule for almost fifteen years.'

'Well now, Master Stanton, you're my seneschal, although you'll still captain the guard. Get them back to their posts sharpish, and the other servants too –

especially the cooks. Tomorrow night there's going to be a feast in my honour. Which is the largest room in the keep? How many can it hold?'

'The great hall, ma'am. It's in the building beside the tower. It can hold nearly two hundred.'

'Send out invitations, then,' Lizzie commanded. 'I want that hall filled. No riff-raff, mind. I want landowners there – rich, important people. Get me the members of the Ruling Council and the Tynwald – as many as possible.'

'I'll go and attend to it right away, ma'am,' Stanton told her.

Lizzie dismissed him. When he'd gone, she stood up and walked down the steps towards me. 'I will rule this island. Do you doubt me, boy?' she asked.

I looked at her warily. 'It all seems to be going to plan,' I agreed.

'Even better than you realize,' Lizzie said with a twist of her lips. 'And don't think that I'm not ready to deal with any tricks. Daniel Stanton has a smooth tongue, but I can see through his flattery. After tomorrow night he'll be too terrified to even contemplate opposing me. And as for you, I'll keep you alive a little longer – you might just prove useful. But one wrong step and it's the end of that blood jar – then the Fiend can have you. Do I make myself clear?'

I nodded.

'Right then, give me your staff. You won't be needing it any more.'

I tried to resist, but the compulsion was still strong, and I found myself laying it at her feet. I knew she wouldn't want to touch it. Witches hated the feel of rowan wood.

'Now get out of my sight,' she commanded, 'but don't leave the keep unless I tell you, and stay away from the dungeons. Go near your master and it'll be the worse for both of you. You'll sleep in one of the rooms up there,' she said, pointing to the steps, 'where I can keep an eye on you.'

Within an hour the keep was a flurry of activity: the

guards were back in position and the cooks were preparing for the feast the following night.

There was nothing for it but to go up the stairs and pick one of the bedrooms; I spent the next few hours in the window seat, watching the bustle below in the courtyard while I tried to take stock of the situation and work out the best course of action. Things looked bleak and I was concerned for my master. And where was Alice? Lizzie hadn't mentioned her absence. Had she been imprisoned in the dungeons too? If so, she'd be beyond the protection of the blood jar.

Things were looking bad. We were like flies trapped in Lizzie's web and I couldn't see how to break free. I just had to wait for an opportunity and, when it came, take it despite the risk.

To my relief, just before dark Alice appeared at the open doorway of my room. She was carrying a plate of cold ham, cheese and biscuits.

'Thought you might like to share some supper with me,' she said, coming towards me.

'Where's the Spook?' I asked.

'He's locked in a dungeon, Tom. Lizzie made me help her carry him down.'

We sat together in the window seat and nibbled at the food. 'Don't eat too much,' Alice said with a smile. 'Leave some room for the queen's banquet tomorrow night!'

'Can Lizzie be serious?' I asked. 'What does she hope to achieve?'

'She's going to release all the prisoners of Greeba Keep and invite them to the feast – all except Old Gregory, of course. Don't know what she wants to do that for. What's her game, Tom?'

'Hard to say why she'd release the prisoners, but if she really means to rule this island, I'd guess she'll be out to impress and terrify her guests tomorrow – show them that resistance is futile. But we've got someone on our side – Daniel Stanton, whom she's just appointed as her seneschal. He'll kill her if he gets half a chance. He served Barrule for years, but now his loyalty is to his next master. The Tynwald will probably appoint somebody next week. But what about Mr Gregory –

she's not going to feed him to the buggane, is she?'

'Not yet, Tom. Lizzie wants to hurt him badly first. After she's had her fun, then it'll be the buggane's turn.'

'What I can't understand is why she's not killed me already – or put me in a cell to feed the buggane. Why risk having a spook's apprentice around?'

'Ain't hurt you yet because I begged her not to,' said Alice. 'And she ain't hurt me because she really means what she said about me uniting the Pendle clans one day. She thinks she can win me over to the dark. She can't, but it don't do no harm to let her think I'm moving her way. That's the only reason you're still alive, Tom. I also asked her to let the dogs go – or have 'em fed at least. She wouldn't hear of it though. They must be starving by now.'

I nodded sadly. Claw, Blood and Bone had suffered cruelly, but at least, unlike some of the other dogs, they were still alive. I'd have to do something about them – and soon.

* * *

The following morning I passed Stanton on the stairs. He thrust a guest list under my nose. There were a lot of names.

'These are the ones we've sent invitations to – all important people, but a lot of them won't come. They see Bony Lizzie as a murderess and a witch and will already be making their own plans to deal with her – maybe even raising some sort of military force to move against the keep. Of course, they can't do much until the Parliament meets next week.

'But there are those who have agreed to attend. Why, I don't know,' the commander went on, shaking his head, 'but some – especially those who don't get their own way at the Tynwald – see her as a route to power. Some are simply coming along to assess the danger she represents. If the meeting turns against her, I might just use the uproar to kill her there and then. Now, tell me – what's the best way to kill a witch, lad?'

'A silver-alloy blade through the heart would be the most effective,' I told him. 'A spook's staff has one, but Lizzie's locked away mine and my master's. Any blade right through the heart might do the trick though – at least for a while . . .'

I didn't like to tell him that he would have to cut out her heart afterwards – otherwise we'd be facing a dead and possibly even more dangerous Bony Lizzie . . . But first things first, I thought.

Guests started to arrive at the keep just after sunset. They were greeted at the gate and escorted to the great hall. Mostly they were men, alone or in groups, but there were a few couples too.

The hall was large and spectacular, its high roof supported on heavy wooden beams arranged in a sequence of triangles such as you found in the very largest County churches. Although constructed on a smaller scale, it reminded me of the interior of Priestown Cathedral. On the walls, rich tapestries depicted scenes from the island's history: there were longboats and fierce-looking men with horned helmets; vessels landing on rocky shores; battles, with houses burning and fields strewn with the dead. Dozens of torches lined the walls to show them off.

Gradually the room began to echo with the low buzz of conversation as servants brought in trays of wine and offered a glass to each guest. The tables were arranged in parallel rows; the head table, where Lizzie would take her place, faced them. To our surprise, Alice and I were seated immediately to the left of the witch's chair, with Daniel Stanton positioned on her right. Yeomen armed with spears stood guard along the wall at the back.

Once all the guests had arrived, another group of yeomen brought in the prisoners and led them to the table right at the back, near the door. I saw that Adriana was amongst them.

Only then did Lizzie enter the room and walk slowly to her place at the head table. The conversation died away as the guests followed her progress. She had clearly raided the wardrobe of Lord Barrule's dead wife; this time she'd helped herself to jewels as well: her fingers were adorned with gold rings, her wrists with gleaming slender bracelets, and set within her hair, which was now clean and lustrous, was a spectacular diamond tiara.

When she reached her chair, Lizzie halted and swept the room with her eyes. Then she gave a smile, but there was no warmth in it. It was the cruel, gloating smile of someone very confident of her power; the sadistic smirk of a bully about to torment her helpless victims.

'Eat your fill!' she commanded. 'We'll dine first and talk later.'

Then, without further ado, waiters scurried into the room with trays of choice cuts of meat. The cooks had worked hard and it truly was a feast fit for a queen. But the guests all ate in silence, merely nibbling at their food, and you could sense the fear and unease that now gripped them. They knew what Lizzie was capable of – how she'd slain the powerful Lord Barrule and killed yeomen from a distance. She'd even bested a spook.

At last, when the tables had been cleared and

everyone's glass filled again, Stanton rose to his feet and called out for silence. An expectant hush fell as Bony Lizzie stood and faced her nervous guests.

She stared at them for a long time without speaking, pursing her red-painted lips. Suddenly I felt a chill in the air. She was using something from the dark already.

'The old ways won't do any longer!' she cried. 'It's time for change!'

There was real authority in her voice: this was no longer the mud-splattered Lizzie who had taken refuge with us in the buggane's tunnels – though she still twisted her mouth and spoke in a heavy Pendle accent.

'You've enemies across the sea to the east. Captured the County, they have, and now they'll be looking this way. They'll want to seize your land and make slaves of you all, there's little doubt about that. This is no time for dithering; no time for empty talk. A parliament ain't needed now. What good is a talking-shop when we need action? Want a strong single voice, you do. Need a different type of rule. It's me you need! I'll be your queen. I'll protect you. Support me and keep your freedom. It's *your* choice.'

Putting emphasis on the word 'your', she extended her left arm and brought it in a slow arc from left to right, pointing her index finger at her audience. The rings on her fingers and the diamonds in the tiara sparkled. She was indeed acting like a queen now – regal, powerful and commanding. She was telling these people that they had but one choice, and that was to obey her.

There was a low grumble of dissent – though one or two men smiled and nodded. Did they actually see her as a future leader, one who would drag them along in her wake?

Lizzie ignored the mutters. 'It's a different life for everyone here now. Let the prisoners go, I have. They were Lord Barrule's prisoners, not mine. His time is over, so I've released them and now the cells are empty – except for the spook, of course. But others will join him in my dungeons – those who oppose me.'

This time the mutters became a rumble, then a roar of disapproval.

'You're either with me or against me!' Lizzie's voice cut through the uproar.

In response, a man rose to his feet; next to him was a very finely dressed woman with silver-grey hair, her gown rivalling that of Lizzie's. An expression of alarm on her face, his wife grabbed his arm and tried to pull him back into his seat. But he shrugged her off and strode forward to stand directly before the high table.

Florid of face and slightly overweight, he looked prosperous and commanding. But here he was dealing with something beyond his experience.

He pointed a finger at Lizzie and opened his mouth twice before any words came out. His hands were shaking and his forehead glistened with sweat. 'You are a stranger to our island,' he told her in a quavering voice, 'an interloper, a refugee – and a witch to boot! How dare you stand before us and assume such a title? What right have you to declare yourself our sovereign?'

Lizzie smiled malevolently. 'A ruler needs to be strong, and I'm the strongest here!' she said, arching her back. 'You're challenging my right to rule, old man. For that, your life is forfeit!'

She stamped her foot three times, muttered something under her breath and pointed the index finger of her left hand straight at the man, whose face was already contorted with terror.

His hands went to his throat, and I could see his eyes bulging from their sockets. He made no sound, but blood started to ooze from each nostril and dribble down over his mouth before dripping off his chin. Then he fell forward and collapsed, striking his head hard against the flagged floor. He lay there perfectly still.

Lizzie had killed him stone dead.

CHAPTER
18
A LOST SPIRIT

The grey-haired woman got to her feet and, with a cry of anguish, rushed forward to help her husband. But she never reached his body.

Lizzie made a sign in the air and chanted the words of a spell. The woman fell to her knees, her hands fluttering in front of her face as if warding off something terrifying.

I was aware of another commotion at the back of the room, where the prisoners had been seated. Someone was trying to force her way towards us but was being restrained by the yeomen. It looked like Adriana. What was wrong with her? If she wasn't careful she'd be returned to the cells.

But Lizzie wasn't finished yet. This was a clear demonstration of her power, its aim to cow her audience so that none would ever dare oppose her again. She stamped her foot three times and, in a loud, imperious voice, uttered more words of enchantment in the Old Tongue. I was still learning that language, a relative novice, and they were chanted so quickly that I could neither catch nor understand them. But the consequences were immediate and terrifying.

All the torches in the room flickered and died down, and we were plunged into almost total darkness. Wails of fear went up from the gathering. Then the huge figure of a man began to form in the air above Lizzie. It looked like a trapped spirit summoned from Limbo. At first I thought she had summoned Bill Arkwright again, but as the apparition took shape, I saw that it was the ghost of the man that Lizzie had just killed. Around him swirled the gloomy grey mists of Limbo.

'I'm lost!' the spirit cried. *'Where am I? What's happened to me?'*

'You're dead and finished with this world for good,'

Lizzie snapped. 'What happens to you now depends upon me. I can keep you trapped in that mist for ever or I can let you go free.'

'*Go? Go where?*' asked the spirit.

'Either to the light or to the dark, whichever your life on this earth has fitted you for. What's your name? What did you do upon this world while you lived and breathed?'

'*I'm the chief miller at Peel, a hard-working man. My name is Patrick Lonan and I'm a member of the Tynwald . . .*'

No wonder Adriana had needed to be restrained by the yeomen. Lizzie had just killed her father.

The witch gave a low, cruel laugh. 'You *were* a member of the Tynwald. Now you're just a lost spirit. You serve me and you'll do my bidding. Return into the mist and await my call!'

The ghost of Patrick Lonan gave a wail of fear and began to fade. The torches flared into life once more, revealing the terrified faces of the guests. Many were on their feet, about to try and leave the hall. The yeomen looked just as scared, in no state to detain any who tried to flee. But Lizzie immediately took control of the situation.

'Be seated!' she commanded. 'All of you. Do it now or join the dead miller!'

Within seconds they had taken their places again. I looked at the table at the back but could see no sign of Adriana. The woman, whom I took to be her mother, was still on her knees, trying to fend off some unseen attacker. Her whole face was twitching, her body starting to convulse. She was muttering gibberish, driven to the edge of insanity by Lizzie's magic.

I looked at Daniel Stanton. He was just as terror-stricken as the rest of the gathering, clearly in no position to make an attempt on Lizzie's life.

'You've seen what I can do,' the witch cried out. 'Death awaits those who oppose me – along with fear and suffering beyond the grave. I will allow the Tynwald to meet one last time in order to dismiss the Ruling Council and declare me ruler of this island. Get ye gone! All of you! Any who wish to serve me may return to the keep at the same time tomorrow night and I will receive your obeisance then.'

The hall emptied quickly and I saw that Lizzie had a triumphant look on her face. She signalled to two of the guards and pointed to the miller's wife.

'Take her home – to die!' she commanded. 'Let her be an example of what happens to those who displease me.'

They dragged Adriana's mother away, still wailing with distress.

'Out of my sight, you two!' she said, pointing to me and Alice. 'Go back to the tower. I want to talk to my seneschal in private.'

I thought briefly about simply following the other guests out of the great hall and over the moat. But then we'd never manage to get back into the keep to rescue the Spook. And anyway, I doubted whether Lizzie would allow it – her power over me was still strong. So I obediently followed Alice across the courtyard to the tower. We went up the stairs and into my room and sat together on the window seat. Outside it was very dark and neither the moon nor the stars were visible; just a few lanterns flickered on the distant boundary wall.

'That was Adriana's father that Lizzie killed . . .' I murmured.

Alice nodded. 'And now Adriana will have been taken down to the dungeons to join Old Gregory. Didn't take Lizzie long to start filling up those cells again, did it? We can't let her just murder anybody she wants. We've got to do something, Tom.'

'If we attack her, she could strike us stone dead with one of her spells. You saw what she did to the miller. She can force me to do things against my will – even smash the blood jar. In a few days she may be in control of this island and then she'll think about taking her revenge on the Spook. We've got to get him out of that cell before she starts to really hurt him. It's risky, but the only way out of this keep is through the buggane's tunnels.'

My words were brave, but inside I shivered at the mere thought of the buggane. To come face to face with the daemon in its own domain would surely mean death.

'You're right, Tom, but we'll have to choose a time when she's not watching us. Soon as Lizzie finds out we're gone, she'll send it after us. Right now she's busy giving orders to her new seneschal, consolidating her power here. And all the guards are on duty at the moment – they won't be in the guardroom! Now – right now, is the time to make a move!' she cried.

Alice was right. We had to strike – and now, when Lizzie would least expect it. If she caught us, she would show no mercy. Trying not to think of the risk of what we were attempting, I led Alice up to the study, where Lord Barrule had studied and practised animism. I opened the door and retrieved both the Spook's staff and mine. As we turned to go, Alice picked up the shaman's notebook.

'What do you want that for, Alice?' I asked with a frown, eager to get away before Lizzie returned.

'Who knows what we might learn, Tom? It might come in useful. Besides, if we take it, then Lizzie can't get her hands on it.'

I nodded – that was true enough. We hurried down

through the throne room and descended the steps towards the dungeons. We passed safely through the guardroom and, taking a lantern from a hook, headed along the damp narrow passageway towards the dungeons.

There were a lot of cells but we didn't need to check each one because the empty ones had their doors open. At last we came to two that were locked. I used my key and opened the first one to find Adriana sitting on the floor in the corner, her head in her hands. When she saw that it was us, she jumped up and rushed over.

'What happened to my mother?' she asked, her eyes full of tears.

'They took her home,' I said. 'I'm really sorry, Adriana, about your father—'

'She killed him then? They dragged me out before I could be sure what had happened.' She looked at me, her dark eyes sorrowful.

'Yes, she killed him,' I admitted, bowing my head. I didn't tell her about Lizzie summoning his spirit from Limbo; it would only have added to her pain.

'My mother will find it hard to live without him,' she said, beginning to sob. 'Father was always so outspoken.'

'He was brave,' I said, 'but he couldn't have known what he was up against – how powerful Lizzie really is . . .'

'We're going to try and escape from the keep down the tunnels,' Alice said, patting Adriana's shoulder sympathetically. 'It'll be dangerous but it's better than staying here.'

We left her cell, and I inserted my key into the lock of the next one. It was stiff, and for a few moments I struggled to turn the key. Eventually it yielded and I opened the door. Alice held up the lantern and we peered inside.

I saw the earthen wall and the tunnel in it. Then something moved. My heart lurched and I stepped back nervously. At first I thought it was the buggane, but then the Spook shuffled towards us, one hand raised to shield his eyes from the glare of the light. He'd been in the dark for a long time.

'Well, lad, you're a sight for sore eyes and no mistake.'

I smiled and handed him his staff. 'I've lots of things to tell you but it'll have to wait till later. The guards could come looking for us at any moment. We're going to try and escape down the buggane's tunnels. It's either that or back up the stairs to face Lizzie. And she controls the yeomen now.'

The Spook nodded. 'Then we've little choice. We don't know where the tunnels lead, so we might as well try up here,' he said, pointing back to the dark entrance in the earth wall of his own cell.

I suddenly wondered why he hadn't already made his escape down that tunnel. Locked in my cell earlier, I'd made the decision not to risk it. But I was still an apprentice and he was the Spook; he must have thought that it would be his only chance to escape before being tortured and killed. Had he lacked the strength and courage to face the tunnel alone? I had little time to dwell on that thought before Alice spoke again.

'We *do* know where one of the tunnels leads,' she said. 'The one from the long room where the dogs fought – it leads to that hollow tree . . .'

'But it's surrounded by a bone-yard, Alice,' I reminded her.

'It's very dangerous, but I might be able to find Lizzie's secret path out. I'm prepared to try.'

'Make a mistake and you'd be crushed to death in seconds, girl,' the Spook said, shaking his head.

'Ain't any better option,' Alice retorted. 'Otherwise we'll be travelling blind through the buggane's tunnels.'

The Spook sighed, then nodded his agreement. 'Right, you lead the way then . . .'

We left his cell and followed the passageway along; soon it widened out and there were dry stone flags under our feet. We helped ourselves to more wall lanterns; we'd need as much light as possible in the tunnel. As we approached the long room, we heard loud barks; the stench of death and animal faeces was overpowering. We saw that the three wolfhounds were

245

still locked in their cages and Lord Barrule's rotting body lay where it had fallen next to the throne.

'We should let the dogs out,' I said. 'They haven't been fed. It might be days before anybody bothers to do anything about them.'

'Take care, lad,' the Spook warned me. 'They've been cruelly treated – who knows how they'll react?'

Warily, we released them. But the dogs neither attacked us nor fought each other. A couple bounded out of the room immediately, but most just wandered about forlornly. Claw, Blood and Bone, however, were pleased to see me. It was good to pat them again and see their tales wagging with excitement; their joy brought a lump to my throat. They were starving and dirty, and I felt angry at the way they'd been treated, but at least the shaman's power over them was broken and they were their old selves again. When we entered the tunnel at the end of the room, they followed us in.

I took the lead, Alice at my heels, and the Spook followed behind Adriana in case we were attacked from the rear. The tunnel was just earth, with no wooden supports like a mine, and the thought of that weight of soil above us was scary. We could easily be buried alive down here; segments of tunnel must collapse all the time. There were roots visible too; sometimes they were twisted like snakes and I had to keep telling myself that they weren't moving.

The lanterns were very much more effective than the candle stub we'd used the first time I came down here with Alice and Lizzie, and it wasn't long before we saw the first of the bones: they weren't lying in large piles, as in the lair of a bone witch, but we never went more than twenty yards without catching a glimpse of some fragment of a human skeleton. Sometimes it was a skull half buried in the side wall of the tunnel, or a fragment of a leg or arm bone, or just a few fingers or toes. However, I did not sense any lingering spirits here; they were just remains. I paused beside an almost intact human foot; only the little toe was missing. To the left of it was a skull; a tree root had twisted its way in through the left eye-socket and emerged from the right before continuing down into the soil.

'Why are there so many bones down here?' I called back to the Spook. 'Do they belong to prisoners who tried to escape from the cells?'

'A few maybe,' he replied. 'But the buggane regurgitates some of the bones it's swallowed after feeding.'

I shuddered, realizing that the foot and the skull had spent time in the buggane's stomach.

For about five minutes we made good progress, but then we encountered a problem. There were thick tree roots ahead of us, completely blocking the main tunnel. Another tunnel went off at an angle, heading downwards. It was new and freshly dug; I didn't like the look of it one bit.

CHAPTER 19
THE GRIM CACHE

'This is the buggane's doing,' I said. 'What now?'

'To reach the hollow tree we need to get past those roots somehow,' Alice replied.

'We could dig round it with our staffs but it'll take ages. I know a better way,' I said, turning to look past Alice and Adriana. 'There are roots blocking our way!' I shouted to the Spook. 'Reverse back down the tunnel a bit. We need to give the dogs room to work. Claw! Blood! Bone!'

The dogs came squeezing past us eagerly as the others retreated. I dug at the earth beside the roots with my hands and pointed ahead. Soon the three wolfhounds were burrowing away enthusiastically, throwing earth backwards with their paws. In fact we got two tunnels instead of one because Claw worked to the left while Blood and Bone dug their own tunnel to the right.

The latter was the larger excavation, and the Spook and I widened it with the blades of our staffs until we could squeeze through.

At last we were moving again. I began to feel optimistic about escaping from the hollow tree. It was dangerous, but if anyone could find the secret way through the bone-yard it was Alice.

But soon we encountered another problem, this one much worse than before. We found the passage ahead completely blocked with hard-packed earth. Once again a new tunnel had been excavated by the buggane; one that headed sharply downhill.

The Spook crawled forward to join me, shaking his head. 'We could try digging again, but the whole tunnel might have caved in behind,' he said. 'I don't like it, lad. It's almost as if we're being herded like sheep. Forced downwards to where someone wants us to be.'

'The buggane?' I asked.

'Maybe – but it could be acting for Lizzie. By now she'll probably know that we've escaped the tower. We either retreat the way we came or go down there,' he said, pointing towards the new tunnel.

'If we go back, they'll be waiting. This time Lizzie will put us *all* in the dungeons,' I said.

The Spook shrugged. 'Then we must go on. I'll take the lead now, lad – who knows what we're about to face?' And with those words he set off, crawling along the tunnel.

The descent got steeper and I was growing increasingly uneasy. I sensed danger ahead.

Then the passage began to widen, and the Spook got to his feet, lifting the lantern. Moments later, we saw a vast space ahead, the walls so distant that the light couldn't reach them. We were at the entrance to a huge cavern.

Even the dogs were silent. They stayed behind us, unwilling to venture in any further and explore. Perhaps they felt as we did: a sense of awe; a feeling that we faced something totally new and beyond our experience.

'I didn't expect this,' said the Spook, his voice hardly more than a whisper. 'I think I know what this place is. I thought it was just a myth – a story. But it's real . . .'

'What's real?' I asked. 'What is it?'

But the Spook just muttered something to himself and didn't answer my question.

'This ain't been done by the buggane,' said Alice. 'Take ten lifetimes to make a burrow this big, even if its claws could dig through rock.'

'This was here already and the buggane chanced upon it,' my master said.

'Or maybe it knew about it,' said Adriana, emerging from the dark tunnel. 'Maybe it deliberately chose to build its labyrinth here because it knew about this cavern.'

'But what would it want something so big for?' I asked, thinking aloud.

'Well, as I've already told you, lad,' said the Spook, 'a buggane takes the animus, the life force of a human, and stores it at the centre of its labyrinth; it was working with the shaman, so it needed lots of space. But this is immense – far beyond what it should need.'

'What does it use the animas for?'

'Well, we know that for a shaman they're a source of magical power, giving him control over animals and allowing him to project his spirit far from his body. But as for the buggane, nobody's ever had a real conversation with such a creature. It whispers, it threatens, then sucks out the animus and kills its victim, but we don't know why. The shaman, Lord Barrule, would know more, but he's dead now . . .

'Well, lad,' my master went on, 'you asked me what this place is, and I'll tell you. It's something I didn't think I'd live to see. Something I've only heard tell of. It's known as the "Grim Cache" after its creator, and it's the largest source of animism in the world. It was first accumulated by a shaman called Lucius Grim many centuries ago. It's said that he was able to project his spirit into the dark itself, but eventually his soul was consumed by a daemon. This is his legacy, no doubt added to by other shamans since – the latest being Lord Barrule. Anyway, let's move on – but keep close to the cavern wall. Who knows – we might find another way out.'

The Spook led the way, the dogs following behind, still subdued. Underneath our feet soft mud gave way to rock. It wasn't long before Alice gasped in astonishment – she had noticed something ahead. 'Something up there,' she said. 'I can see lights moving. Don't like the look of 'em.'

We looked up to where she was pointing. Tiny points of yellow light like distant stars were combining to form intricate patterns, moving more like a shoal of fish than a flock of birds. I tried to count them; it was difficult, but I thought there were seven. Suddenly one detached itself from the rest and floated down towards us. As it approached, I saw that it was a glowing sphere.

'Fire elementals!' cried Alice. 'Just like the ones we saw in Greece . . .'

We'd faced different types of fire elemental there,

ranging from fiery orbs to asteri, which looked like five-pointed stars. They were all deadly and could burn you to cinders in moments. They'd certainly done for Bill Arkwright.

However, the Spook shook his head. 'Nay, girl, whatever they are, they won't be fire elementals. It's too damp in this cavern. In fact this whole island has a wet climate very similar to the County. It's no place for entities like that. They couldn't survive here.'

As if to prove him right, rather than attacking us, the glowing orb backed away, drifting upwards, and once more became a distant point of light, having rejoined its companions in their strange dance. It was as if it had taken a close look at us and decided we were of no interest.

It was then that the Spook first noticed that Alice was carrying a book. 'Where did you get that, girl?' he demanded with a frown. 'Did it belong to the shaman?'

Alice nodded. 'It's his notebook. Brought it so that Lizzie wouldn't get her hands on it and learn new things about the dark. Best that we have it, don't you think?'

My master looked unconvinced but said nothing, and we continued to follow the curved wall of the cavern. Once again it was Alice who brought us to a halt. She sniffed loudly, three times. 'There's something ahead and coming this way,' she warned. 'Something from the dark . . .'

No sooner had she said that than all three dogs began to growl; they had sensed the danger too. We held our lanterns aloft and saw a figure approaching us.

'It's the abhuman,' Alice said as he moved into the arcs of light.

She was right. Horn was alone. The two holes in his ears where they'd attached the chains still appeared inflamed, and his blind, milky-white eyeballs moved as if he were assessing each one of us in turn.

The union between the Fiend and a witch could produce a wide range of different offspring. Grimalkin, the witch assassin, had once given birth to a perfectly human baby boy; the Fiend had killed it on the spot for just that reason. Then there was Alice, born fully human but with the potential to become a powerful witch. Here, at the other end of the scale, was this daemonic figure, a horned beast like the father who'd sired him.

The Spook readied his staff and approached the creature.

The abhuman hissed at him through his teeth, then spoke in a harsh voice. 'Follow me,' he rasped.

'And why should we do that?' demanded my master, raising his staff threateningly.

'Follow me,' Horn repeated. He turned and headed into the darkness.

I didn't like the idea of leaving the relative safety of the rock wall. I had a bad feeling about venturing out into the vastness of the cavern: you could get lost; or just be swallowed up by the darkness.

'Wait!' cried the Spook, no doubt thinking the same thing. 'You need to give us a good reason to follow you – otherwise we stay here!'

The abhuman turned back to face us, and his face twisted in anger, the glare of a feral beast rather than a human being. 'You *must* follow. You have no choice.'

'There's always a choice to be made,' said the Spook. 'Aye, there's always that. Suppose we choose to stay here . . .'

'Then you will stay here in this cavern until you die. There is no escape from here unless I wish it. Now that my master is dead, I control the buggane. Despite all the efforts of the witch, it still does as I command – at least for the moment.'

'He could be lying,' Adriana said, lowering her voice. 'It's safer to stay here.'

'Not if all the entrances and exits are made by the buggane,' I replied.

'And I suspect that's exactly what we'll find,' said the Spook. 'I fear that the wisest option for now is to do as he asks.'

So we reluctantly followed the abhuman into the cavern. Soon the walls were far behind us and we continued in the pool of yellow light cast by our lanterns, beyond which nothing seemed to exist. Darkness extended in every direction. Our footsteps echoed in the silence and I grew increasingly nervous.

The situation soon became even worse: our lanterns all began to dim until, after a few moments, they gave off only the faintest of glows. This had to be the work of dark magic, and the Spook immediately held up his hand, motioning us to halt. No sooner had we done so than the lanterns went out completely, plunging us into absolute darkness.

Was it a trick? I wondered fearfully. Had Horn lured us out here to our deaths?

CHAPTER
20
IMMENSE POWER

I stood there, preparing myself for some sort of attack at any moment, but nothing happened.

'Keep moving forward,' Horn commanded from up ahead in the darkness. 'We are almost there . . .'

We shuffled along very slowly; it was so dark that I couldn't even see the Spook in front of me. But for the sound of his boots on rock, he could have vanished. Then I saw a faint glow.

As we got nearer, the luminosity grew; not in intensity but in size. It reminded me of the glowing sphere that had descended from the cavern roof to take a look at us. But whereas that had been small and yellow, this was red and immense. Neither was it a true sphere; it flexed and shifted its shape, as if under pressure from invisible internal or external forces.

From a distance it had appeared to have a definite outline, but as we approached, we saw that it was more like a mist in a forest dell, diffuse on its perimeter but far denser within. Already the abhuman was walking into it and becoming more indistinct. We followed – on my part, with increasing reluctance: I wondered if everybody else felt the same. The skin on my hands and face was tingling, my sense of danger increasing with every step I took. Then the abhuman came to a halt and turned to face us – just a horned silhouette against the radiance.

'This is indeed the cache of Lucius Grim – I was right,' said the Spook.

'It presents no danger to you,' Horn told him. 'At least, not in itself. It's the place where the buggane stores the life force that it steals from the living. It's energy, that's all – a vast store of animas reaped over centuries.'

'Think of the hundreds of people it's murdered.' The Spook shook his head in disgust.

'Not just hundreds – thousands upon thousands,' said the abhuman. 'Other bugganes have added to the cache; the process has gone on for centuries. This cavern is now a great source of energy and a meeting place for all those who are skilled in animism magic – not only shamans in spirit form, but Romanian witches. At present a coven of seven have temporarily projected their spirits from their distant homeland. They saw you enter the cavern and warned me of your whereabouts.'

The seven lights were now dancing high above our heads – they must be the witches' spirits, I realized. I remembered reading an entry about such things in the Spook's Bestiary. They were dangerous: a group like that could suck the life force from a human victim in minutes.

'Come on then! Out with it,' demanded the Spook, an edge of impatience in his voice. 'What do you want?'

'Revenge,' said the abhuman, his cruel face

contorting in anger. 'I want revenge upon the witch who killed my master, Lord Barrule. I want her destroyed!'

'Aye, we'd also like to put an end to her,' said the Spook. 'But have you brought us here just to tell us that? If so, it would have been better to let us go on our way.'

'I needed to show you this – and to give you vital information,' Horn went on. 'Information that might help you to stop her in her tracks before she rules this whole island. You see, without realizing it, the witch is using my master's thumb-bones as a conduit and drawing on the power stored here. And it will get worse, much worse. I'm using that same power and trying to resist her. But she is stronger than me, far stronger, and will soon have the buggane in her power. Then this vast reservoir will be at her disposal!

'At the moment she knows nothing of this cache, but once she has made the buggane her creature, she will quickly learn the truth. Then she'll realize what she's capable of. And she won't stop here.

Eventually nations beyond our shores will be at risk.

'My master was obsessed by gambling and never bothered to harvest more than a fraction of the magic that is available here; the witch is sure to seize it all and use it against those who cross her. You must act quickly before it's too late!'

The Spook nodded. 'We need to get those bones away from her – though that's easier said than done. How long can you resist her? Just how long can you keep her away from the buggane?'

'It's impossible to say. All I know is that it's getting harder with each day that passes,' Horn replied. 'There's no time to waste. I'll show you a tunnel which will take you up to the forest above. You needn't face the witch's bone-yard.'

As the abhuman led us across the darkness of the cavern, our lanterns flared back to their full brilliance. He guided us to a freshly dug tunnel before retreating back into the gloom. It went up at a steep angle, and it was indeed clear; within minutes we had emerged among the trees. It was still dark, but the sky was growing lighter on the eastern horizon and we could see Greeba Keep in the distance, lanterns gleaming on its battlements; the guard would be on full alert.

'That tower's too close for comfort,' said the Spook. 'The more distance we can put between it and us, the happier I'll be.'

'Nowhere's safe now,' Adriana said. 'I'm heading home to Peel – I need to see to my mother. The shock of Father's death may have been too much for her. You're welcome to join me.'

'We're strangers to this island, so we'll be glad to accept your invitation,' said the Spook, 'but first we'd better retrieve our bags.'

They were still where we'd left them. I took the shaman's notebook from Alice and put it in my bag, which I then picked up, along with my master's, and we set off west, this time with Adriana leading the way. After a while Alice moved up to walk alongside her and they began to chat.

It was a miserable misty morning, with cold drizzle drifting into our faces out of a grey sky. Our progress was slow because we avoided the main lanes and tracks and cut through woods and along dripping hedgerows. I was soon ready for something to eat and a bit of warmth and shelter.

'Where is Romania?' I asked, picking up my pace to walk with the Spook.

'It's a forested land to the north-west of your mam's homeland, Greece, lad. Why? Are you thinking about those seven witches?'

I nodded. 'They came a long way to visit the cavern,' I said.

'True, lad, but they didn't come in person or we'd really have been in trouble. What we saw was their spirits projected from their bodies by the power of animism, drawn there by that cache. They were co-operating with that abhuman, so they didn't pose a threat. But we have a big task on our hands. Even if we deal with Lizzie and the buggane, leaving all that stored power there is dangerous. Some other denizen of the dark might find and use it for their own ends.'

'So why hasn't it happened before?'

'Maybe it has, lad, but it takes a lot of skill to control such a cache. Even Lucius Grim didn't properly understand its power – and that ultimately led to his own destruction. Luckily Lord Barrule was too distracted by his gambling to fully benefit from that resource. However, in time someone with great dark strength is bound to make use of it. There are other bugganes on this island who might add to it; like boggarts, they can use ley lines to travel from place to place. Aye, we have to be wary of that. A big task awaits us.'

We arrived at Peel Mill early in the afternoon. As we emerged from the woods, we saw ahead of us the huge wheel, slowly turning under the force of the water streaming across a long multi-arched aqueduct. But we soon discovered that no flour was being ground. On hearing of Patrick Lonan's death, as a mark of respect the mill workers had gone home.

The miller's large house flanked the wheel: we were made very welcome there. After first attending to her mother, Adriana ordered the servants to prepare baths, hot meals and beds for us all. Her poor father might be dead, but she insisted on business as usual, sending word to the workers to report for duty the following morning.

The abhuman had urged us to attack Lizzie quickly, but we stayed at the mill for two days, resting and gathering our strength, wondering how best to proceed. The Spook was very quiet, and it seemed to me that he had very little hope to offer us.

How could we win now? Lizzie was in control of Greeba Keep and I saw no reason why the whole island should not soon be hers. And if she learned of the full power at her disposal . . . well, that didn't bear thinking about.

However, we knew we couldn't stay at the mill for long. It would be an obvious place to search: before long the bone witch would send her yeomen after us.

On the morning of our third day there, I awoke at dawn and went for a walk with Alice. It was a bright, cold morning with a light ground frost. Alice seemed very quiet and I sensed that she was troubled.

'What's wrong?' I asked her. 'I can tell something's bothering you. Is it Lizzie?'

'Lizzie's bothering all of us.'

I said nothing for a while and we walked in silence. But then I decided to question her further. 'Lizzie's your mother, Alice – and everyone wants her dead. That must upset you . . . Tell me – don't just keep it to yourself.'

'Hate her, I do. She's no mother of mine. A murderer, that's what Lizzie is. She kills children and takes their bones. I'll be glad when she's dead.'

'That night I fought her, when you were in the cage, I had her at my mercy. But I couldn't kill her. It wasn't just that I couldn't bring myself to do it in cold blood; it was also because she was your mother. It just didn't seem right, Alice.'

'You listen to me, Tom. Listen well to what I say. Next time you get the chance, kill her. Don't hesitate. If you'd killed her that night you'd have saved everyone a lot of trouble!'

But no sooner had she said that than Alice started to

sob uncontrollably. I put my arms around her and she buried her face in my shoulder. She cried for a long time, but when she was quiet, I squeezed her hand and led her back towards the house.

As we emerged from the trees, I saw Adriana throwing crumbs to a small flock of birds near the front door. When she spotted us, she clapped her hands, and the birds immediately took flight, most of them landing on the roof. She came across the frosted grass to meet us.

Her face was grave: her mother was still suffering from the effects of her encounter with Bony Lizzie and there was still no news of the whereabouts of Simon Sulby; both he and Captain Baines seemed to have disappeared without trace.

'How's your mother today?' I asked.

'She seems a little stronger,' Adriana replied. 'After a little persuasion she managed to sip a few mouthfuls of broth this morning. But she's still confused and doesn't seem to know she's back home. Mercifully, she's forgotten what happened to my father. I dread having to break the news to her . . .

'And I'm afraid I have some bad news for us all,' she continued with a frown. 'I suppose it's only what we've been expecting since we arrived. One of our millers was riding to work across the fields this morning, and he spied a large party of yeomen assembling on the road north-west of St John's. It looked like they were preparing to march in this direction. If so, they could be here soon.'

CHAPTER 21
PREPARED TO FIGHT

'We need to go into hiding,' Alice said. 'Or maybe head south down the coast.'

'Yes, you should, but I won't be able to go with you,' Adriana said. 'My mother's too ill to move. I'll have to stay here.'

'Let's see what Mr Gregory thinks,' I suggested, and we headed back to the house. But before we reached it, Alice spotted a runner – a yeoman – in the distance. At that moment the Spook came out of the house to join us; he must have seen the man from a window. He stood beside us, holding his staff diagonally in a defensive position.

The yeoman approached us, but seemed unarmed.

He stood there for a few moments, head bowed and hands on his hips, gasping for breath. Then he reached into his pocket and held out an envelope. 'It's for a Tom Ward,' he said.

I took it and tore it open, unfolding the letter within and starting to read.

> Dear Master Ward,
>
> I have left the employment of the witch. In truth I was lucky to escape with my life. I am now recruiting a force with which to oppose the new ruler of Greeba Keep and we are on the road to Peel. We will meet you at the mill. To help defeat our enemy I need the expertise of you and your master.
>
> Yours,
> Daniel Stanton

'Well, lad, don't keep us waiting,' said the Spook. 'Read it aloud!'

I did as my master asked. When I'd finished, he scratched at his beard and glared at me. 'Do you trust this Daniel Stanton?'

I nodded. 'He's a soldier and probably hasn't lived a totally blameless life, but that's true of all of us. Yes, I do trust him.'

'Right, then we'll wait and see what he has to say.'

'I wonder how he knew I'd be here at the mill?' I asked.

'Well, it's not too difficult to work out, lad,' replied the Spook. 'He knows that we escaped with Adriana and that she'd be desperate to be reunited with her mother.'

'Well, if he knows where we are, it's pretty certain that Lizzie will too.'

'Aye, lad, she'll know for sure. But she's probably too busy with her new-found power to bother about us for a while. She's confident she can deal with us easily when the time comes. Right now she'll be devoting all her energies to seizing control of this island. She'll come for us eventually – you mark my words.'

* * *

Just over an hour later, Stanton arrived with his men. There were perhaps no more than fifty in all, but they were armed with pikes and clubs and looked formidable.

Adriana, the Spook, Alice and I sat round the kitchen table with him while he explained the situation.

'The witch has got over three hundred men under arms while I've barely a sixth of that so far. More will join me – and they're prepared to fight, make no mistake. Two days ago Lizzie led raiding parties against some of the local landowners and farmers – those who'd refused outright to pledge their support. Some families – men, women and children – were murdered in cold blood. But I was already away by then.

'Lizzie's sent me to St John's with some of the men you see here now. Our task is to seize the area and prepare for the meeting of the Tynwald in a few days' time. The witch wants to dissolve the Parliament and have power handed over to her. She's planning to go there herself once I have it under control.

'But I talked to some of the lads and a few Tynwald members too, and we've decided to try and tackle her. We're not standing for it. We've never had to answer to anyone before and we never will.

'That's where you come in,' he went on, looking at the Spook and me. 'I've been close to the witch and she terrified the life out of me. All the strength seemed to drain out of my body. She kills people without even touching them – how do we deal with that?'

'It's something I'm still pondering,' said the Spook. 'The power she wields – killing from a distance with such ease – is more potent than anything I've encountered before in a single witch. But now we know its source we'll find a way to stop it eventually, don't you worry.' My master sounded more determined than he had for some time.

'The only problem is that Lizzie has supporters – lots of well-armed yeomen bought with bribes of wealth and power – and it won't be so easy to get her on her own again,' Stanton told us.

'You said that you were lucky to escape with your life . . . What happened?' I asked him.

'That night when the witch killed your father' – he nodded towards Adriana – 'I'd already decided to make an attempt on her life. But I was as helpless and terrified as the rest of that gathering and my blood just turned to water. And she sensed something. It was almost as if she could read my mind.

'Later she questioned me. Wanted to know how loyal I was. She said she was starting to have doubts about me and ordered me to tell her the truth. I could feel her right inside my head, twisting and prodding. I began to shake and sweat, and it took all my will power not to admit that I'd planned to kill her. It was close – very close.'

'Well, it seems to me that a lot will depend on just how much support you can muster,' said the Spook. 'With enough men you could attack when the Tynwald meet. In the confusion we might be able to put an end to her. If Lizzie was distracted, she could still be bound with a silver chain.'

'Or I could put my sword through her heart,' Stanton said. 'I'm going to send runners to the nearest towns and villages to drum up support. Anyone who can carry a weapon and wants to fight for the freedom of our land will do.'

Although word had already been spread to the surrounding villages, by noon only about a dozen new men had rallied to Stanton's cause. Most were farm labourers who had brought nothing better than clubs – though three boasted pikes and one had brought a spear. These latter had once been yeomen, but they were no longer young and their weapons were rusty. Despite that, Stanton had greeted each man warmly and accepted his pledge of loyalty.

And then another arrival brought a delighted smile to Adriana's face: a young man carrying a stout stick. It was Simon Sulby.

'Any news of Captain Baines?' the Spook asked him when he could finally extract himself from Adriana's embrace.

'I'm afraid he was arrested at St John's,' Simon replied. 'He wasn't supposed to leave Douglas, so they took him back to his ship under guard. And there he'll stay until they need him to return those refugees to the County.'

Early evening brought a fresh band of about twenty armed yeomen, which swelled our supporters to over eighty – along with several women who had followed their menfolk. They in turn had brought a number of children, including at least three babes in arms.

The sun sank rapidly, as if time itself was moving faster and faster. Soon a dozen fires were lit by the mill; fires that grew brighter as the dusk thickened into night. One of the yeomen hung a flag, with its emblem of three legs, from the roof of the mill. It fluttered in the breeze, and the makeshift camp echoed with laughter, the talk filled with optimism. Someone produced a fiddle, and the women kicked off their shoes and the grass was suddenly awhirl with dancers, Simon and Adriana quickly joining in. Some of the locals arrived and watched from a distance. They were clearly afraid of getting involved.

Stanton now prepared to march his men east towards St John's under cover of darkness. He planned to hide them in the forest at the foot of Slieau Whallian and attack at noon, when the Parliament assembled. Scouts had already reported that the route was clear, so we would take the main road for the majority of the way.

The Spook, Alice, Stanton and I followed behind the yeomanry, but the women and children were staying at the mill. Adriana reluctantly remained to care for her mother. After the doctor's medicine had failed to bring about any improvement, Alice had treated her with herbs and potions, but to little effect.

The Spook handed me his bag to carry. 'The odds are certainly stacked against us,' he said to Stanton, shaking his head. 'A witch like Lizzie can sniff out approaching danger. More than likely she'll know that we're coming and use *dread* – the spell that terrifies her enemies. If she does that, brave as your men are, they'll take to their heels.'

But Stanton refused to be daunted by the Spook's words. 'I've seen what she's capable of but we have to try. If we don't make a fight of it, she's won,' he told us.

Some hours before dawn we were hidden deep in the forest but within easy range of St John's. Stanton posted guards, and the rest of us grabbed the chance to rest.

Dawn brought drizzle and grey skies, but we couldn't risk lighting fires so had to make do with a cold breakfast; for the Spook and me that meant cheese, and he grumbled as he ate a small portion. He liked to fast before facing the dark but always kept up his physical strength with a little cheese.

'This isn't a patch on our County cheese, lad,' he commented. 'I prefer it yellow and very crumbly!'

I had no appetite and ate little. I was nervous and my stomach was in knots. I'd a very bad feeling about what we were about to attempt. Lizzie's new-found powers were so strong, and she had too many men. We had no hope of getting near her. If we weren't killed in the attack, we'd be taken prisoner again. If that happened, I dreaded to think what Lizzie would have in store for us all – especially the Spook.

CHAPTER 22
THE BATTLE AT TYNWALD HILL

Daniel Stanton was a capable commander and it was clear that his men trusted him and obeyed his orders without question. The first stage of the attack went well.

We advanced through the trees in a thin arc towards St John's, the yeomen spread out to deal with enemy patrols. They encountered three: two surrendered without a fight; the third put up only token resistance. If this had been a straightforward military engagement, the element of surprise would have been with us. But Lizzie was different.

Back in the early days of my apprenticeship to the Spook, Lizzie had moved into the Chipenden area and been staying in a cottage only a few miles from the village. She'd snatched a child to take its bones. I managed to rescue it and, enraged, the local men set off with clubs and sticks to get her. Using long-sniffing, she'd sensed the danger and fled. The mob had then burned her cottage to the ground.

But this time Lizzie was the one in the position of power. She'd sense the threat we posed, then use her superior forces to swat us as easily as you would a fly. To counter this we planned a lightning raid that would strike straight at the witch herself, taking her unawares.

Under Stanton's orders, the yeomen re-formed, the thin crescent becoming a compact wedge, to drive through any resistance and make directly for the witch. As we approached St John's, the Spook, Alice, Simon and I were to the rear of the yeomen.

My master turned to me and Alice. 'Use these lads as cover for just as long as you can, then go straight for her!'

I nodded, and we released the retractable blades in

our staffs. Alice didn't usually carry a weapon but Simon had given her a knife. She now wore it at her belt. I wondered if she'd be able to use it against her own mother. Somehow, for all her harsh words about Lizzie, I doubted it.

'Stay close to me!' I told her, concerned that the battle might separate us, and that she'd lose the protection of the blood jar.

My mouth was dry with fear and excitement. We were near the edge of the trees now: I could see buildings and a large green straight ahead. A big gathering of people stood there, some holding pikes and spears. Our yeomen readied their weapons.

'Now!' cried Stanton, and led the charge. We broke into a run, still holding our tight wedge formation. I couldn't see much through the press of men, but in the distance I spotted the four-tiered grassy mound known as Tynwald Hill, where the Parliament was already gathered. Lizzie might be addressing them right now; she had to be somewhere close by.

Then I heard shouts and cries of pain as our yeomen

made contact with the enemy. Our forward movement was starting to slow as the resistance hardened.

Whether we would have reached the centre of the green or not I'll never know, because at that moment, just as we'd expected, Lizzie used the spell called *dread*. I felt a sudden overwhelming fear; the strong need to turn and run from some terrible unseen threat moving towards us. I resisted the urge, knowing that Alice and my master would be doing the same. But our yeomen were powerless in the face of such a spell, and they broke formation immediately, scattering to every point of the compass – as did Simon Sulby. How could he do otherwise? He'd never before been subjected to such a feeling of terror.

But it wasn't all bad: such a spell isn't selective, and it affected Lizzie's own troops as well as our own. Had she not realized that would happen? The spell had surely failed to gain her any advantage at all, I thought. Perhaps the power had gone to her head.

There were yeomen running in all directions across the green, along with members of Parliament and other dignitaries, their gowns of office flapping around their ankles. But where was Lizzie?

'There she is!' cried the Spook, pointing with his staff.

She was standing near the hill, staring at us malevolently. For a moment her eyes locked with mine and a new tremor of fear and anticipation ran through my body. I now faced something more dangerous than *dread*, which I had already brushed aside. Lizzie had the power to kill us from a distance, and I was the most likely candidate. She wouldn't slay the Spook outright; she owed him a long, lingering, painful death. Alice was her daughter, and I wasn't sure what she'd do with her. But I was just a thorn in her side, the one responsible for the destruction of Mother Malkin, Lizzie's grandmother.

We were still running towards her, weaving our way through the thinning ranks of yeomen, when suddenly the sky grew dark. In an instant the sun vanished as angry clouds raced in from the west and the trees began to shake and moan. Torrential rain drove right into our faces, making it difficult to see. This was more powerful dark magic being conjured by Lizzie.

I bowed my head and wiped the water out of my eyes, my left hand gripping my staff. I was near her now, and when I raised my head, I saw her face twist into a cunning, lopsided smile, which widened into an evil grin of pure triumph. Suddenly I realized that this was what she had intended all along. She didn't care that her own forces had been scattered by her spell. All she wanted was to face the Spook, Alice and me and take her revenge. She truly believed that she was a match for the three of us together.

I was ahead of the Spook, ahead of Alice; another dozen paces would bring me within striking distance. I raised my staff, holding it like a spear. Lizzie was now gripping two long blades and getting ready to use them on the first to come within range.

I was almost upon her when someone surged past me, sword held aloft.

'She's mine!' cried Daniel Stanton. Somehow his courage had managed to counter the witch's spell.

But as he reached her, thrusting the sword towards her heart, the witch knocked it aside with the blade in her left hand; using her other weapon, she cracked the handle down with great force on the back of his head. Stanton staggered and fell, rolling over and over, the sword flying out of his hand.

Why hadn't Lizzie used the blade? I wondered. Immediately my question was answered, for she spoke right inside my head:

There'll be a slow painful death for him – for you and your master too!

In an instant I was upon her. I stabbed down at the witch with my staff, but at the last moment I slipped on the wet grass and she struck me a glancing blow with the handle of her dagger. A light flashed inside my head and I don't remember hitting the ground.

I must have lost consciousness briefly, because the next thing I knew, the Spook was slowly approaching Lizzie, his staff held diagonally across his body. Alice was standing to one side, her face fearful, watching the encounter between the witch and my master. Lizzie was grinning again, almost gloating. I looked at the Spook and I could see his fear. No, it was more than that. His whole face was twitching, and his eyes told me that he was already defeated. No doubt Lizzie was speaking inside his head, telling him that he had no chance against her; telling him what she would do to him after taking him prisoner.

The sight of my master in that situation horrified and dismayed me. He had always been such a tower of strength. Even when temporarily defeated by the dark, he had always been brave and optimistic. All that was gone now – I turned away, unable to bear the sight of him brought so low.

Suddenly the Spook lowered his staff and fell to his knees at Lizzie's feet. She smiled and raised her dagger high, about to bring the handle down on his head and knock him unconscious. I sat up and staggered to my feet, but a wave of dizziness and nausea immediately washed over me. I wanted to intervene but knew I couldn't reach my master in time.

But there *was* an intervention. Alice suddenly

shouted out – it was a word in the Old Tongue. I didn't know what it meant but guessed it was some sort of spell. Something seemed to dart between Alice and Lizzie; something small and dark. Alice didn't throw it – whatever it was came straight out of her open mouth.

The effect on the bone witch was immediate. Lizzie staggered backwards and the dagger fell from her grasp. And then Alice attacked, holding her dagger aloft – though she didn't stab Lizzie. She used her other hand to draw her nails right down the witch's face. Lizzie screamed and fell back.

This was my chance and I stepped forward, raising my staff to drive my blade into her heart. But though I tried with all my strength, I could not hurt her as Alice had done. I was no match for her power. The staff froze in my hands.

'Quick, Tom!' Alice cried, dragging the Spook to his feet. I picked up his staff, took his other arm, and we started to pull him away. I glanced back and saw Lizzie still clutching her face. Whatever Alice had done, I knew its effects wouldn't last long.

Somehow we got clear, losing ourselves in the throng of terrified people. As we headed back through the trees, we saw people still staggering about, both yeomen and members of the Tynwald, their faces showing bemusement and terror. Of Simon Sulby there was no sign.

As we made our way into the forest, the Spook shrugged us off almost angrily. 'I can walk! I don't need dragging!' he snapped, and immediately started off ahead of us. At first he seemed unsteady on his feet, but then he pressed on with more vigour. Alice and I dropped back a little so we could talk.

'He's not angry with us, he's angry with himself,' I told her.

'Old Gregory's pride's hurt,' Alice said. 'Lizzie bested him again – no mistake about that.'

'But you bested Lizzie. How did you manage that when she's so strong?'

'It was something that my aunt Agnes once taught me. It's a spell some witches call *talon*. You bite off a small piece of the nail of your forefinger and spit it at your enemy. Then you scratch her face and stun her. Took Lizzie by surprise, it did. She didn't know I could do that. Only gave us a few moments though. I'll never be able to repeat that spell. She'll be ready for me next time.'

The aunt Alice had mentioned was Agnes Sowerbutts, whom Alice had once lived with briefly in Pendle.

'But I thought you told me that Agnes was a benign witch, a healer?' I said to her.

'She is, Tom – wouldn't lie to you, would I? But any witch who lives in Pendle needs some spells to defend herself with. Never know when some other witch might try it on. Agnes would only use something like that in self-defence. Same goes for me.'

Soon we were well clear of St John's and the sun was shining again. When we reached the mill late in the afternoon, Adriana was distraught to hear that Simon had gone missing. She feared the worst.

However, to her relief he was back before noon the

following day – though the news he brought was mostly bad. Within the hour, the Tynwald had assembled again and had appointed Lizzie ruler of the island; the Parliament was dissolved, leaving her in full control.

'It was over so quickly,' Simon said. 'Everyone was scared of her. They just did what she wanted, then went home. Who can blame them?'

The Spook nodded. 'What then? Did Lizzie stay in St John's?'

'No, she left immediately for Greeba Keep.'

'What about Daniel Stanton's forces? Did she take prisoners with her?'

'Just one – Stanton himself. She was in a great hurry to get away – she seemed excited about something, and I don't think it was just about becoming ruler of Mona. She took no other prisoners. That was the only good thing about the whole business: all the yeomen had been comrades once and they weren't keen to fight each other, so there were no casualties. Only half a dozen were wounded, and none seriously. Those who didn't return to Greeba with Lizzie simply went home.'

'I wonder why she rushed back so quickly,' muttered the Spook thoughtfully.

'Do you think she's found out about the cavern and what it contains?' I asked him.

'It's possible, lad. If so, she'll take some stopping, that's for sure.' He looked across the table at Simon and Adriana. 'I think you two will be safe enough here,' he told them. 'But as soon as Bony Lizzie gets her hands on that cache of power, she'll come looking for the three of us. We'll take the dogs and make ourselves scarce.'

'There's an abandoned cottage south of here in Glenmaye,' Adriana said. 'It's not been lived in for years but you'd have a roof over your head.' Suddenly she blushed. 'It's where I used to meet Simon – a place Father didn't know about. Simon would go and wait for me there and I'd join him if I could get away from the mill. Trust me, you'll be safe there.'

CHAPTER 23
NIGHTMARES

Adriana gave us a sack of supplies: hams, potatoes, carrots and cheese. It was heavy, so I handed our bags to Alice and carried the sack over my shoulder. Adriana also sent one of the mill workers, a young lad, to guide us.

The cottage stood on the edge of the glen just inside a wood; although the trees had lost their leaves, it was well hidden and could only be reached by a narrow track that twisted its way between the hills. We arrived just before dark and spent an uncomfortable night sleeping on the damp flagged kitchen floor. The following morning we set about making ourselves more comfortable. It was a simple cottage – two up and two down – and every room was full of rubbish: broken furniture, mildewed blankets, and piles of leaves, blown in through the open doorway – the front door had come off its hinges.

Alice crafted a broom of twigs and set about sweeping the place clean. I laid four big fires, one in each room, so that we were soon warmer and the cottage was starting to dry out a little. I hadn't the tools to put the door back on its hinges, but I propped it up in the doorway, supported by heavy stones. There was still a draught but it kept most of the chill out.

However, the kitchen was where we felt most comfortable. That night, after a meal of boiled ham and potatoes, we sat cross-legged on the flags close to the fire. We were all tired and the Spook's head kept nodding forward onto his chest. Soon he was fast asleep. After a while he started to groan and mutter to himself. He sounded scared. At last he opened his eyes wide and woke up with a gasp of terror.

'What was it – another nightmare?' I asked.

'It was more than a nightmare, lad. Lizzie was right

inside my mind, taunting and threatening me. Telling me what she'll do to me when I fall into her hands once more.'

It saddened me to see my master in this state – and to be powerless to help him. 'It's not worth worrying about,' I told him, attempting to be optimistic. 'She may be able to torment your mind but she's a long way away. We're safe for now.'

The Spook stared at me angrily. 'Not worth worrying? I've every right to be worried. In all my time as a spook I've never felt so low and close to defeat. My library and house are gone and I'm exiled here on an island ruled by a witch who'll only grow more powerful with each day that passes. I've never failed to bind a witch before, never missed with my silver chain. And now I've failed not once but twice. Lizzie's proved to be too strong for me. Everything I've worked for all these years has been overturned. I never thought it would come to this.'

'We'll find a way to deal with Lizzie,' Alice said. 'There might be something in that shaman's notebook that could help. After all, he worked with the buggane to build that cache of magic.'

'Using the dark to fight the dark again?' My master shook his head sadly.

'No,' Alice contradicted him. 'It ain't that at all. You once asked me to tell Tom what I'd learned from Lizzie so he could write it down in his notebook. You do remember saying that, don't you?'

The Spook nodded.

'Well, this is the same. I'm just trying to get information. I'll start reading at first light.'

'As long as it's only reading, girl,' he warned. 'Remember, no spells or you'll answer to me!'

The following morning, after breakfast, Alice started on the shaman's notebook, but she didn't find it easy going. Some of it was in code and impossible to decipher. Even the parts that could be read used terms she'd never even heard of. It seemed that animism was a very different type of magic to that taught by Bony Lizzie. However, Alice was not one to give up easily, and she returned again and again to her study of that notebook. Sometimes she looked excited, as if she'd made some progress, but when I questioned her about it, she shook her head and wouldn't discuss it with me.

Then, three days after the Spook's nightmare, I had one of my own.

I was in a dark forest, alone and unarmed. My staff lay somewhere nearby, but I couldn't find it. I was desperate, because in a few minutes, at midnight, something would be coming after me – something terrible.

Later, when I woke up, I couldn't remember what it was – dreams are like that sometimes – but I knew it had been sent by a witch seeking revenge for something I'd done to her.

In my dream, a church bell began to chime somewhere in the distance. I froze, petrified, but on the twelfth note I began to run towards it. Branches whipped at my face as I sprinted desperately through the trees. Something was chasing me now, but it wasn't footsteps that I heard: it was the beating of wings.

I glanced back over my shoulder and saw that my pursuer was a large black crow. The sight of it filled me with terror, but I knew that if only I could reach the church I'd be safe. Why that should be I don't know – churches aren't usually places of refuge from the dark. Spooks and apprentices relied on the tools of their trade and the knowledge they'd gained. Nevertheless, in that nightmare I knew that I had to reach the church or die.

I suddenly tripped over a root and sprawled headlong. Winded, I struggled to my knees and looked up at the crow, which had alighted on a branch. The air shimmered in front of me and I blinked furiously to clear my vision. When I could finally see again, I was confronted by a figure in a long black dress. She was female from the neck down but had the huge head of a crow.

Even as I stared, the crow's head began to change. The beak shrank, and the eyes shifted shape until the head was fully human. And I knew that face. It was that of a witch who was now dead.

I must have cried out on awaking from that dream. The Spook was still fast asleep, but as I sat up, shuddering, Alice's arm went around my shoulders.

'You all right, Tom?' she whispered.

I nodded. 'Just a nightmare – that's all.'

'Want to tell me about it?'

I gave Alice a short account of what I'd dreamed. 'I think the crow was the Morrigan, the dark goddess worshipped by Celtic witches,' I added. 'No doubt it harks back to the time when Bill Arkwright and I faced a Celtic witch who'd travelled to the County. She summoned the Morrigan, who attacked me in the shape of a crow, but I somehow managed to drive it off. The witch warned me then never to visit Ireland. She said the Morrigan was much more powerful there and would seek her revenge on me.'

'Well, that explains your nightmare, Tom. Don't worry, we're not in Ireland. We'll be heading back to the County once we've dealt with Lizzie.'

I knew that Alice was just trying to comfort me, but I felt gloomy about the future. 'There's little chance of that while it's still in enemy hands,' I observed.

'As Old Gregory once said, wars don't last for ever,' Alice remarked cheerfully. 'Anyway, what happened to that Celtic witch?'

'Bill Arkwright killed her with his knife. Right at the end of my nightmare, the crow took on her dead face. That was the scariest thing of all.'

The Spook had become very quiet and withdrawn, giving me just an hour of instruction a day, studying the Old Tongue. Then, using the large notebook that he always carried in his bag, he spent the rest of the time writing. I noticed that he was making sketches as well.

'What are you doing?' I asked, curiosity getting the better of me.

'I've got to start somewhere, lad,' he told me in one of his rare talkative moments. 'All that's left of my library is the Bestiary, so I'm going to try and rewrite some of the other books that were lost. I've got to do it before I forget. I'm starting with *A History of the Dark*. The lessons we learn from history are important – they keep us from repeating past mistakes.'

I felt that we should be using this time to work out how to deal with Lizzie. Most days we discussed it briefly, but the Spook seemed lost in thought and contributed little to our discussions. Yes, the books did need to be rewritten, but it seemed to me that he was distracting himself from the real problem – a witch who was growing more and more powerful.

Exactly seven days after our arrival at the cottage, we had a visitor: Alice opened the kitchen door to throw out some food scraps and a bird flew straight into the room – a grey pigeon. But instead of flapping about in panic, it landed on the table.

'Bad luck for a bird to fly into a room!' Alice said. 'It means someone's going to die soon.'

'Well, you're not always right, girl. Besides, I think this one has a message for us,' said the Spook, pointing to a piece of paper tied to the pigeon's leg.

He held out his hand and the bird hopped onto it. Carefully he took it in his hands and held the creature out towards me. 'Untie the message, lad. Be as gentle as you can . . .'

I did as he asked. The piece of paper was tied on so that it wouldn't come loose, yet one gentle pull on the end of the string, and the pellet of paper dropped into my hand. While the Spook gave the bird some crusts of bread and water, I unfolded the small square of paper and smoothed it out on the table. The writing was very small and difficult to make out.

'It's from Adriana,' I said. 'She says it's safe to return, but there's bad news as well.'

'Well, read it out, lad!'

So I did as my master commanded.

'*Dear Mr Gregory, Tom and Alice,*
Soon after you left, the yeomanry searched the area, but I stayed hidden close to the house and they passed me by.
The witch is still at Greeba Keep: I hear strange tales of what is happening there, and I have much to tell you, so

please hasten back immediately.

I have bad news too: five days ago my mother died. So the witch killed both my parents. I owe her for that and intend to repay her fully.

Yours sincerely,

Adriana.'

'Poor girl,' said the Spook. 'Well, let's get back to the mill and see what the latest news is. I fear the worst.'

Within the hour we were on our way back to Peel.

CHAPTER
24
TERRIFYING THINGS

We arrived just in time for the evening meal. Adriana had sent the cook home early and prepared a lamb stew herself. Simon helped serve us. It was the best food I'd eaten in weeks, and she'd provided each of us with a large cup of mead, a delicious drink made from honey, the sweetness tempered with aromatic spices.

When the Spook had offered his condolences for the death of her mother, Adriana had wept bitterly.

'Well,' said my master now, sipping from his cup of mead. 'I've tried to be patient but I can't wait any longer. What are the strange tales from Greeba Keep that you mentioned in your letter?'

'Terrifying things have been seen in the surrounding woods – all manner of monsters and daemons—'

'The buggane can take on many different shapes,' interrupted the Spook.

'These things weren't seen in the buggane's domain,' Adriana replied, 'but much further to the north. Sheep and cattle have gone missing too. All that remained was small fragments of bone.'

The Spook pulled at his beard. 'What about the sightings? Were the witnesses reliable?' he asked.

Adriana shrugged. 'Some are more reliable than others, but one was a forester, a dour, plain-speaking man not given to flights of fancy. He also saw strange dancing lights – he counted seven. When they approached him, he fled. Could they be the same lights we saw in the cavern?'

'He did well to run,' said the Spook. 'That coven of witch spirits could have drained his life force in minutes. This is all very bad news. It means that denizens of the dark visiting the cache of animas can now use its power to wander far beyond it. They're a threat to your whole island and possibly beyond.'

'Can anything be done?' asked Adriana.

'Aye – killing the buggane would stop it. The cache is only attractive while it continues to grow. Without an active buggane, such power soon starts to diminish. What else?' asked the Spook. 'Is there any more news of the bone witch?'

'She took her force of yeomen back to Greeba, but then paid them off and dismissed the majority within a few days, retaining only about fifty for guard duty.'

'Well, Lizzie's made a big mistake there,' the Spook said. 'Those men had permanent jobs under the Ruling Council. They'll be disgruntled now and could become a force that can be used against her.'

'It's no mistake,' said Alice, shaking her head. 'I know Lizzie better than anyone, and that's the scariest thing I've heard so far. She had lots of money; and even if she'd emptied that chest, she could have raised taxes if she needed some more. Ain't bothered then, is she? Don't need 'em. That's how powerful she is now.'

The Spook didn't reply but his expression showed that Alice's words had disturbed him.

'Since then some of those guards have deserted, terrified by the things that were happening in the keep,' Adriana continued. 'They heard voices when there was nobody there, and footsteps following them that stopped when they stopped, and strange shadows that could only be seen out of the corners of their eyes. Nowhere inside the keep was free of them. It was worse after dark, but these things could be heard and felt even in daylight. There were spots of intense cold too . . .'

I knew that was bad. The Spook and I, being seventh sons of seventh sons, feel a strange coldness when something from the dark is near; other people are not usually aware of it. If those men were aware of intense cold, then very powerful dark magic was involved.

'By now the witch has probably no more than a dozen men with her – ones more scared of leaving than staying,' Adriana went on. 'She made threats – said that anyone else who left without her permission would die in their sleep, and sure enough, two were found dead ... So what are we going to do now?' she asked. 'Lizzie's got to be stopped.'

'I've been racking my brains to come up with a plan,' said the Spook. 'With the reduced guard it'll be easier to get near her, but what can we do in the face of such power? The first time I couldn't even cast my chain true, and at St John's she brought me to my knees. I was helpless.' I'd never heard my master sound so hopeless, so defeated.

'But it's my duty to put an end to her' – the Spook sighed – 'and I'll do that even at the cost of my own life.'

'We need to distract her,' said Alice. 'Get the shaman's thumb-bones away from her and she'll be a lot easier to deal with.'

'Horn said they were a conduit for her to tap that stored power. But that was then. By now, she may have direct access to it,' the Spook pointed out. 'She may not need them any longer.'

'We have to do something,' I said. 'Distraction is a

good idea. We should split up and come at her from different directions. It's worth a try.'

'Different directions?' asked the Spook, draining his cup of mead. 'We've only two. There's the main gate or the buggane's tunnels. The first will still be guarded. As for the second, the buggane will surely be Lizzie's creature by now. I for one don't relish the idea of confronting it down there. It doesn't even need to attack directly. It could just collapse a tunnel and suffocate us.'

We were all tired and went to bed very early without having come up with a proper plan. I'd only just dropped off to sleep when I jerked awake, aware that someone was standing beside me. I sat up and some-one whispered, 'Shhhh! It's all right, Tom. It's just me, Alice . . .'

'Something wrong?' I asked.

Her hand found mine in the darkness. 'Just wanted to talk, that's all. Old Gregory ain't going to do any-thing. Losing his house and books, and now failing twice to deal with Lizzie – it's just about finished him off. He's past it, Tom. He's scared. I think you and me should sort her out. We'd be better off without him.'

I suddenly felt as cold as ice. 'Don't talk like that, Alice. He's been through a bad patch, that's all. He'll recover and be back stronger than ever – just you wait and see!'

'No, Tom. You got to face it: he's finished. Still be able to teach you, he will, but it'll be you doing the real work, the dangerous work, from now on.'

'What are we supposed to do? None of us can think of a way to deal with Lizzie – it's not just Mr Gregory.'

'I can, Tom. I know a way. But Old Gregory wouldn't approve. He'd never go along with it.'

'Does it involve using dark magic?' I asked.

Alice squeezed my hand again. 'Not actually using it, Tom – just knowing how to counter it. Old Gregory wouldn't understand. That's why Adriana put something in his drink. He'll sleep until long after dawn. We could be back by then – with it all done and dusted.'

'You've put something in his drink? That's crazy!

What will he say when he finds out? I can't do it, Alice. He would never forgive me.'

'You've got to come and help – otherwise Adriana will try to deal with Lizzie by herself. She told me so. Without us she'll be dead or fed to the buggane in no time. She's already set off for the keep with Simon – she'll attack Lizzie whether we join her or not. Ain't going to risk the buggane's tunnels. Going in through the front gate, we are. Adriana can get us in!'

'How can we get past the guards? There'll still be several men inside that keep and the portcullis will be down.'

'There'll only be about half a dozen, that's all: they change over at eleven. None of 'em want to stay in there at night, so they take turns. Lizzie's agreed to that. We'll strike as the guard changes.'

'How will Adriana help?' I asked.

'Remember she said she was a bird witch? Thought it was nonsense then. Well, I still don't think she's a witch. Nobody would think so in Pendle. But you wouldn't believe what she can do with birds. She's going to use them to distract the guards. Just you wait and see.'

'There's one big problem though. We know that Lizzie won't be able to long-sniff me or you. She won't know we're on our way. But she'll sniff out Adriana and Simon for sure. She'll sense the danger before they get anywhere near the portcullis.'

'Talked to her about that too. If we go in and tackle Lizzie, she and Simon will stay outside. If we don't, they're both going in together – Adriana is set on taking revenge on Lizzie.' Alice shook her head and sighed. 'But she's no good against her, Tom, so we have to go. It's our one chance.'

'But when we get inside, what exactly will we do?' I asked.

'I've been thinking about that. We'll need to make for that room where the shaman kept his books. I've spent a long time trying to make head or tail of his notebook – can't understand a lot of what's in it, but it refers to pages in the grimoires. If you know where to look, there'll be stuff on controlling the buggane. Even mentions that cache of animas. Tells you how to use its power.'

'Will you be able to read those grimoires? They'll probably be in the Old Tongue. You know I've been studying it for months now and I'm making slow progress.'

'I practised it for nearly two years. Lizzie had a small library – most of her stuff was in English, some in Latin, but the most powerful spells of all were in the Old Tongue. I'm still slow, but I can work it out given time. It's worth a try, Tom. What do you say?'

So, very reluctantly, I agreed to accompany Alice. I said goodbye to the dogs and managed to keep them quiet. The Spook was still snoring loudly. I dreaded to think what he'd say when he found out. But under the circumstances, what choice did I have?

CHAPTER
25
THE BEATING OF WINGS

I t was a cloudless night; the moon wasn't up yet but the stars were very bright. We were walking through the trees, approaching the keep, when I heard an owl hoot three times somewhere ahead.

'That's Adriana,' Alice whispered, leading us towards the sound.

As we got nearer, I had a sudden strong feeling of being watched. Everything seemed very still and there wasn't a breath of wind. And then I glanced up and saw hundreds of eyes staring down at me intently. The branches above were covered with birds. There wasn't enough light to identify the different species, but they ranged in size from sparrows to large crows. They should have been roosting at this time of night; yet here they were, wide awake – it was unnerving to see them watching us like that.

Adriana was waiting with Simon under a tree. She put her finger to her lips to indicate the need for silence. Through the trees beyond her I could see the entrance to Greeba Keep. The portcullis was down, and five men were striding towards the gate.

Adriana stepped forward and placed her left hand on Alice's shoulder, her right on mine. Then she looked up to where the birds waited silently, opened her mouth and gave a strange cry; it was something like a bird's call – though none that I recognized. In response the flock seemed to move as one. There was a rustling of feathers, a settling, then silence again.

'You'll be safe now,' Adriana whispered. 'They won't touch you. I only wish we could come with you . . .'

'Ain't worth the risk,' Alice whispered back. 'Lizzie would sniff you out for sure. Once we've dealt with her, we'll meet you back here. No knowing how long. Could be hours – or even a day or more.'

The men had almost reached the gate now. We heard the grind of metal on metal and the clank of chains as the portcullis was slowly raised.

'Simon and I will wait here, no matter how long it takes. And we'll watch the keep. Now go down towards the wall directly ahead,' Adriana told us, her voice still low. 'When the birds attack, slip in through the gate.'

We did as she instructed and started heading down the slope. The portcullis was fully raised now and the guard was about to change. There were about dozen men there. In a few moments the old guard would set off home. If they glanced our way, there was a danger that we might be spotted.

Somehow we reached the wall without attracting their attention. Half the yeomen were heading towards the trees, and there was a clank of chains again as the others began to lower the gate. In a few moments it would be too late. But then there was another noise – the beating of wings. I looked up and saw that the stars were eclipsed. Like a black cloud, a huge flock of birds descended upon the two groups of men. I heard curses, shouts, and then a loud cry of pain.

Alice and I began to run along the wall. Adriana had talked about distracting the guards, but as we reached the gate, I realized that this was no minor diversion to allow us into the keep. Those men were fighting for their very lives. Some were running around, arms flapping desperately to ward off their attackers. One was on the ground, rolling over and over, covered in birds; the air was thick with feathers.

They were all too preoccupied with their own survival to see us go through the gate which had now ceased its descent. And it was clear that the birds were driving them away from the keep. Of course, the guards' fear of Lizzie might well make them return later – that's if they were in any condition to do so.

Just as I'd hoped, the inner portcullis – the one that gave access to the tower – was also raised, and moments later Alice and I were safely inside.

We were now faced with two threats. The most dangerous, of course, was Lizzie herself: she might well kill us outright; at the very least she could take the blood jar or even make me smash it. We might also encounter the threatening creatures we'd heard about, drawn to the area because the witch had meddled with the cache of animas, making it unstable. It would now act like a baleful beacon – a fire lit by witches, summoning powerful entities from the dark.

We began to climb the tower steps, trying to make as little noise as possible. I knew that the odds against us reaching the shaman's study without being detected were high. I was carrying my rowan staff with the blade at the ready; the silver chain was in the left pocket of my cloak, and I'd filled my breeches pockets with salt and iron. Who knew what we might encounter?

After passing the doors that led to the kitchens and bedrooms, we came at last to the throne room. It was quiet, deserted and dimly lit; just two torches flickered on the wall. We walked along the crimson carpet past the throne to the door and up the flight of steps. In the circular antechamber we paused to listen out once more. Again there was no indication that anyone was around, so we opened the door to the shaman's study and stepped inside. The room was in darkness but there was a candle on the table. Alice strode forward and picked it up. It ignited immediately, filling the room with a flickering yellow light.

'Alice!' I exclaimed in annoyance. She'd used dark magic to light the candle; the first time I'd ever seen her do that.

'Ain't no time to waste, Tom! Don't worry,' she told me. 'It's just a useful little trick, no worse than using a mirror.'

But I did worry; she seemed to be using the dark more and more – and where would it all lead?

There was evidence here that Lizzie had been poking around. The rows of books had been disturbed; there were gaps on the shelves. Three grimoires were now stacked on the table next to the skull. But the large chest still lay in the corner.

'She's been searching through these books,' Alice muttered. 'Good job I took the notebook, ain't it? Even if I can't do anything with it after all, at least I kept it from her. Better get busy . . .'

With those words, she sat down at the table and looked at the covers of the three books in turn. That done, she selected one, opened it and began to leaf through.

'Where's your list of pages to refer to?' I asked.

'Don't be daft, Tom. I wouldn't bring 'em here in case Lizzie got her hands on them. Pendle witches read stuff once and commit it to memory. All their spells are learned by heart. What I need is in my head.'

I left her reading, went over to the window and peered out into the dark night. The moon was up, and now, below me I could see the courtyard and a section of the wall. Unfortunately this window didn't overlook the gate so I couldn't tell whether any of the guards had returned to the keep.

Where was Lizzie? I wondered. If she wasn't in the tower, maybe she was in one of the other buildings? I suddenly realized that I'd be better off watching from the top of the stairs. Then I'd hear if anybody was on their way up.

'I'm going to keep watch, Alice,' I told her.

She nodded, turned over a page and then, head in hands, frowning in concentration, returned to her reading. I went out into the antechamber, leaving the door open. The seven other doors were all closed. One was where the gowns were stored. Another was the bathroom. So there were five bedrooms. A sudden chill ran down my spine. Perhaps Lizzie was asleep in one of them? It would give me the chance I needed. I could bind her with my silver chain.

And suddenly it was as if a flash of light had gone off inside my head. *Always trust your instincts* – that was what the Spook said. At once I was certain which was Lizzie's room. Certain also that she was inside.

I leaned my staff against the wall and eased my chain onto my left wrist, ready for throwing. Then, with the other hand, I opened the door very slowly. The room was in darkness, but the torch outside lit the bed, and I could see Lizzie lying there. She was flat on her back on top of the bedclothes, wearing the purple gown.

I moved cautiously towards her.

But the moment I stepped inside I realized my mistake . . .

It wasn't Lizzie lying on the bed after all. It was her empty gown!

My limbs felt like lead. It hadn't been my instincts at all. I'd been lured into a trap. Some spell of compulsion had drawn me to the room. I sank to my knees. What was it – something like a bone-yard? I was finding it difficult to breathe, my body growing heavier by the second. I seemed to be melting right through the floor. As I lost consciousness, I felt myself being lifted up and carried down, down, down . . .

I heard a groan nearby and opened my eyes. I was lying on my side on damp flags.

There were chains bound tightly around my legs and fastened to an iron ring set into the stone wall. I sat up slowly and manoeuvred myself until my back was resting against the wall. I felt stiff and my head ached. I looked around. I was in a cell that was much larger than the one Lord Barrule had put me in, though it had the same three stone walls and one of earth. There was a torch high up on each of the walls to my right and left, flickering in the chill draught that came from the round hole in the earth wall directly ahead. It was another of the buggane's tunnels – I realized I was down in the dungeons again.

Where was Alice? I wondered. Had she been taken prisoner too? Had Lizzie found her in the shaman's study? Or had she been more interested in capturing me?

To my left sat another prisoner, also shackled to the wall; but his head was bowed forward, chin touching his chest, so I couldn't make out his face – though it was definitely a man, not Alice. Then I realized that there was another figure beyond him, and at the sight of him I gasped in horror, the bile rising up into my throat. I choked, struggling not to be sick. It was a dead yeoman, lying in a pool of his own blood. One of his arms and both legs were missing, his face a ruin; the buggane had been eating him.

I squeezed my eyes tight shut, my whole body trembling. I took deep, slow breaths and tried to calm down.

I glanced to my right and saw that there was someone else chained directly under the torch. I immediately recognized the milky eyes; the two short horns protruding from the thatch of dark hair. It was Horn, the abhuman. When he sensed me looking at him, he growled deep in his throat. He sounded like a wild animal. Despite those blind eyes, I remembered, he somehow had the power to see.

I tried to speak, but my throat was parched and the words only came out at the second attempt. 'I'm not your enemy,' I croaked. 'You're wasting your time threatening me.'

'You'd kill me or bind me if you got the chance!' the deep, feral voice accused.

'Look, we're both in the same boat here,' I said.

Horn let out a deep moan. 'I thought I'd live

my days serving Lord Barrule. He was a good master.'

'Was he?' I asked. 'He killed your mother, didn't he? That's what I was told.'

'My mother? My mother!' Horn spat on the earthen floor. 'She was a mother in blood and name only. She treated me cruelly and gave me pain beyond endurance. But I hate the Fiend even more than her, for it was he who fathered me; he who made me walk this world marked as a beast for all to see! Lord Barrule was the only person who's ever showed me any kindness.'

Kindness? I remembered how Barrule's guards had controlled him with the lengths of silver chain through each ear. That hardly seemed like kindness, but there was nothing to be gained from enraging the creature further.

'I suppose the witch now controls the buggane?' I asked.

I saw his head nod, the sharp horns glinting in the torchlight. 'I fought with all my strength, but to no avail. She rules the buggane but struggles to control the animas in the cavern. She doesn't fully understand my master's ways. It is not her kind of dark magic.'

'Who's this, do you know?' I asked, nodding to where the other prisoner was slumped.

'Commander Stanton. He was cruel. My master listened to him, not me, and allowed him to bore the holes in my ears for the silver chains. Said it was the only way he could control me. Ask me, he's got what he deserves. His mind has gone: he's empty – the buggane has drained his animus. Soon it will come for his flesh and blood. After that it will be my turn . . .'

Commander Stanton! He had paid the price for his opposition to Lizzie.

My thoughts turned to Alice once more. She had done well to deprive Lizzie of the shaman's notebook – it might have made all the difference. I didn't know exactly what Alice hoped to achieve, but she'd once made a pact with the Bane, an even more powerful daemon than the buggane. It had almost led to her destruction, but she had managed to control it for a while. With the help of the shaman's notebooks and the grimoires, maybe she could do the same here?

I felt weak with hunger and thirst, but worse than all that was a growing terror within me that I struggled to control. If Alice didn't help me, I was soon going to have my life force sucked out of me. At least then, I thought gloomily, I wouldn't be here to see Lizzie's blades when she took my thumb-bones. It was a terrible thing to have to depend for my survival on Alice being involved with dark power like this, but for a moment it gave me some hope. Then I remembered that Alice might have been captured too . . .

My arms weren't bound and I was able to check my pockets, which I found still filled with salt and iron; even my silver chain hadn't been taken. It might be that Bony Lizzie couldn't bear to touch it. Or maybe now, supremely confident of her power, she didn't care. My special key was there too. It would open almost any lock, but when I tried my shackles, I couldn't even get it in the keyhole. My sudden flare of hope was extinguished.

At least an hour passed while I worked through all the possibilities – all the things that might give me some hope of escape or of being rescued. Finally I thought about the Spook. Eventually he'd wake up and maybe work out what had happened. But he'd been powerless against Lizzie. The truth was, I had more faith in Alice.

From time to time Stanton gave a groan as if in pain, but it was just his body crying out, a reflex action; his mind was long gone, his flesh and bones now just an empty shell. Perhaps his soul had also fled.

Suddenly I heard a new sound. A sound that sent fear running down my spine. Someone or something was moving down the earth tunnel towards our cell.

I trembled as soil cascaded down onto the flags. Then the huge hairy head of the buggane emerged. Its large close-set eyes peered at each of us in turn and its wet snout sniffed the air before it pulled its bulk down into the cell. But it was not alone. Someone else crawled out of the tunnel behind it, a bedraggled figure with dirty clothes and mud-caked hair. It was a woman and she looked a sorry sight. It was only when she got to her feet and I saw the pointy shoes and wild glaring eyes that I recognized Bony Lizzie. Her tiara was still in place but almost invisible under the coating of dirt on her hair.

The witch ignored me and went over to look at Daniel Stanton. She knelt before him and I saw the knife in her hand. I averted my gaze as she began to cut away his thumb-bones. The commander cried out as if in agony, and I had to remind myself that it was just the reaction of his body; that his mind was no longer there to feel the pain.

Then Lizzie came across and crouched down to face me. She smiled, her hands covered in blood, still gripping the knife, hard eyes filled with malice. 'It's your turn next, boy. Right now I need all the help I can get. The bones of a seven times seven could make all the difference.'

I had to think fast. 'I thought you wanted to be a queen,' I said, trying to distract her, easing my hands into my pockets to grab some salt and iron. 'I thought you wanted to rule this island. What's happened to you?'

At that, Lizzie appeared bewildered, and an expression of pain and loss flickered across her face. Suddenly I could see Alice in her; the girl that the witch had once been. Then her face twisted into a sneer, and she leaned nearer so that her foul breath enveloped me.

'There's power here, boy, power beyond my wildest dreams; power that could give me the whole world if I wanted it. But first things first. In order to rule above, I need to control what's in the cavern. It'll take time, but it'll be well worth it. And your bones are going to help . . .'

CHAPTER
26
CORRUPTED BY THE DARK

For a moment I thought Lizzie intended to cut away my bones there and then, and my arms tensed, ready to envelop her in a cloud of salt and iron. But instead she returned the blade to the sheath on her belt and rose to her feet.

'I'll let the buggane take what it wants first,' the witch said, turning and heading towards the tunnel again.

I relaxed, breathing out slowly. Even with the salt and iron I'd still have been chained; I'd still have been at the mercy of the buggane. The witch would have recovered all too soon.

Lizzie disappeared into the tunnel, but the buggane had unfinished business. I saw its mouth open wide to reveal the sharp triangular teeth within. It bit deep into the throat of Daniel Stanton and drank his blood with relish. When it had drained him, it began to tear at his flesh. I covered my ears to shut out those awful shredding sounds, but then it began to crunch his bones. I thought it would never end but, sated at last, the buggane finally padded away, leaving bloody footprints on the flags. It climbed back into the tunnel and was soon out of sight.

How long would it be before the dream came back for me in spirit form? I wondered, fearful.

I didn't have long to wait. Within moments, the whispering began inside my head and my heart raced with terror. At first it was almost too faint to hear, but gradually I could make out individual words, such as rot, blood and worms. Then I experienced a sensation that I hadn't expected – no one had ever described a feeling like this. It was as if a dark cloud had floated down from the ceiling and covered me like a thick cold blanket. The distant sound of dripping water faded and was gone; but even worse than the loss of hearing was the rapid dimming of my sight. I could no longer see the torches; everything grew dark. I was blind.

My heart was thudding in my chest, the beats becoming laboured. I began to shiver with cold as the buggane slowly drew the energy from my body, stealing away my life force. The whispering grew louder. I could still make no sense of the words, but painful images from the past began to form inside my head, as if I was actually present at the scene.

I was on a mountain path. It was evening and the light was beginning to fail. I could hear a woman sobbing and voices raised in anger. I seemed to be gliding rather than walking and had no control over the direction I was taking. Ahead a rock jutted up like a giant rat's tooth; around it stood a group of people, amongst them one of Mam's old enemies, the witch, Wurmalde. I heard a series of heavy rhythmical thuds and saw someone with a hammer. At each blow there was a cry of pain.

Anguish squeezed my heart. I knew exactly where I was; what was happening. I was witnessing the moment when Mam's enemies had nailed her left hand to a rock. Blood was dripping down her arm and onto the grass. Once she was nailed, they bound her naked body with the silver chain, wrapping it around the rock. I saw her flinch with pain, the tears running down her cheeks.

'In three days we'll return,' I heard Wurmalde say, her voice filled with cruelty and malice, 'and then we'll cut out your heart.'

They left her waiting alone in the darkness – waiting for the sun to come up over the sea in the east; the sun that would burn and blister her body.

I wanted to stay with Mam. I wanted to comfort her; tell her that it would be all right. That my dad would find her in the morning and shelter her from the sun with his shirt and his shadow, and they'd get married and have seven sons. That she'd be happy . . .

But I couldn't move, and I was plunged into absolute darkness once more. Happy? On this world, happiness never lasts long. Neither did Mam's.

In the blink of an eye Mam's life was over, and now

I was witness to how it all ended. I was back in the Ord, watching her fight with the Ordeen. I'd seen Mam swoop down to attack, her white feathered lamia wings making her more angel than insect. I'd seen her grapple with her salamander-shaped enemy. She'd told me to leave and I'd obeyed, escaping from the Ord with the others – all except Bill Arkwright. I'd seen the destruction of the citadel from a distance, the towers collapsing as it was drawn back through the fiery portal into the darkness waiting beyond, carrying with it poor Mam, and Bill too.

But here I was, at close quarters, watching Mam's feathers burn, hearing her scream in torment as she held the Ordeen in a death grip.

Fire was all around me now, and I felt physical pain. Flames were singeing my own flesh, but even worse, I could see Mam's flesh bubbling and burning and hear her long anguished howl as she died in agony.

Once more I fell into darkness.

Suddenly there was light again, and I found myself standing in the kitchen at the farm. There was a row going on upstairs. Next thing I knew I was at the top of the stairs. Three men were holding my brother Jack. One of them was hitting him, spattering his blood over the wall and floorboards. I was now witnessing what had happened when the witches had raided the farm. They had wanted Mam's trunks, but she had protected the room against the dark and they couldn't get in. They'd made Jack go and bring the trunks out.

He was crying out in terror and pain but I couldn't help him. I was just a silent invisible presence, forced to witness his suffering.

So it went on. The buggane forced me to visit all the agonizing memories of the last few years. I looked down at Dad's grave again, and felt the pain of loss. I'd even missed his funeral. I visited these painful scenes again and again. It was a vortex of suffering: I kept returning to the same points in my life and I could do nothing to change them.

Darkness again; I was numb, and getting colder and colder as my life force was drawn from me. I felt myself moving closer to death.

But then . . . something new. I heard a voice:

Get harder or you won't survive. Just doing what Old Gregory says won't be enough. You'll die like the others!

It was Alice's voice. She'd said those words to me when I'd stopped her from burning Old Mother Malkin. Burning her had seemed too horrible. I just hadn't been able to do it.

You've got to match the dark, Tom. Stand up to the buggane. You can do it! You can do what needs to be done!

The moment Alice cried out those words, I had a new vision: another fragment of my life. After the first weeks of my apprenticeship to the Spook, I'd returned to the farm. Mother Malkin had appeared there, undead, soft and pliable. She'd oozed into Snout, the pig butcher, and possessed him, controlling his body, directing his every action. Now he was holding a knife to the throat of Jack and Ellie's baby daughter, Mary.

I relived those awful moments when I thought the child was about to be murdered; every second of anguish and horror. Alice ran forward and kicked him hard, her pointy shoe burying itself so deep in his belly that only the heel was showing. My heart in my mouth, I watched as he dropped baby Mary. Just before she hit the ground, Alice caught her and carried her away to safety. Now it was my turn: I hurled salt and iron at him. With his head enveloped in a cloud of the mixture, he fell senseless at my feet.

It was happening all over again. Snout was unconscious on the ground, his eyes rolling up into his head, his apron stained with the blood of freshly slaughtered pigs. I watched Mother Malkin slither out of his ear and take shape again. She'd shrunk to a third of her former size and her gown was trailing on the floor. She started moving away.

I was filled with anger; a terrible rage at all I'd been forced to see over and over again. Previously, I'd let the witch go. Alice had run after her with a burning brand and I'd caught her and pulled her back. It seemed too terrible to burn Mother Malkin. I couldn't allow it. But this time my anger transformed me. As before, I caught Alice as she ran by, but this time I snatched the burning brand from her and chased Mother Malkin across the farmyard.

Without hesitation, I set fire to the hem of her gown. It caught at once. Seconds later she was burning; shrieking as the flames consumed her. It was a terrible thing to do but I didn't care. I had to get harder to survive; to become the spook I was destined to be. Then I heard somebody speak: this was no whisper. The voice was loud and insistent.

'There's darkness inside me too!' it cried. 'I can match *anything* you do. I'm the hunter, not the hunted!'

Only slowly did I realize that I was the one who'd cried out. And I knew that what I'd said was true. The abhuman had been right. I'd become corrupted by the dark and there was indeed a sliver of darkness within my soul. It was a danger to me, but also a source of strength. As Mam had once promised, the day was fast approaching when I would become the hunter. And then the dark would fear me.

* * *

An age seemed to pass while I floated on the edge of consciousness. Finally I opened my eyes.

I was shivering, my brow burning with fever, my throat parched. The buggane hadn't drained me fully: I'd survived my first encounter with it, but how long would it be before it returned?

I felt weak and lethargic. I couldn't think clearly. Painful images swirled sluggishly inside my head like a whirlpool that was sucking me down into its dark, churning spiral. It was then that I heard a voice from my right.

'You're the lucky one,' Horn said. 'It'll be over for you soon. You'll be dead. I have to sit here watching you and waiting my turn.'

Wearily I turned my head to look at the abhuman. He was naked from the waist up, but even in the dim light from the torch above him I could see the powerful muscles bunched at the shoulders. And suddenly I had an idea.

'Do the iron manacles give you pain?' I asked.

He shook his head.

Not all creatures of the dark were vulnerable to iron. It seemed that Horn had some resistance to it. So much the better . . .

'Then why don't you free yourself?' I suggested. 'You're strong enough to do that . . .'

'For what purpose?' he asked. 'The cell door is too thick for me to break through.'

'Once you've freed yourself, free me too. Then we can venture into the tunnels together. I have weapons against anything that might threaten us – salt, iron and my silver chain. It's better than waiting here for death.'

'Free you? Why should I trust you? You're my enemy!'

'For now we need each other,' I told him. 'We'd be stronger together. Once we're free we can go our own ways.'

For a long time there was silence. Horn was obviously considering my suggestion. Then I heard a long groan. Only when the sound was repeated did I realize that it was the noise of exertion rather than physical pain or mental anguish. He was tearing the links apart.

I licked my dry lips and my heart pounded. I was suddenly filled with hope.

Horn stood and came across to where I was chained. I could smell stale sweat and a rank animal odour. But there was no chill; no warning that I was close to something from the dark. Horn was nearer to the human than he appeared. Nonetheless, I had to be wary. Despite our fragile pact we were natural enemies.

Without hesitation, Horn reached down and seized my chain close to the iron ring in the wall. He groaned again as his muscles tensed, then stretched it until the links first elongated and then snapped. With the end free, it was the work of moments to unwrap its length from my legs.

'Are you not blind?' I asked, wondering about his seemingly sightless eyes and how he had reached directly for the chain.

'I can see better than most, but not with these!' he

said, pointing at each of his milky eyeballs in turn. 'I have a third, spirit eye. With it I can see the world, and even things beyond the world. I can peer into the darkness within people.'

I jumped to my feet, and my heart began to pound even harder. I felt weak and shaky, but I was free! We stood face to face. My enemy from the dark was now my temporary ally. Together, with the help of Alice, we might have a real chance against Lizzie.

My tinderbox was in my bag but I still had my candle stub, so I reached up and lit it from the torch. Carrying the candle in my left hand, I led the way into the tunnel, suddenly realizing that it might not be necessary to follow the buggane's tunnels for very long: I remembered how cells that didn't contain prisoners usually had their doors left ajar.

When I'd reached the end of the short tunnel, I turned right. About twenty yards on, I reached the access tunnel to the next cell and turned right again into it. The moment I emerged into the empty cell, my hopes soared. The door was ajar! We could reach the steps that led up to the tower.

Of course, it meant passing through the guardroom. Had the yeomen returned after being attacked by the birds? I wondered. If they hadn't, who was it who had carried me from Lizzie's room down into the dungeon?

CHAPTER
27
I'LL TAKE YOUR BONES NOW!

The passageways were now in total darkness; nobody had been renewing the torches. Without my candle it would have been difficult to find our way.

We hadn't gone far when I suddenly felt the special coldness that told me that something from the dark was near. I came to a halt and I heard Horn hiss. He'd sensed it too. There was a clicking, crepitating sound directly ahead, and then a deep menacing growl. Something was moving towards us. I held up my candle stub, and saw that there was a place low on the wall where the light seemingly couldn't reach; a shadow darker than the other shadows. It moved towards us and started to grow.

What was it? I'd never encountered anything quite like it before. The growl came again, deeper and much more threatening. This was some dark entity drawn here by Lizzie's meddling.

I had to act – and fast. Quickly I handed the candle to Horn, reached deep into my breeches pockets and filled each fist with the substances waiting there: salt in my right, iron filings in my left. I hurled both handfuls straight at that threatening shadow. They enveloped it in a cloud. There was a sudden agonized shriek, and then only the scattered salt and iron remained on the flags. Whatever had threatened us was no more. It had either fled in agony or been destroyed. But there might well be other similar dangers ahead.

I looked upwards fearfully. Would that noise have alerted the guardroom? The cry had certainly not sounded human. Perhaps it would be more likely to cause any there to flee than descend into the darkness and investigate.

Horn now took the lead. We passed through the section of tunnel under the moat, where the water was cascading down the wall and dripping from the ceiling, and then headed for the steps. We began to climb, pausing now and then to listen. When at last we reached the guardroom door, we put our ears to it, but there was no sound from within.

Horn handed me the candle, then eased open the door. The room was empty. There were pitchers of water on the far table and I seized one and took several desperate gulps, then helped myself to a crust of stale bread, which I softened with some of the water before swallowing. My body had an urgent need for energy, to replace what the buggane had taken. When I'd finished, the abhuman walked across to face me.

'We should attack the witch now,' he growled.

'It's probably better if we find Alice first,' I told him. 'She'll be able to help.'

Horn nodded in agreement and we left the guardroom together and continued upwards.

We found Lizzie sitting on the throne, a smug look on her face. She clearly knew we'd escaped and had just been waiting for us to come to her. We were like two trapped flies going round and round in circles; we'd never even left her web.

Then I noticed the body of a yeoman behind the throne – and the blood on Lizzie's lips. He must have been the one who'd carried me down to the dungeon. Now she'd killed him and drunk his blood. Although primarily a bone witch, Lizzie liked human blood too. She preferred children's but would drink an adult's if she was thirsty enough.

As Horn and I walked down the carpet towards her, I readied my chain, wondering if I'd have the strength to bind her this time. But before I could attack, Lizzie sprang to her feet and glared at Horn. She looked wild, close to insanity, and a mixture of blood and saliva dribbled from her mouth to ooze into the slime on her chin.

'*You've* crossed my path once too often. You were meant to die a slow and painful death, but now you'll die fast!' she cried, raising her left hand, palm towards Horn, fingers spread wide. Then she closed her hand into a fist as if crushing something within it, while muttering an enchantment in the Old Tongue.

The abhuman screamed and buried his face in his hands. To my horror, I watched his head begin to crumple and collapse in on itself, rupturing and sending out gouts of blood. Horn dropped to the ground at my side like a sack of stones, his shrill, agonized scream giving way to a final gasp and then silence. His head was reduced to a bloody pulp.

I struggled to hold down the contents of my stomach and my knees began to tremble.

'Now, where's that daughter of mine?' Lizzie demanded, a scowl furrowing her brow.

I found it hard to believe that she hadn't found Alice. Where could she be? I took a deep breath to calm myself and shrugged. 'I don't know. I'm here to look for her,' I said.

Lizzie pulled a sharp knife from the folds of her gown. 'The buggane will have to manage without this time,' she said. 'I've had enough trouble from you so I'll take your bones now. *Come here!*'

Against my will, I found myself moving towards her. I tried to draw the silver chain from the pocket of my cloak, but my arm was paralysed! I began to sweat and shake with fear. I took a deep breath to calm myself, but my legs were no longer under my control. I took another step, and then another, until I was so close to the witch I could feel her foul breath warm upon my face and I almost retched again.

Lizzie seized my left hand with her right and lifted it before me. 'Take a last look at that thumb, boy. It'll be boiling and bubbling in my cauldron soon!'

Was this it? Was I to die here after all I'd been through?

With her left hand the witch brought the knife down towards my thumb. I tried to break free of her grip but was powerless. I flinched, expecting to feel an agonizing pain. But the blade failed to make contact with my skin. Instead the torches flickered and died down, and a shimmer of light appeared. Suddenly, to my utter astonishment, Alice was standing there, in front of me, holding one of the shaman's grimoires.

353

All at once I noticed that tell-tale shimmer of an apparition – it wasn't Alice in the flesh; it was her spirit. She'd projected it here from somewhere else. I was filled with sudden hope. Was this a result of her study of the shaman's books?

'If you hurt Tom, you'll never get your hands on this!' Alice warned, her image flickering. 'I took Barrule's notebook and studied it. I learned that the really useful stuff is in this grimoire here!'

'Might have known you were up to something, girl,' Lizzie snarled.

'Tells you in here how to tap the power of the cache directly, but he wrote it down in code. You've got to take bits from lots of different pages and link the spells together,' Alice said. 'Without this book and my know-ledge you'll never know what to do. You'd study for years and get nowhere. Ain't that so?'

Lizzie's face twisted with anger but she didn't reply.

'If you want this book and what I know, come and get it. I'm down in the long room where Lord Barrule and his gambling cronies used to have their fun and games. Bring Tom with you, but don't you dare hurt a hair on his head or you'll never get your mucky hands on this.' Alice raised the book towards her mother.

She vanished and the torches flared up again.

Lizzie turned to me. 'Looks like you'll live a little longer, boy! At least until I get my hands on that book . . .'

Keeping a tight grip on my arm and holding her knife at the ready, Lizzie dragged me down the steps of the keep, through the guardroom and along the underground passages. As we passed the cells, I noticed that all the doors were now shut, as if they contained prisoners.

The long room was almost in darkness – just a couple of torches were flickering in their rusty wall brackets. Lord Barrule still lay there on the stone floor, and the place reeked more strongly of death than ever.

Alice appeared, walking out of the shadows to face Lizzie. She was carrying the grimoire in her left hand and my staff in her right.

'Let Tom go and then I'll tell you what I know and give you the book,' she said calmly, the corners of her mouth twitching up into a grin.

Lizzie pushed me roughly towards Alice. 'Give me the book and start talking! Make it fast. My patience is stretched to breaking point!' she snapped.

'You're welcome to the book,' Alice said, and she tossed it towards her.

Lizzie reached out to catch it, but before her fingers closed on it, with a loud *whoosh*, it burst into flames. The witch flinched away and it fell at her feet, the pages curling and blackening.

Her expression was now black as thunder but Alice was smiling, a look of triumph on her face. The witch arched her back, pointed her finger straight at her daughter and muttered some words in the Old Tongue. For a moment I was horribly afraid for Alice, but nothing happened and her smile grew even wider.

'Used the cache to protect myself,' she said to Lizzie. 'You can't hurt me, and now Tom's at my side you can't hurt him either! But I can hurt you. Push me and I can hurt you really badly. If you weren't my mother, I'd kill you now! But you're going to do as you're told and do it right away. Give me the shaman's thumb-bones! Hand 'em over now!'

Lizzie began to shake, and beads of sweat broke out on her forehead. Her face was twisted with the effort of trying to resist Alice's command but she wasn't strong enough. I remembered how she had controlled us, but now things were reversed. Now she was forced to do Alice's bidding, reaching into the pocket of her dress and pulling out the bones that she'd cut from the dead body of Lord Barrule. They were white now, clean bones, the flesh boiled off as part of the ritual to tap into their full power.

Alice held out her hand to receive them, and once more Lizzie tried to resist, her whole body shaking with the effort, but then, with a gasp, she finally let them fall into Alice's palm.

That done, with a shriek, the witch ran towards the underground tunnel and scrambled inside.

CHAPTER 28
THE BUGGANE

'We must go after her, Alice,' I said, heading for the mouth of the tunnel. 'We can't let her escape. It's my duty to bind her.'

Alice shook her head. 'Sorry I let her go, Tom. Could have killed her then but despite what I said, I wasn't hard enough to do it. She's my mother after all. What kind of girl would kill her own mother . . . ?'

'It ain't safe to follow her through the tunnels now. Even though I was stronger just then, Lizzie still controls the buggane. She'll be able to find a way to the surface but she can't return to the keep. Locked all the cell doors, I have, just to make sure she don't try to double back. I'll lock the door to this room too,' she said, holding up a key.

'Then we should head to where we left Adriana and Simon and try to cut her off!'

Alice nodded but her eyes were fearful.

'What's wrong?' I asked her.

'The further we get from Greeba Keep, the less I'll be able to draw on the power of the cache. After a few miles it'd just be me against Lizzie, and she's bound to be stronger.'

'All the more reason to deal with her before she gets too far away,' I said.

We hurried out of the keep; it was deserted and we headed directly for Adriana and Simon. They were still waiting at the edge of the trees, so we quickly explained what had happened and made our way towards the chapel, watching closely to see if Lizzie emerged.

But we watched and waited in vain. Two hours later there was no sign of the witch and we began to grow dispirited. Had she already escaped?

'Can't you sniff her out, Alice?' I asked.

She shook her head. 'Been here before, she has, and her stench is everywhere. Can't tell what's fresh 'cause there's so much of it.'

It was then, as the light began to fail, that I saw a figure approaching in the distance and my heart sank right down into my boots. There'd be a reckoning now all right.

It was the Spook, and as he drew nearer, I saw that he was scowling.

It was Adriana who spoke first. She stepped forward, placing herself between him and us. 'It was my idea,' she said. 'We had to try and deal with Lizzie. I knew you'd never agree. It's all my fault.'

The Spook nodded. 'Aye,' he said angrily, 'you've put a bad taste in my mouth in more ways than one. But we'll deal with all that later.' He turned to me, his expression grim. 'We need to get down to practicalities: tell me what happened and make it quick . . .'

After I'd finished, my master shook his head. 'It's a bad business. We need to follow the witch and deal with her once and for all. But now that she's gone and no longer has access to the power here, our first priority is the buggane. I've been thinking – and if we can destroy it, eventually the tunnels will collapse and the cavern with that cache of power will be buried. That'll stop servants of the dark from visiting it in spirit form. They'll no longer be able to tap into it directly. And that includes you, girl!' he said, turning on Alice. 'Deals with everything nicely.'

'That's not fair! I'd be dead by now but for what Alice did,' I shouted.

'She still used dark power – and not for the first time, as you well know. But we won't speak of that now. We'll go directly to the chapel – that's at the centre of the buggane's domain. It'll sense us there and attack.'

'What about the dogs – won't they help us?' I asked my master.

'There's no time for that now, lad. I left them at the mill, and we've got to deal with this creature.'

The Spook turned and began to walk away. Alice and I were at his heels, with Adriana and Simon close behind. Suddenly my master spun round to face them.

'This is spook's business,' he said, holding up his hand. 'Dangerous work for just me and the lad. It's best if you wait here until we've dealt with the daemon. And that means you too!' he said, glaring at Alice. She opened her mouth to protest, but then shook her head. There would be no arguing with my master after what had just happened.

So the Spook and I headed directly for the chapel. Despite his wishes, I hoped Alice wouldn't be very far behind. She couldn't afford to distance herself from the blood jar. We arrived at the ruins and waited just inside the trees, within sight of those crumbling dark stone walls. The minutes passed but nothing happened; Lizzie would be getting further and further away with every second, I thought.

It was a cold, crisp, clear night and the grass was white with hoar frost. Half a waning moon cast dappled shadows on the ground. Occasionally an owl hooted, but apart from that all was silent; there wasn't even a breath of wind.

'Why doesn't the buggane attack?' I asked.

'It's nearby – I can feel it in my bones – but it's not showing itself,' the Spook answered. 'Most likely it'll be down the slope close to the water's edge – a place we want to avoid. It'll take the shape of a worme on that marshy ground, and wormes are hard to kill. But what choice do we have? Let's get it over with!'

I followed my master towards the incline. I was gripping my staff nervously. The last thing I wanted was to face a worme again. I remembered the way they could spit poison and bite off an arm or leg with those rows of sharp teeth.

As we descended, the slope became steeper and our boots squelched in the soft ground. I soon found it hard to stay on my feet. Below, the murmur of the river was ever louder, though as yet I couldn't see it through the trees. They grew closer together here, interspersed with dense bushes and saplings, making our progress difficult and forcing us to make frequent detours.

'Spread out!' the Spook commanded. 'Giving it more than one target will distract it.'

JOSEPH DELANEY

I did as he said, obeying without question and moving away to the left. My master was the expert here and, having already faced a worme, I knew it was the same advice that Bill Arkwright would have given: he'd been the specialist on all creatures that lived in marsh and water.

We were very close to the riverbank now, and the Spook was hidden from view by bushes and tall reeds, though I could still hear the suck and squelch of his boots.

It was then that I heard another noise in the reeds; a heavy wet slippery sound, almost as if someone had fallen onto their back and was sliding down the steep slope towards the water. But the sound was getting louder and moving closer – *up* the slope, directly towards us. My heart lurched with fear.

All at once something burst through the reeds directly ahead of me and lunged for my head. I threw myself sideways, catching a glimpse of something above me before it withdrew back into the reeds: a long, sinuous body like a fat snake, small fierce eyes and a mouthful of fanged teeth.

It certainly wasn't a worme – at least not the type that I'd once fought – and the only snakes I'd ever seen were small grass snakes and, more rarely, adders. But this was huge. It had to be the buggane, and it had taken the form of a great serpent.

In a blind panic, I struggled to my knees. I was only just in time. It attacked, and this time I jabbed at the creature with my staff. It hissed and retreated again. I came cautiously to my feet and heard a scuffle to my right. Then the Spook shouted something – I didn't catch it the first time, but when he repeated it, I realized it was a cry of warning.

'Hydra!'

From what my master had taught me, I knew that we were in serious trouble. There were many forms of hydra, some real, some just fantastic creatures made up by storytellers. The one referred to in the Spook's Bestiary was a creature called a Scylla, which had seven heads. All hydra certainly had several heads – and this one was attacking my master and me simultaneously.

Again I heard that slithering sound, and the snake-like head surged towards me along the ground, parting the reeds before rearing up towards my throat. But this time I was ready, and I used my staff like a spear, ramming the blade past its teeth and right down its throat with all my strength. It screamed and convulsed, and blood sprayed in an arc from its fanged mouth. It retreated immediately, almost dragging the staff out of my hand, but I held on tight and the daemon's head slid away, its mouth gushing blood.

I followed it through the reeds towards the water's edge. Once on the riverbank I could see the buggane by the light of the moon. Its body was hidden underwater but its many heads reared and writhed, lunging towards me. I quickly counted to nine, but then gave up because they were moving too quickly. The one nearest me hung limp, dark blood issuing from its gaping mouth and swirling away in the current. That was the one I'd just speared. The Spook was now on the riverbank too, jabbing furiously with his staff. But there were so many heads, all roaring and howling eerily. How could we deal with them?

'To me, lad!' cried the Spook, plunging into the strong river current. 'Its heart – we need to cut our way to its heart! I'll go for the body while you tackle the heads!'

I splashed along to his side. The water reached our waists and it was a struggle to stay on our feet. The grey body of the hydra surfaced briefly before submerging again. That sight filled me with hope because it didn't seem to have the hard defensive scales of a worme and would be vulnerable to our blades. No doubt the daemon had sacrificed that defence in favour of the attacking capability of those many fanged heads. I kept swinging my staff in an arc and jabbing directly at any ravening mouth that came too close.

The Spook began to attack the hydra's body, driving his staff in deep and leaning against it while I defended us both against those heads with their dangerous teeth.

How long that struggle went on I don't know. All I

remember is the water, dark with blood, and those daemonic heads shining silver in the moonlight as they sought to put an end to us. At one point I was almost overwhelmed – teeth and ravening jaws were all around me – and the Spook had to halt his attack on the body and help me fight off the heads. But then I heard a cry from the bank, and saw Alice standing there, waving the short blade and shouting at the buggane, trying to attract its attention.

Several of its heads immediately lurched towards her. I was afraid for her, but the daemon was distracted and it gave us our chance. Furiously the Spook renewed his attack. Within moments his silver-alloy blade had found the daemon's heart. There was a blast of foul air, and then water rose up before me in a high wave and I went under, still gripping my staff. Moments later I floated up to the surface.

Eventually the Spook and I dragged ourselves wearily out onto the riverbank. Alice's face looked full of relief. I stood there beside her, shivering and dripping wet.

'It's gone, lad. Not one bit of it remains,' said the Spook, bending over, exhausted. 'And as for you, girl – will you never do as you're told?'

'If Alice hadn't disobeyed we'd probably both be dead now,' I pointed out indignantly.

My master gave a grudging nod but didn't comment further. He knew what I said was true.

'Now it's time to deal with the witch,' he muttered.

CHAPTER
29
ONE FOR SORROW

Once we'd rejoined Adriana and Simon, the Spook wasted no time looking for signs of Bony Lizzie.

I knew he was an expert tracker, but with only moonlight to rely on, would he find Lizzie's trail when even Alice couldn't sniff her out? We watched him pace around the wood, checking it systematically, bit by bit. Every so often he paused and knelt down, studying the ground. Maybe there wasn't anything to find? Maybe Lizzie was still hiding in the tunnels?

It was almost an hour before my master found something and waved us over. There were three footprints in the mud. They were fresh and made by pointy shoes . . .

'They ain't mine, that's for sure,' said Alice. 'Got big feet, Lizzie has. Much bigger than mine.'

'So she's heading south-west,' said the Spook. 'That's the way we should go—'

'I'd like to know something . . .' Alice interrupted.

'What is it, girl?' demanded the Spook impatiently. 'We've not got all day, so speak up!'

'You ain't going to bind Lizzie – you're going to kill her, aren't you?' she asked. It wasn't really a question. I could tell from her face that she knew the truth of it and she didn't look happy.

The Spook nodded in confirmation, his expression grave. 'I've no choice, girl. She's murdered too many innocents. I can't leave a witch like her at large – especially one with such ambition. If she'd had her way, this whole island would have been plunged into her rule of darkness. Who knows what else she might attempt in the future? Best thing would be for you to stay here until we return. She is still your mother, after all. No need for you to be there. You've done enough, girl. Get yourself back to the mill with Adriana until it's over.'

But I knew Alice would refuse. I'm sure she didn't want to be a witness to her own mother's death, but if she waited here, she'd be beyond the protection of the blood jar. She had to accompany me.

She shook her head. 'I need to be there,' she said quietly.

'I'm going after Lizzie too,' Adriana told the Spook. 'You might need my help – are you with us, Simon?'

Simon Sulby nodded. 'Yes,' he said, looking determined. 'We're going to spend the rest of our lives together so we'll do this together too.'

We went as fast as we could, but after half an hour we'd seen no sign of the witch; my master was getting worried.

'We've got to catch Bony Lizzie, lad,' said the Spook, 'and put an end to her once and for all.'

'Perhaps we should go back to the mill for the

dogs now,' I suggested. 'They'd soon hunt her down.'

'No time. She's already got too much of a head-start.' My master knelt down and searched the ground nearby before shaking his head. 'Wait here. I'll see if I can find her tracks again . . .'

He wandered off into the trees. As before, he kept pausing and looking down to scrutinize the ground, but there was more cloud now and the moonlight was intermittent.

'Can he find her again?' Adriana asked me.

'He's an excellent tracker but it's really hard,' I said. 'The Pendle witches can cloak themselves, using dark magic to conceal their trail. A seventh son of a seventh son can still follow them but it's not easy. If he doesn't pick up her tracks soon, she'll get clean away.'

The Spook was now out of sight, but within five minutes he reappeared on the edge of a copse of trees and beckoned us over. When we reached him, he gave one of his rare smiles and pointed down at a patch of mud close to a tree trunk. There were two clear prints. Pointy shoes again . . .

'At least we've got confirmation of her direction. She's still heading south-west,' he said. 'No doubt she hopes to make her escape by sea – compel some poor fisherman to carry her west towards Ireland.'

We set off even faster. Twice more the Spook found Lizzie's tracks, but then he lost the trail.

Adriana thought she'd probably be making for either Port Erin or Port St Mary, where there were vessels capable of making the trip westwards even in a rough sea.

We were pressing on through the dark as fast as we could when a sudden vivid flash of lightning in the distance turned night into day. This was followed by a low rumble of thunder, and then the wind began to freshen. A storm was heading our way. And what a storm! Within minutes torrential rain had driven us to take shelter in a grove of trees, while a fury of thunder and lightning erupted from the clouds above.

'If I didn't know any better, I'd say that Lizzie had sent this storm to hold us at bay!' said the Spook as we waited for it to subside.

Cut off from the cache of animas, she was unlikely to have had the power to unleash such a storm, but she was still strong – as we soon discovered to our cost.

The storm now abated just as quickly as it had arisen. The clouds were scurrying away to the east, and we were suddenly bathed in moonlight.

We were just about to leave the shelter of the trees when, in the silence after the storm, we heard a cacophony of squeals and shrieks approaching from the west.

'Rats!' Simon shouted.

Moments later he was proved correct. A horde of huge, fierce rats with long whiskers and sinuous tails surged into view. I knew a witch could summon rats and drink their blood, but I'd never heard of them being used to attack her enemies. We were soon fighting for our lives. We laid about us with our staffs, beating at the ground to squash the rodents and desperately plucking them off as they raced up our legs, biting and scratching as they made for our throats and faces.

I heard Alice scream and turned to find her covered

375

in rats. She was trying to protect her head, but she was losing the battle. I tore a big rat off her head, hurled it to the ground and stamped it underfoot.

Wave upon wave of grey rodents continued to attack us; then, suddenly, they were fleeing, leaving behind a mass of dead and dying bodies.

Luckily we were more exhausted than hurt. 'That was Lizzie's doing,' I said.

'Aye, lad, there's little doubt about that,' replied the Spook. 'But why they broke off and fled we can only surmise. Maybe Lizzie doesn't want to use up too much of her power. Could be she's saving the worst for later.'

At dawn we halted and rested for a couple of hours. Simon offered to keep watch while the rest of us grabbed some sleep. The Spook was the only one who managed to doze. His nap didn't last long either; he awoke groaning and sweating. Lizzie had been speaking inside his head again.

Adriana suddenly started to shiver; Simon turned to her, concerned, and put his arm around her. 'What's the matter, love?' he asked her.

'I've got that feeling again,' she said. 'A premonition that I've not got long for this world.'

'But you felt like that before they rolled you down the hill – and you survived the barrel, didn't you?' I pointed out.

'I did, but this time it's stronger than ever. I'm certain that I'm going to die soon.'

Needing to keep up our strength, we bought bread and cheese from a cottage. It was then that Adriana offered to try her powers again. The Spook didn't like it, but he had no better suggestion to offer.

She cupped her hands and gave a high whistling cry. Within minutes, in answer to her summons, a pair of sparrowhawks dropped out of the sky to land on her shoulders. She stroked them gently with the tip of each forefinger and whispered to them, her voice so low that, even though I was standing close, I couldn't catch what she said.

They flew off but returned within the hour. This time they circled overhead before flying off in a different direction. When they repeated the manoeuvre exactly, Adriana pointed in the direction they'd taken.

'They've found her,' she said. 'That's the way. She's making for Port Erin.'

Adriana was a bird witch all right – her magic had succeeded in tracking down Bony Lizzie.

Not long after, the Spook discovered another pointy footprint in the mud. We were hot on the witch's trail again. And then Alice confirmed it: she could now sniff her mother's presence. Finally, at twilight, we saw Lizzie in the distance, and despite our exhaustion, increased our pace.

She was somewhere ahead of us in the gathering dusk: we glimpsed her once more, little more than half a mile away, but it was now almost dark, and a sudden shower exploded from the heavens, soaking us to the skin in the five minutes it took to blow itself out.

Adriana and Simon were sprinting alongside me and Alice, the Spook just behind us, and we were closing in on the bone witch with every stride. Soon I heard the angry roar of the sea in the distance, and the rhythmical pounding of waves against the rocky shore. At last the moon came out from behind a cloud, bathing the scene in silver light, and I saw Lizzie less than a hundred yards ahead of us. Then Simon noticed something on the ground: a pair of pointy shoes lying in the grass. Lizzie had kicked them off in a desperate attempt to gain more speed.

'She's running straight for the headland. We've cut her off from the port. She's nowhere to go now but the salty sea!' shouted the Spook.

He was right. Lizzie was running directly towards the cliffs. Very soon we would face the last of her power. How strong was she still? Would the five of us be able to overcome her? It was far from certain, but we had to try.

It was then that disaster struck. Alice slipped on the wet grass and went down hard. I stopped and helped her up, but when she tried to put weight on her left foot, it buckled under her and she fell to her knees. As the Spook raced past us, he turned to shout at me: 'Leave the girl, lad! We'll come back for her later. I need you with me! Now!' He ran on towards the cliffs, his footsteps fading into the distance.

'Yes, leave me, Tom! My ankle's sprained. He's right – he'll need all the help he can get to beat Lizzie. She's still strong.'

'No, Alice, we stick together,' I told her, putting my arm under her left shoulder and lifting her back onto her feet. 'You know why we can't risk being separated . . .'

Alice could only limp forward slowly, grunting with pain.

The witch had nowhere left to run. She turned her back on the sea to face the Spook, Adriana and Simon. They'd slowed to a walking pace but continued to advance along a narrow spur of grass that jutted out above the sea. The waves crashed onto the rocks below before drawing back to surge forward once more.

At first nothing happened; then, very suddenly, like a blow to my solar plexus, I felt Lizzie's power again. It took my breath away, almost stopped my heart. But it wasn't *dread* or any other spell designed to immobilize us while she took our lives with her blade. It was a spell of compulsion. I was consumed by a strong urge to run forward and throw myself off the cliff. I wanted to fall onto the rocks and break into little pieces; to become nothing – as if I'd never been born.

I fought back but she was too strong. I saw the waves far below. I had never wanted anything so much.

Far ahead, the Spook had fallen into a crouching position, his staff still in his left hand. With his right he was clutching a tussock of grass as if that would somehow anchor him to the cliff-top. But then, to my dismay, Simon suddenly sprinted directly towards the cliff edge. I realized that he was going to throw himself over!

I heard Adriana scream, a long wail of anguish and loss. Simon had jumped out into nothingness, and was gone. Under the compulsion of Lizzie's dark magic he'd hurled himself over the edge to his death.

Ahead, Adriana was stretching her arms above her head and pointing towards the sky, arching her back just as Lizzie had earlier. Then she began to chant, hurling her words up into the firmament. She was speaking in the Old Tongue, gabbling far too quickly for me to understand.

In answer came a peal of thunder and a flash of sheet lightning, and suddenly, far above us, the heavens were filled with birds. There were crows, ravens, blackbirds, finches and swallows – and a single magpie . . . one for sorrow.

Alice and I had almost reached the cliff, and I heard Adriana utter four more words very slowly and clearly. Even with my poor command of the Old Tongue, these were easy to translate. It was a command: 'Peck out her eyes!'

From the smallest to the largest the birds obeyed, swooping down in unison to attack the witch. For a moment Lizzie was hidden from our sight, buffeted to and fro by the frenzied, screeching birds.

But she was not to be defeated so easily. There was an intense flash of light and a blast of hot air that made me close my eyes. When I opened them again, the birds were screaming, falling out of the sky, wings aflame.

Some dropped, blackened, burned and twitching, onto the cliff-top; others fell down towards the sea, trailing smoke. Lizzie had blasted them out of the sky.

Adriana let out a great sob and rushed towards her, but the bone witch seized her by the throat and lifted her off her feet.

I knew what was going to happen: I let go of Alice and stumbled forward to try and help her, but the world was still spinning about me and I was forced to my knees, hard pressed just to stay on the cliff-top, still consumed by the desire to throw myself onto the rocks.

As I watched, horrified, Lizzie hurled Adriana over the cliff. As she fell towards the rocks, she gave a shrill cry like a bird. Then she was gone.

CHAPTER 30
A FULL RECKONING

A gloating smile settled over Lizzie's face.

'Do you know why the boy stayed behind with the girl instead of coming to help you?' she asked the Spook. 'Do you know why he disobeyed you? He needs her more than anything else in the world, and she's just as soft on him. Your apprentice sold his soul to the Fiend, and now the only thing that's keeping him and the girl safe is a blood jar. That's why they have to stay together. He's using dark magic to save the both of them. That's just one step short of belonging to the dark!'

The Spook staggered to his feet and looked at me, and as our eyes met, I saw on his face a mixture of sadness and disappointment. I'd let him down. I wasn't the apprentice he thought I was.

Lizzie laughed long and loud, and the ugly sound was filled with triumph, with the knowledge that the dark had won.

But the battle wasn't over yet. Adriana was dead, but her final cry hadn't merely been one of pain and shock; it had been a command. Fresh raucous caws sounded overhead, and I saw a large flock of circling seagulls – the fierce aggressive birds that Alice had once called 'rats with wings'.

Suddenly they swooped towards the witch, their harsh piercing screams filling the air. Bony Lizzie waved her arms to scare them off, whirling them about like a windmill in a gale. Perhaps she'd exhausted her power, or maybe there were just too many of them and she never had time to gather herself to withstand the attack. The gulls dived straight for her, eager talons outstretched. Soon all I could see was birds, a chaotic turmoil of beating wings and stabbing beaks.

For a moment I glimpsed Lizzie's head again. Her hands covered her face and blood ran down between her fingers. She staggered towards the cliff edge, leaning back at an impossible angle. Her eyes were black sockets in the moonlight, her mouth wide open in a scream, the sound lost amongst the shrieking of the birds. The seagulls obscured her again; when they soared upwards, she was gone.

I ran to the cliff and peered down. For a moment her broken body was visible below. Then a big wave engulfed her, its ebb dragging her into the sea's salty embrace. The bone witch was no more.

'Well, that's the end of her, lad,' the Spook said, walking up to stand beside me. 'If she's not dead already, that salty sea will kill her quickly. Then she'll be food for the fishes. They'll eat the heart and everything. She won't be coming back.'

'Poor Adriana and Simon have gone as well,' I said sadly. I could see no trace of their bodies on the rocks below. The sea had taken them too.

My master nodded. 'Aye, that was a bad business,

lad – but that girl helped to save our lives. She was a witch all right – no doubt about it!'

'But what kind of witch was she?' I asked. 'She didn't use blood or bone magic and didn't have a familiar.'

'She was something new to me, lad. I've certainly never met her like before. Maybe she simply had a special ability, one that can't be learned and passed on to others.'

'Adriana was a *benign* witch,' I insisted.

My master didn't reply. I knew he didn't agree. Adriana had used some kind of magic to kill. To his way of thinking, the fact that she'd killed Lizzie, a malevolent witch, was irrelevant. She had still employed the dark.

I heard a noise behind us, and turned to see Alice limping along. The Spook looked at us in turn. 'What Lizzie said about you selling your soul and employing a blood jar . . . please set my mind at ease and tell me she was lying,' he said quietly.

'I can't,' I said, bowing my head. 'It's true. I owe the

Fiend my soul. Alice made a blood jar, and that's the only thing keeping him away. That's why I couldn't leave her behind. If I do, the Fiend will claim her in revenge for saving me.'

'Why did you give him your soul?' he asked, frowning at me. 'What sort of a fool would sell his soul to the Fiend?'

'I did it at Meteora, in Greece. It's a long story, but without that we'd all be dead now, and the whole world – not just the County – would be at risk . . .'

The Spook sighed; it was a sound filled with sadness and a hint of despair. 'We'll find somewhere to rest,' he said quietly. 'I'm weary. We'll talk in the morning.'

His head bowed, he turned and began to walk away, heading back towards the mill, where we needed to collect our bags. Once he had his back to us, Alice put her hand in the pocket of her skirt and drew out some objects, flinging them over the cliff and into the sea. They gleamed silver in the moonlight as they fell, the same colour as the tears that glistened in her eyes.

They were the thumb-bones of the shaman.

* * *

Luckily we quickly stumbled upon the ruin of a cottage. There were just three walls standing, and no roof, but it provided some shelter, and fortunately it didn't rain again, so we settled down there for the rest of the night.

We awoke at dawn, cold and stiff, and the Spook set about building a fire while I went off to catch rabbits for our breakfast. I only managed to get one, which I skinned and gutted before Alice cooked it. There wasn't really enough to go round but it took the edge off my hunger.

As we ate, it began to drizzle, and dark clouds gathered from the west. There was worse weather to come.

At last there came the full reckoning.

'Right, it's time to talk!' commanded the Spook. 'Don't leave anything out. I want to know everything. I don't care how bad it is, I want to know it all. Let's start with you, girl. Tell me about the blood jar. Did you fashion it?'

Alice nodded.

'Am I right in thinking you've put your own blood in it – the blood of a daughter of the Fiend – and the blood of my apprentice, Tom?'

Alice nodded again and bowed her head.

'Well, lad, I'm finding this hard to believe. You actually gave your own blood for the purposes of a dark magic spell?'

'No!' Alice cried defiantly. 'Ain't true, that. Tom was unconscious when I took it. Back in Greece, there was a rock-fall in a cave. Knocked out, he was, so I took three drops of his blood and added them to mine in the jar. Tom didn't even know about it. It was only later, when the Fiend came for him, that I pushed it into his hand. After that Tom had to keep it on him to stop the Fiend coming back and dragging him off to the dark. I have to stay close to Tom as well, else he'll take his revenge on me!'

'So tell me what you got for your soul,' the Spook asked.

I explained how the Fiend had given me three

things: the location of our terrible enemy, the Ordeen; a delay of one hour before she awoke; and, finally, the lives of him and Alice, who were facing imminent death.

'Not only that, he showed me the future,' I said. 'Thousands would have been massacred that day – men, women and children. Had the Ordeen won, the County would have been the next place to be destroyed. In the past I've resisted the temptations of the dark – even when the lives of my own family were at risk. This time it was the County in danger. And you've always taught me that we protect it, and that our first duty is to the County and its people. So in the end that's why I did it. Not for Alice, not for you – for the County. It seemed worth my soul at the time.'

'Show me,' the Spook said quietly.

I reached into my breeches pocket and pulled out the small jar. I held it in my open palm so that he could see it properly.

'Give it to me,' my master ordered.

'It's dangerous even to let it out of my possession—'

'Hand it over, lad!' he commanded angrily, raising his voice.

Nervously I did as he asked. He peered at it closely, and for a moment his fingers gripped the stopper. One twist and it would be open, and he could pour away the drops of blood. My heart was in my mouth.

'What if I were to smash this now, or drain it of its contents?' he asked me. 'Could the girl make another?'

'Ain't possible to make another to save Tom,' said Alice. 'You can only use a spell like that once.'

'And it would be the end of me and Alice,' I added. 'The Fiend would come for us. We'd be dead and our souls dragged off to the dark. You too probably – he wouldn't spare the life of a spook.'

'Don't try to scare me, lad. I'll do what's right, whatever the cost.'

'I wasn't trying to scare you. Just telling you how things are. I've thought about it a lot,' I retorted.

'Would he come right away?' asked the Spook, looking thoughtful. 'Tell me that, girl. You made it, so

THE SPOOK'S NIGHTMARE

you should know. I've never encountered this type of jar before.'

'Could be here in the blink of an eye,' Alice told him.

'What a miserable existence you've got ahead of you,' said the Spook, shaking his head. 'Living in fear with just this little jar standing between you and a terrible fate. Then, when you die, which is inevitable, the Fiend will be waiting for you. He'll collect your soul the minute you draw your last breath.'

'Not if Tom manages to bind or destroy him first—'

'And how on earth is he going to manage that?' demanded the Spook.

Alice shrugged. 'Tom's mam believed he would do it one day—'

'Did she ever say *how* it could be done?'

'Perhaps the secret is buried amongst her papers and notebooks in Malkin Tower,' I suggested.

'Well, lad, that might be so, but the last time I was there I found nothing like that. And Malkin Tower is a long way from here, across the sea and now behind enemy lines. I can't help thinking that if your mam

393

really *had* known how to bind or destroy the Fiend, she'd have told you before we went to Greece. After all, as her letters told us, she thought she'd have to sacrifice her own life to defeat her enemy. No, I think she hoped that you might discover a way to do it yourself.'

There was a long silence, and I thought about what I'd seen within myself: maybe that would help me to find a way . . .

Then Alice spoke up. 'I can think of someone who might know – someone who's thought about it long and hard: Grimalkin . . .'

'The witch assassin?' My master scratched at his beard in irritation. 'It just gets worse!'

'She once told me how much she hates the Fiend. She said she thought he could be bound with silver spears,' Alice went on.

'What? Bound in a pit?'

'He'd be impaled on the spears,' she explained. 'Then maybe you could bury him beneath a stone like you do with boggarts. Wouldn't that work?'

'Maybe, girl. When a daemon such as a buggane or the Bane takes material form and you pierce its heart, it's usually destroyed. I can't see that being enough to finish off the Fiend – he's much too powerful. In any case, where would we get silver-alloy spears from?' asked the Spook, shaking his head.

'Grimalkin would make them. She's a skilled black-smith. We should send for her; bring her here.'

'You'd use a mirror, no doubt,' said the Spook, his face grim. 'More dark magic . . .'

'What's done is done,' Alice snapped, 'but the main thing is to keep Tom safe. And Grimalkin's resourceful. War or no war, she would find a way to get here.'

'I need time to think this through,' said the Spook, handing the jar back to me. 'Get out of my sight for a while – both of you!'

I nodded and we wandered slowly off into the trees, Alice still limping badly. I was relieved to have the blood jar back in my pocket. For a long time Alice was silent, her lips pressed tightly together, her face a mask. Then she began to cry, great sobs racking her body. I put my arms around her, offering comfort as best I could.

'Ain't crying for Lizzie,' Alice said at last as her grief began to subside. 'Not even crying for poor Adriana and Simon, although I'm sorry that they lost their lives like that and can never enjoy the happiness they deserved. No, I'm crying for what I never had. Crying for the mam every girl should have – someone who'd have loved me and cared what happened to me.'

After a while she smiled and wiped the tears from her eyes with the back of her hand.

'Thanks for saving me back there in the dungeons, Alice,' I said softly. 'The buggane was draining me. I could feel my life slipping away. I was so cold and weak.'

Alice squeezed my hand. 'In the shaman's study, as soon as I worked out how to control the cache, Lizzie's power started to wane. I used a spell to cloak myself. Walked right past her and she didn't see me. I went into the tunnels and started to work on the buggane. It was in its spirit form, whispering to you, when I finally reached it with my mind. I was just in time, Tom. It was planning to drain you in one go – as Lizzie had ordered. So I called out to you; told you to fight it – and, just in time, you started to resist. Then I went looking for Lizzie again and managed to stop her taking your bones. By then I knew we'd won. I was stronger than her . . .'

'Have you still got that power, Alice?' I asked. 'Is all that dark magic still at your service?'

'Still got a bit left, but it's fading fast. Power's still there down in that cavern, but I can't reach it no more.'

'What do you think the Spook will decide to do?' I asked.

'Old Gregory will send for Grimalkin, mark my words. He wouldn't have dreamed of such a thing once, but now he hasn't any choice. He's not the man he was. Too much has happened: his library's burned to the ground, the County ransacked, and now this – being defeated by a powerful witch not just once but three times over. But for Adriana, I think Lizzie would have killed us all – Old Gregory included.

'From now on you'll get stronger and he'll get weaker. It happens to us all eventually. He's had a long life fighting the dark, but now it's coming to an end. You'll be the new spook and you'd best get ready to replace him.'

I nodded. There was some truth in what Alice had said, but I wasn't ready to take over from my master just yet. I put my arms around her and hugged her again. Once more we'd survived, and two more enemies of the light were no more.

As we walked back towards the cottage, we saw the Spook waiting for us in the doorway. What had he decided to do? His face was grim, and I thought it looked like bad news.

But I was wrong.

'Find yourself a mirror, girl, and summon Grimalkin,' my master said. 'We have no choice now but to attempt to bind the Fiend.'

Once again, I've written most of this from memory, just using my notebook when necessary. We are still on the island of Mona in the cold, dark, stormy heart of winter, staying at the abandoned cottage Adriana showed us. Over the last two months we've been busy with spook's business.

My master has almost finished rewriting a book about the Pendle witches, and Alice has volunteered to add to the beginnings of his new library. She's started on an account of the two years she spent being trained in witchcraft by Bony Lizzie; it will add to our knowledge of the dark.

The tunnels beneath the chapel have collapsed, closing off all access to the Grim Cache. So my master, Alice and I have hunted down and slain every other known buggane on the island – five in all – to prevent one burrowing down to find it again. Now Mona is a safer place for those who work for the light.

Grimalkin agreed to join us in an attempt to bind the Fiend once and for all, but she has not yet arrived and Alice is no longer able to contact her by using a mirror. She now fears that something has happened to the witch assassin. Without her we can do nothing, and the blood jar is our only defence against the Fiend.

There is no good news from the County. It seems that it is in the iron grip of the enemy. And here on Mona, the Ruling Council are assembled again and started returning refugees across the water; there is no news of how they were received – or of Captain Baines. The yeomen are still searching for those who have avoided their net, and the island is less safe for us with each passing day.

The Spook was right. The people have reverted to their old ways.

At least with Lizzie's death, Bill Arkwright will have finally found his way to the light.

I long to go back to the County, but the Spook's plan now is to escape westwards, to Ireland. We go within the week. But whenever I think of that land I remember my nightmare and the threat made by the Celtic witch; I remember the Morrigan.

In just over two years I'll finish learning my trade. My master tells me that he might take it easier then and let me do most of the work. As a young spook, he worked alongside his own master, Henry Horrocks, until he died, and it was to the advantage of both.

It's his decision. He's the Spook and I'm still just his apprentice. Soon we sail to take refuge even further from the County's shores. No doubt we'll be heading into even greater danger.

Thomas J. Ward

Joseph Delaney is a retired English teacher living in Lancashire. He has three children and nine grandchildren, and often speaks at conference, library and bookshop events. His home is in the middle of Boggart territory and his village has a boggart called the Hall Knocker, which was laid to rest under the step of a house near the church.

Most of the places in the Spook's books are based on real places in Lancashire, and the inspiration behind the stories often comes from local ghost stories and legends.

You can visit the Wardstone Chronicles website at
www.**spooksbooks**.com
where you can find Joseph's blog
and more information on the books.